Mark of Ravage And Ruin

Jacyn Gormish

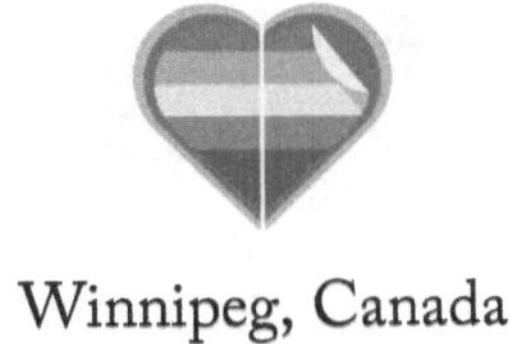

Winnipeg, Canada

Developmental editor: Craig Gibb
Proofreader: Sanford Larson

Published March 2022 by Deep Hearts YA, an imprint of Deep Desires Press and Story Perfect Inc.

Deep Hearts YA
PO Box 51053 Tyndall Park
Winnipeg, Manitoba R2X 3B0
Canada

Visit deepheartsya.com for more great reads.

Mark of Ravage
And Ruin

Chapter One

BARLI KNEW THE MOMENT she opened her eyes where she was.

It smelled like refuse and coriander. The air tasted of garlic and mint. The competing and overwhelming assaults on her nose nearly made her want to barf. Instead, she breathed through her mouth. It was slightly better that way.

Her wrists hurt, which wasn't a surprise. She tried to move them but found she was tied down. Clamps pressed along her arms.

The Asylum. There was one on every island, with more than one on the largest two. Her arm throbbed and she pulled at the restraints, putting pressure on the cut, sealed up and bandaged.

She was never getting out of here.

She would never see Visea again.

"*Kitadu*," she muttered.

Barli stopped fighting her restraints—it only hurt more—and studied the room. It was simple, barren aside from the restraints, a glass of some liquid on a bedside table, and a single chair. The liquid reminded Barli she was thirsty. She stretched her head out, forcing herself up by the strength of her abs alone. Her neck forced itself closer. And closer. And...

She fell back. Tried again. Fell back again. The glass was mocking her. She was strong enough to reach it. She had to be that strong. She pulled against the restraints harder, wriggling just a touch closer. She was almost there. She could smell it—smell it like she could smell a hundred other unpleasant odors. It smelled clean and cool, a welcome change.

Her nose nudged the glass. Barli surged back, feeling like a rocking horse as she tried to use the momentum to stretch just that tiny little bit more. Her throat was raw. She'd been screaming. She knew she'd been screaming. Her nose brushed the rim again. Just a little farther and she could get her teeth around it...

It stuttered, stammered, and fell. The liquid bled from the glass, rolling away, and Barli leaned forward and licked the table where the smallest rills tumbled toward her.

There was the clang of metal on metal and Barli lay back as the keyhole turned. They'd restrained and locked her in? Just how dangerous did they think she was?

The door swung open and a young, relatively short man dressed in mustard yellow robes entered the room. His eyes were impassive, his face one that could not be picked out from a crowd. Even with a face, he was nearly faceless. His features bled into each other like a child's watercolor. Dislike curdled in her stomach until she realized what she was doing. Stopped. Then realized who she was, and that it was okay now if she didn't like men like him. She hated him again.

His gaze flicked over to the fallen cup. "You are resistant still," he observed. His voice was like slack in a belay.

Barli hated him more. "I'm *thirsty*."

He picked the glass up, turning it over in his gloved hand. Aside from his face, no part of his skin was visible. His getup was complete, with no holes in his defense. She wondered if she could spit in his face. No, he was too far away—and she couldn't gather any saliva anyway. "I expect someone like you to be belligerent," he said, "but generally when someone is facing death they are a tad more graceful." He sighed. "I expect it is the demon in you."

She shut her mouth. Barli didn't *want* to die. Not right now, anyway. Barli was not good at keeping quiet. No one had *told* her what to do in situations like this. No one she knew had ever been in this situation, though. She supposed the Priests liked that. No one could be coached. It was a fresh new terror for every victim.

He set the glass back on the table. "I see hatred in your eyes. Some of our residents are grateful, you know. You should be too. No one else will care for you anymore."

That was why her face ached, pained with a thousand fires. Barli closed her eyes, hating the nearly faceless man still more. There was no getting out of this. There never would be. "*Kitadu!*"

"Don't you want to be taken care of? If you want to

die…it can be arranged. But we prefer not to kill." The Priest shook his head. "We're nearly overrun as it is."

Barli thrashed against the straps before settling. It was hopeless. The man watched her impassively for several long minutes, waiting.

Finally, she unhinged her tense jaw. "I don't want to die," she said through gritted teeth.

"Good. I assume you want to be given freedom too. I understand that our way of life here can be confusing to those not accustom to its peculiarities. We try to let the residents handle their own matters. We have far too many things to do than tend to your needs. So. Unless you need a Priest, do not look for one unless you are called."

She had to crane her next to keep a good view of him. "When do I get out of here?" she asked, her arms tugging at their chokepoints.

"You are a dangerous one," he said. "We have to be careful with you. We have a locked ward for new arrivals. You'll begin your time there. If you manage not to kill anyone, you will be released into the rest of the Asylum, be given a job, and expected to do your work for the home we provide. It's only fair, given what you are."

He hadn't answered her question. Soon, she hoped. "And if I do kill someone?"

"We try to keep our residents alive, so we'd be forced to remove the danger."

They would kill her. Not surprising. But—"What if someone tries to kill *me*?"

"Consider it for the best," he said, "but it only happens about once a year. You're probably fine."

Barli lay in insufferable silence for several minutes. If someone tried to kill her, she was not going down. Assuming she wasn't locked in shackles, she was sure she could find a way out, if she had to. The only problem was surviving once she did so. "Can I have water?" she asked.

The Priest appraised her quietly. "I will send one of our residents in to help you. If he feels comfortable, he may free you. Otherwise you will wait here, longer."

She hated the words coming out of her mouth, but she did not want to jeopardize her situation. Besides, she was incalculably thirsty. "Thank you."

"You'll do fine here, as long as you remember what you are."

She shouldn't be upset. Why would she be? It was hard to deny the fact that she belonged here. She should be glad she was alive—that she even had a second chance. But…but what if she'd held things together a little better, a little longer? Maybe she wouldn't be here now. Now and forever. She closed her eyes, letting her head sink back against the hard pillow. The scents were less overwhelming now, but she still hated them. There were too many and the ones that could be picked out clashed.

Barli heard the door swing shut again. This time it was left unlocked. No good to her, of course. She was still restrained. Perhaps the reason it had been locked was not for the other's safety, but for her own.

She tried to turn over in the bed, but it was impossible. She couldn't get comfortable, though her back ached from the stillness. Barli did not like to stay still. Even less, she was quickly finding, did she like to be bound into stillness.

Her discomfort grew until her anger was far less tempered. If that Priest had waited too much longer before showing up, she would have been far sourer to him. And she might be dead now too, if that was the case. If she'd been too sour with him, he might have tipped her fate the other way.

Finally, she heard the door opening again. A young boy walked into the room. He couldn't have been more than twelve. The telltale brands on his face marked him instantly for what he was: a Sin. Some of her anger dimmed—she wondered how long he had been here. He looked perfectly comfortable, though his gaze flicked uneasily to her wrists.

At least he wasn't staring at her face.

Barli's face flushed. No one would want to again—and she knew why he wouldn't want to. She looked toward the empty glass. "W-water?" she asked hopefully.

He held it out to her, face flushing when she didn't take it. "Sorry," he said quietly. He extended the glass to her lips, carefully letting her drink from it. She sipped at the water eagerly, gulping down what he offered her. She drank the whole glass.

He offered her a little smile as he set it down. "Hello," he said.

"H-hello. Could you—I mean can you release me?" she said. She didn't want to yell at a child, though it was certainly tempting.

The boy tilted his head. "Are you going to hurt me?" he asked seriously.

Barli swallowed. "I—"

"That's why you're here, isn't it? You were hurting."

"I—"

"And when you're hurting, sometimes other people get hurt too."

Her fist clenched. "I won't hurt you," she promised.

He lifted his chin. "Good. You know they say the demon doesn't want to attack itself, but sometimes it can't recognize itself for what it is."

"You seem like you've studied an awful lot."

He shrugged, gesturing to his leg. She realized his foot was somehow deformed. So he'd been here a long time— probably for years, if not his whole life. No wonder he seemed comfortable here. "There's not much else to do after so much time." He slowly went to the straps around her wrist. "Do you mean your promises?"

"They're promises, aren't they?"

"Yes," he said, "but some people don't mean them."

"My mother said, if you're to have any honor at all, you must mean what you promise." Her mother had also said she would always love her, but that was clearly inaccurate. So did her mother have no honor either? The thought drew her brows together.

He undid them gently, turning her arm over to look at the thick bandage wrapped around it. She tugged away from him, sitting up as soon as she was capable.

Barli touched her wrists, rubbing her blood flow back. "What's your name?"

The boy gave her a strange look. "No one has a name," he said. "Or we all have the same one."

"How do you tell anyone apart then?" Barli asked. She

wasn't about to give her name up! Her parents had given it to her.

He leaned close to her. "Well, I suppose we do have names, or nicknames, but we're not allowed to have them. But we're Sins, so who cares if we break a rule or two, right?"

"I'm Barli," she said.

"You have a real name."

"You don't?"

"Maybe I did, but I don't know it. Farren calls me Ginsun," he said in a conspiratorial voice, "but don't tell anyone."

She smiled sadly. This was her life now—full of nameless people who knew the rules need not apply to them. Part of it was thrilling. More of it was frightening. "Okay," she agreed.

Ginsun stepped back, picking up both of the empty glasses. "Do you want me to show you around?"

Barli nearly growled. "I'm sure I can figure it out. It's locked, anyway, isn't it?"

He nodded.

"Do you live in the locked ward all the time?"

Ginsun tilted his head. "They let me out," he said. "I'm not the most dangerous sort of demon."

And who was? And who might be dangerous to always live in the locked ward? Barli wondered how dangerous she was.

She got to her feet, though her ankles felt weak. How long had she been unconscious? Her wrist smarted and the pain radiating from her face was irritating. It was also a constant reminder—as if this place couldn't manage that on its own.

Barli threw the door open and hurried out into the hallway. There was no escaping this place—but it didn't mean for a moment she wouldn't try. Ginsun followed more slowly behind her, his uneven gait echoing in the hallway.

The hallway was short, a few assorted doors before the hallway opened up into a far larger main room. There were two small couches. It almost seemed…cozy. There was a kitchen adjoining the room, where some of the less horrific scents were coming from. A young girl stood on a stool, stirring the pot. An older woman stood behind her, watching critically.

"A little slower, tai," the woman cautioned.

Barli glanced around, surprised. Were there only children and elders here? "Th-this is where they keep the dangerous ones?"

"You're the most dangerous one here," Ginsun informed her. He hurried over to the girl, looking into the pot she was stirring.

Barli looked down at her wrist. Was she truly so dangerous? Were they really afraid of her? Was no one else here so wrong? "There's no one else?"

"Except Farren. We had a few others, a while ago. But they're gone now."

Dead, he meant. "And how long has Farren been locked in here?" Farren—the one who had given Ginsun a name. How long had Ginsun been here? His face looked healed. It must have been quite some time.

"Farren?" Ginsun shrugged. "Longer than me," he said.

"*I* won't be here that long, will I?" The Priest hadn't said.

Ginsun shrugged. "Probably not."

The girl stopped stirring, looking up and meeting Barli's eye. She smiled widely. "Who's the new girl, Ginny?"

Ginsun stuck his tongue out. "None of your business, Walunata."

"No fair!" She jumped off the stool and ran up to Barli. This place certainly didn't seem intimidating. And with a bunch of young kids around, they were almost cute. The girl tilted her head, staring at Barli's wrist. "Does it hurt?" she asked.

Barli held her arm to her chest. Then again, kids could be pretty obnoxious. "No."

Walunata pursed her lips, sticking her chest out. "I don't believe you," she said.

These were not normal children, Barli thought. They did not act with the proper poise—perhaps that was because it was not expected of them. They did not have the manners Barli had been instilled with—not that she'd been the best at following them. Still, she would never have been so blunt.

There was nowhere to go—there was nowhere to hide. How did she escape these little people? She stepped around Walunata and up to another door, blinking to see another hallway beyond. She tried the door, but found it locked.

Locked in. Locked in with nowhere to go. She ran to another door and tried it. Locked again. How many locks were there in this place?

She flung another door open. Empty. She ran down the hallway, pulling the rest of the doors open. There weren't too many: the space was small. She felt like she couldn't breathe. There wasn't enough room to move. There were too few people. It was all too little.

She crashed into several small rooms. One was clearly storage of some sort, while yet another was an empty room like hers. Still another had some possessions, and even had a small window. But it was still a dead end. She slammed all the doors she had opened shut again.

One led out into the air, and Barli hurried into the courtyard. It was a substantially sized garden and Barli finally stopped her rapid rush. She took in the fresh new air. This was where all the herbal smells were coming from— this garden, full of plants in bloom and unidentified greenery sweeping out of carefully constructed containers— overflowing and yet there were no dead branches or wilting flowers. It was well maintained.

The air still smelled. Barli thought she would choke on the air here, so full of flavor and too much of it foul. Barli walked the perimeter of the courtyard, but the walls were high and unscalable. There was no chance of escape here— she could not even get a good look at the rest of the Asylum. The walls carried on upward for a good twenty feet. They were massive, thick, and sheer. A few small peepholes, more like arrow slits for archers, were all that gave access to the outside world.

Barli pressed her eye against one of the slits, looking at the street sweeping down from the Asylum's summit. The Asylum met the mountain, but the fishing town met the water. The Asylum lingered between shore and hill, an untouchable middle ground no one wanted anything to do with.

She could see a few people wandering the streets, their faces plain, their presence ordinary. They were just people.

If she was just a person, she wouldn't be like that—caught up in the drudgery of daily life where simply doing your job and being with your family was enough. How trite and selfish!

But that was how normal people were. And that was how she'd known, in her heart of hearts, that she wasn't one of them. Her parents would likely say she had gotten demon-touched, some horrific accident had landed her this way, but Barli knew there hadn't been a moment when she had become decidedly different. It had been a gradual sureness in her character. She thought it had always been there, just less obviously so.

The look was not enough. Even knowing it was populated only by dreariness, Barli wanted to run through the streets, ride old Masanu's poor heifer, and jump off the docks into the water. Her hand crept to the wall and she tried to find some crack to jam her fingers into. She wanted *out*. The world was much too large to be contained like this. She was much too large. People did not belong in containers.

She hoisted herself up on the window slit, but could get no further traction to boost herself higher. She scrambled at the wall until her limbs were weak—an embarrassingly short time—and fell backward into a patch of plants.

"New girl, what are you doing? Farren's going to be mad!"

The little girl had followed her. She had wide eyes, like two ripe tomatoes just waiting to fall from the branch. Her long hair was braided neatly down her back, though as Barli stared at her she took the strand and fit the dead ends into her mouth, chewing furiously. "He won't like it," she said through the hair.

Barli sat up slowly, feeling a slight twinge in her ankle as she stood up. She had crushed several of the plants. Barli growled lowly, making her way past the arrogant girl once more.

The rest of the ward met with similar resistance— anything that led to something further was locked. The other doors swung into useless rooms…though there weren't enough of them. Other people lived here, though they seemed to be out and about. There was one door that was also locked, but it didn't seem to lead anywhere else. It just looked like another bedroom.

Like a storm, she found her way back to the main room with the adjoining kitchen. The older woman was stirring that same pot. It couldn't have been too long. Barli threw herself on the couch, feeling as though her body was crawling.

"Would you like some stew, dear? It'll be for dinner later, but you've been sleeping for a while."

Barli gave her a blank stare. She was hungry. "I want a key!"

"Now, child, that's not the way you'll get out of here," the woman cautioned.

"You have one, don't you? You have to be able to get out." She fought the urge to go up to the woman and shake her out, just to see if something would come falling out.

"Haven't you noticed, tai? The doors lock from the outside. We're all just as trapped in here as you."

She opened her mouth for several seconds. "But…but you get out, don't you?"

"When they let us."

"How do you stand it?"

The older woman shrugged. "It isn't so bad, once you get to know the people here. You'll find you don't much want to go anywhere else. The rest of the world's not likely to be kind to you." The older woman had no obvious defects beyond her face, which had been branded just as the children's had.

Barli reached up and touched her face for the first time since she'd awoken. The skin was irritated and painful, but she could feel the ridges and uneven rises of her damaged skin. There was no changing it now. She was marked.

"So that's it, then?"

"You're a Sin, child, what did you expect?"

Barli had no answer for that.

She spent the rest of the afternoon exploring the rest of the rooms she had access to—a grand total of about six, plus the garden. Most were nothing but empty bedrooms, just like the one she'd awoken in. One of the doors she realized must have led to a similar bedroom was inexplicably locked.

Ginsun and Walunata had been called back into the kitchen with the older woman, who they called Parsley. They helped her—or at least they tried to. Running around the kitchen, sometimes spilling the ingredients she asked for, they were more a hindrance than help.

Barli rubbed her wrist and resisted the urge to kick at the locked doors. "How long?" she asked. "How long until they let me out?"

"You cannot seem eager for it, tai, or they will know they cannot keep you. They cannot have you running away."

Where would she run? But she would try. She knew she would try. It was better than being trapped here. Besides, she needed to see Visea again. "Will you tell them?"

Parsley's wrinkles pulled at the corner of her eyes. "I will."

"Why?"

The old woman dipped her head, smelling the stew she had steaming. "I know you will understand in time."

"I won't! It's not right."

Parsley sighed. "Many feel that way, when they first arrive. But they learn—as will you. You'll stay on your own accord and you won't ask such questions."

"Ginsun, where's Farren? Has he seen the garden yet?" Walunata asked.

There was a knock on one of the locked doors that looked out into the hallway. Parsley wiped her hands. "Go on, you two. On the couch. Child," and now she was addressing Barli, "you must go back to your room now. I'll come for you, when they've gone."

"You're going to lock me in? You *do* have a key."

"Please, child, or no one will eat."

Barli's mouth opened slightly. "No one?"

Ginsun stuck his chin out. "They won't open the door

till you're separated. They don't want you getting out just yet. Everyone comes here to eat. Except Farren."

"I don't want to." How could they make her go back, become trapped in an even smaller space? How could she escape?

"But Li-li! I'm hungry," Walunata groaned. "I don't wanna wait!"

The children continued whining and Barli could see the hallway filling with people. How many were there? She wanted to know—but Parlsey was firm. That door was not opening until Barli was locked away.

Barli slunk back down the hall, slamming the door behind her. She sat on the bed, listening as the door swiveled locked. She sat on her hands, rocking back and forth slightly.

She stood and went back to her door, leaning against the locked handle. She listened to the sounds in the hallway, but she couldn't quite hear anything coherent. Barli slammed her hand against the wall.

Barli wished there was a window, or *something* she could use to get more of a view. She needed more than this limited view: four walls all around. Dull.

Her fingers groped for her wrist, still throbbing slightly as she slowly undid the bandages. The bandages clung to the cut, the healing scab melded to the fabric. She hissed as she pulled it free.

Fresh blood seeped up from the edges of the wound, but she noted that they had done some stitch-work to keep it mostly closed up. For a moment she contemplated biting the stitches free – but then she certainly wouldn't have seen

Visea again. If she wanted that chance, she had to watch herself. She had to behave. And she couldn't be ripping herself apart. Barli had told the Priest the truth, at least for the time being: she wanted to live.

She rewrapped the wound, sighing. Someone who would do a thing like that was clearly crazy. She deserved to be here, didn't she? She was nothing special; she was only a Sin, like the rest.

The door finally clicked open again. "There's food, if you want some, tai."

Barli didn't move, but let the old woman walk away. Once she no longer had to be kept, it didn't seem as bad to stay. In fact, the quiet had its high points. There were no children to bother her here.

She finally got up, walking into the kitchen slowly, her shoulders hunched and every footstep sinking into the cold stone floor. The two children and the older woman had disappeared as well. There were few enough places for them to go—was she all alone now?

Barli stepped up to the pot, hunting around the kitchen until she found a bowl. There was some other food out too, and she stuck her fingers into an orange mashed substance, licking them to find a surprisingly sweet morsel on her fingers. She found a plate and piled it with the orange mush, forgoing the hardy-looking stew. Parsley could cook, but not all of it looked appetizing.

She sat down on the couch, glancing around dully. There was nothing to do here, and nothing to see. She found a small bookshelf hiding in the corner, though it was almost entirely fully of texts about demons, all written by the Priesthood. She rolled her eyes. The literature was all dull religious tomes.

Barli ate with her fingers, licking them clean. Finally she set the plate down, noting the large stack of dishes to the side of the large washtub. Were they left for the next day? Surely one of the Sins did the dishes. A janitor—a maid—someone must come through here. But everything was quiet. Eerie.

Had they left her all alone here?

Barli got to her feet, walking down the two small hallways. There was no one in sight. She sighed, pulling the doors open again just to check them. They were empty, one after the other—until she found that one of the locked doors gave way. She thrust it open, nearly slamming her shoulder into it.

A dark-eyed boy glared up at her. His face was made up of soft lines, but the look he was giving her was anything but kind. "What are you *doing* here?" he asked. "This isn't your room." He had long black hair that reached down to his shoulders, rough and uneven. His eyes were more black than brown.

"I…" Barli was so startled she shut the door again. The boy would have been around her age, fourteen or fifteen. Farren—it must have been. Somehow she'd thought Farren would be older, the way Ginsun talked about him.

And why was his door open now? It must have been locked before. How dangerous was he? Barli examined the door. It, too, locked from the outside. So they'd kept him in the whole day? Trapped in that tiny room? And now he was staying in there? What sort of crazy person was he?

He definitely belonged here—not like her.

Barli swallowed. His hair had covered part of his face, but she could still easily see he was branded, like they all were. But that wasn't what had struck her most about him. He seemed impossibly sad. She didn't think she'd ever seen a look like that on a person's face before, and it disturbed her.

She let go of the knob and found her way back to the main room. Her hands were itching. Alone with Farren in a locked ward. Alone with a boy furiously wilted. He was like half a man, and not because of his age. There was a piece of him missing and for the first time she thought maybe the Priests really were on to something: that was the look of a demon if she'd ever met one. Perhaps it wasn't surprising he was kept in a locked ward.

Her fingers were still itching, the way they did sometimes where she couldn't bear to be still. She would have run, if she could have. Instead, Barli moved to the washtub and picked up a rag, dipping it into the water.

Before she'd meant to, the dishes were washed. She couldn't figure out where to put them, so she left them scattered out across the countertop to dry. She went around and tried the rest of the doors, the ones she hadn't gotten to. She went about it more carefully, scared that someone else might lie behind those doors to surprise her. But they were still all empty.

She wandered out into the courtyard garden. The night was fresh with a subtle chill permeating the area. She looked through the small window slits again. The streets were empty. There were no other people to even watch. What sort of misery was this? To be so fully alone, isolated. She hated it.

Barli wandered back to her room. She shut the door, for the first time afraid. She didn't like the idea that Farren could get into her room. Even less did she like the knowledge that he was the only one who possibly could on short notice. He was locked in here because he was dangerous, right? So why had they kept him locked up during the day but unlocked it for the night?

Was he too dangerous for the children?

But Ginsun and Walunata certainly spoke as if they knew him. Farren had named Ginsun. Walunata had warned her about disturbing the garden. So he wasn't always locked away. Or had they only talked through locked doors?

Her head hurt trying to work out the puzzle. Part of her wanted to go back to his room and demand answers. But she did not want to risk disturbing him again; his response had been so fierce the first time.

Barli groaned, flopping onto her stomach as she tried to get comfortable on the mat. Would the Priest be back tomorrow? When would they let her out? They had to eventually, right?

She turned again, staring up at the ceiling. The roof was high, but it wasn't high enough to match the walls of the garden. There had to be another floor above them— possibly more than one.

Barli had never thought much about the Asylum, but now that she was here, there wasn't much else to think about. Besides, to think about something besides the Asylum would mean dwelling on an old life that was no longer open to her. The brand on her face changed everything.

Her fingers went to the ginger swelling. She knew it would only get better with time. She was surprised any of them would look at her right now, with the way her face was swollen and disfigured.

Her mind would not keep quiet and the night was not a restful one, but in time she managed to fall asleep.

Chapter Two

THE NEXT THREE DAYS were almost exactly the same. Within limits, it seemed, Barli had no problem limiting herself—as much as she might dislike her current boundaries, having now explored them she saw little reason to mingle in the main room with the two younger children and the older woman. It wasn't that she disliked them, but rather that she had no interest in getting close to anyone in this place. They would have to let her out eventually.

The only other place she spent time besides her room—and doing a load of dishes in the evenings once all the others were gone—was the small courtyard garden. She liked the feeling of air and sun on her skin. Once a day, after making sure the children and Parlsey weren't watching, she attempted to scale the wall. It was, of course, an impossible task. With nothing to grab onto, it was virtually impossible to get any higher off the ground than whatever one could manage clinging to a windowed slot.

Barli didn't like asking questions—she didn't like not

knowing things, but she disliked admitting that fact more, so she didn't say anything. The children were precocious devils. Half the time they were playing tag, running around and hassling Parsley. Walunata wasn't there one day, and Ginsun took the opportunity to badger her, trying to get her to play games. In the end, she was so bored she decided to indulge him.

Although they played tag, Ginsun never went toward Farren's room, and Barli never checked whether it was locked or not. The look in his eye had been enough to scare her off for the time being.

From Ginsun's rambling, she figured out a few things. There were about fifty residents in the Asylum. They cooked the food for them here, in the locked portion of the ward. The day Walunata was gone, she was apparently assisting in some other task the commune took upon for itself. They lived mostly independently, though on rare occasions they were let out for short excursions, to see about important matters they needed to attend to. If she was lucky, someday she could get assigned to tasks that would let her out of the Asylum's walls and give her a glimpse back into the world she had once known. It would be different— but at least she would have some freedom. At least she would not be caught so deeply in this place.

So, it had become her goal—when Parsley and the others were around, she behaved. She was quiet. She followed Parsley's advice and made no mention of her desire to be free of this place. For whatever reason, Parsley believed she would eventually come to not want to leave, and although Barli was certain the older woman was touched in the head, she was the closest thing to authority Barli had to go on.

It was the fourth night she couldn't seem to get to sleep. She sighed for a substantial amount of time, turning aimlessly. She was tired of being alone. She had never spent so much time in isolation. Was she getting any closer to being let go? Barli hadn't seen a priest since she got here—except on occasion from through the windows.

The windows. They were her saving grace. She could spend hours looking out them, watching people pass. They were always so busy—none of them cared to take a glance and see who might be looking through the window at them.

Unable to sleep, she found her way to the courtyard, pushing the door open and out into the night. She stared up into the night sky, looking up at the stars. The empty streets were dull, but she found them more entertaining than her ceiling.

Barli wasn't sure how long she spent staring out the window before she was finally too tired to stay outside in the cold air. She found her way back to bed, finally falling asleep. Sometimes she thought she heard noises outside, but for the most part she ignored them.

The next day Barli woke up late. She had no official duties, as far as she could tell, and the emptiness of all of it was unnerving. She had never been so without something to do. Her parents had always kept her relatively busy—it was that way in every family, she guessed. Though she was actually used to confined spaces, having taken several trips on sea, sailing between the islands. Those trips were never longer than a few hours, however. This was a whole new level. Besides, when she was on a ship, she could see they were moving.

When Barli finally came out of her room, Ginsun was playing marbles in the hallway. The moment he saw her, he scrambled to his feet. "Barli! Come play with me," he said, dragging her back toward the small balls.

"Walunata's gone again today?"

He nodded sadly. "I want to get out too," he huffed. "You're boring."

Barli opened her mouth. "Hey! I can be fun."

"Oh yeah?" Ginsun asked. "Prove it!"

"I don't have to—" Barli rolled her eyes. "There's nothing to *do* around here. What do you expect?" She hadn't known they had marbles—and she had searched the place pretty carefully. Ginsun must have brought them in with him.

"And you smell," he said.

"What do you expect?" Barli snapped. "It's not like there's anywhere to get clean."

Ginsun stuck his tongue out. "Not my fault."

"Well, I'm pretty good at marbles. Unless you think the smell's going to be too much for you to take, I'm pretty sure I can take you."

"Yeah right!" Ginsun replied, scampering back to his marbles. "I've been playing for forever!"

Barli knew it would be the nice thing to let Ginsun win, but he wasn't too terrible and Barli hadn't played a real game in a long time. Besides, Barli didn't lose. "That's three for me," she said when Ginsun groaned once again.

"Ginsun, I need your help!" Parlsey called from the kitchen.

"I'm going to beat you next time," he promised as he scampered away.

From the smell in the kitchen, it wouldn't be long until she was locked away again. Barli wandered over to the courtyard. To her surprise, when she turned the handle, it didn't move.

Her eyes widened as she tried the door again. Still locked. Barli took a step back, staring through the thin window out into the small garden. Weird. Barli looked more carefully and finally saw a black head between the tender herbal garden fronds.

Farren. It must have been Farren. So he was here now, locked in the outdoor space instead? She backed away from the door slowly. There was no going outside today, it seemed.

"Why's the door locked?" she asked as she wandered back to the main room.

"Cause Farren wanted to be outside," Ginsun said with a shrug. "He usually spends several days a week out there, when the weather's good."

Parsley pulled a long pan from the oven. Fresh, warm bread. It smelled good. "He picked a good day for it too. There's a bad wind on its way." She took on a tired look to her eye, while Ginsun laid the plates out. "Best get back to your room, Barli. You can eat later."

Ginsun tossed her a marble. "I don't want to have an unfair advantage," he said. "You better keep practicing too, or I'm going to beat you!"

Barli barely caught it, running the glass through her fingers. "You won't," she said as she made her way back to her quarters. She sighed as she heard the lock click into place.

When Barli awoke the next morning, there was only silence. She wandered into the kitchen to find it barren. Not even Parsley seemed to be there. The loneliness unsettled her. There was absolutely no one else around.

She walked around, testing the doors again. The main door was still locked. Barli tested the garden door and found it unlocked again. Barli couldn't find anyone there either. It was just her—just her and Farren. And she would let him stay in his no doubt locked room.

Barli sighed, throwing herself on the couch. Didn't they have to make food here? Or was someone going to come later on? Was there another kitchen? Then why would they have been using this one?

She had spent a night alone—a bad enough state of affairs. Was she supposed to spend the day in isolation as well? Barli pulled the books off the shelf, in search of anything that might give her a good diversion. None of the titles were interesting in the slightest. Barli threw one of the books against the wall, growling. Even if Ginsun was irritating, she was quickly finding he was better than nothing.

Barli huffed, stacking and unstacking the books in a frenzy of disquiet. Barli's eyes drifted back down toward the corridor where Ferran's room was.

She slunk down the hallway toward his room, finally sitting outside his door, her back to the wall. Barli took out

Ginsun's marble, rolling it through her fingers. At least he'd left her something to play with. She laid the marble on the ground and flicked it against Ferran's door.

It didn't take long before she was bored of that too. What else was there to do here? Her mind flashed back to the kitchen, but she quickly shut that path down. It wasn't likely to help her get out of here.

"Hey," she said.

There was no response.

"Hey!" She couldn't take the silence or the emptiness. "Hey, Farren!"

The door remained still. She flung her marble against it again.

"Come on, you've got to be as lonely as me! So talk to me!"

The silence was insufferable. She wanted to break it. She needed to hear another voice beside her own.

"Shatung!" she cursed. "Just say something to me! Come *on*!" She pounded her fist against the door. "At least tell me you want to be left alone! Something!"

Cursing to herself, she stood up, turning her back on the stupid door. Parsley had to come eventually, right? Barli wondered if this wasn't some test to see if she could be let out. They were that sort of crazy, weren't they?

"Who are you?"

She stopped dead. The voice was quiet, caught between her and a thick door. Another voice! Finally! "What?" she asked instinctively.

"Who are you?"

"I-I'm Barli." She walked slowly back to the door,

putting the palm of her hand against the door, as close to human contact it seemed she would be.

"What's a name tell me?"

"Hh…"

"I can't see you. I don't know you. So what does a name tell me? It's only a way to differentiate between voices that mean nothing at all."

Barli's eyes widened. "Well, I'm here, doesn't that tell you something more?"

"Everyone I know is here, so no, not really." Farren said.

She wasn't sure whether she was irritated or excited by the boy's oddity. "Well, then…tell me who you are." She didn't know what to say.

There was soft quiet on the other side of the door.

"What? If you want to know, you've got to tell me something too. I've never told someone who I am before, not like that." Barli complained.

"I've heard that people describe themselves, by comparing them to other people. But I've only known a few people to know how I am like and unlike them. So…I don't really know who I am."

"Then I guess we'll just have to figure it out as we go, right?"

There was silence from the door. Barli growled.

"Hey! What else have you got to do?" she yelled, quickly getting irritated again. "And where is Parsley and the others? Why is no one else here?"

The door creaked open and Barli took a step back. It

wasn't locked? She'd just assumed it was, but if no one else was around…

"No one else is here," he said, "because today is my day to cook."

Barli's eyes widened.

She had only caught a quick look at Farren before. Now he stood before her and she couldn't seem to look away. There was no obvious reason to call him a Sin: it was not some physical ailment that had sent him here. At least, not one she could see. Farren had surprisingly small eyes. He was thinner than her, and smaller too. His body seemed as though it had been grown in a space too small for it, and that had caused what might have been a heavily-built powerful person to end up stunted and scrawny. It was unsettling and contradictory—he was someone who had been forced to fit in a place too small for him.

His long hair was unkempt and seemed to be cut at odd angles. Part of it had been roughly braided, teased into something unrecognizable.

Ferran's face was heavily marred by the branding. In addition to the usual brand, he had an extra one on his other cheek, so that no matter which side you looked at him from, you would be sure to know. The brand was larger than usual too, and across his forehead was another brand that Barli didn't recognize. She had never seen it before. He was obviously a Sin—even more inescapably so than others.

His clothes were at once too big and too small for him. The sleeves of his shirt went halfway past his elbow while the fabric was loose around his chest, falling so far down that he looked as though he was wearing a dress.

It was his eyes that were the most riveting portion of his appearance. They seemed small, but perhaps it was only because there was so little reflected back in them. Dark enough to be black, they were little pits, all the more powerful for their diminutive size.

He didn't look dangerous. He looked like a kid with no one who cared about him to show him how to take care of himself.

Barli's heart thudded. "F-farren."

"That is what the others call me," he said. He stepped out into the hallway, closing the door softly behind him. "I don't know what it means or who it says I am."

Barli took another step back. Now that he was there in front of her and they were face to face, she wasn't sure what to say. "You cook?" she asked finally.

He nodded. He awkwardly skirted around her, as though not sure how humans were supposed to respond to being in close quarters to another person.

She trailed after him, watching as he started pulling pans from cupboards. "Why wouldn't you talk to me, before?"

He did not seem to have any directions, but he never hesitated, making his movements with practice. "I don't really want to talk to you now, either."

Ouch. "Why?"

"You'll be gone soon, like everyone else. They come for a few days and then they leave and they never come back. So I don't bother to get to know anyone anymore."

Barli rolled her eyes. "So what? Maybe if they did, they

would come back and see you. And even if they didn't, isn't something better than nothing?"

Farren ignored her, going back to his work, quickly chopping up vegetables.

She narrowed her eyes. "So. You think they'll let me out?"

"If they don't kill you," he said.

Her heart thudded. "Do you think they would?"

He glanced up at her and she took another step back. His eyes swept over her—over her face, her chest, her arms, her wrist. "As long as you don't do anything crazy, they have no reason to."

"What would you know about that?" Barli snarled.

He turned around, stoking the fire that always made the room toasty during the day.

"Huh? What do you know about anything!"

"Do you think it's surprising?" he asked quietly.

"What?"

"That I wouldn't want to talk to you. You're volatile. If you speak to a Priest like that, they'll certainly kill you."

"And you wouldn't mind that at all, would you?"

"Why would I? You messed up my garden."

And for the first time, she saw a dangerous glint in his eye.

She swallowed. "I-I…well it's not like I meant to."

"And how much of any of this do you mean?" He frowned. "And how can I trust anything you say or do, when you do things you say you don't mean."

Barli's eyes widened. She turned and stalked off, kicking the wall angrily. Where did he get off saying things like that? Everyone said things they didn't mean! She was hardly unique in that fashion. It didn't mean anything at all.

She slammed the door, returning to her room and flopping onto the bed. Farren. He was still a mystery, and now she felt she had even less to go on than before. She had learned several things—he was ornery, protective of his garden, and could apparently cook something. But none of that seemed particularly helpful. She had known two of those things already, given the way he'd pressed her out of his room.

Barli fumed. What right did he have to question her anyway? She really hadn't meant to do anything to those stupid plants. And it had been her first day, anyway. Didn't he give her any slack? What was his *problem*? She snarled at the door, though she was sure he was not outside it. He had little care for her, after all.

Her fingers twitched impulsively, the way they often did when she was about to do something…unadvisable.

Barli's scowl lengthened and she passed from her room, through the main room where Farren was cooking, and on to Ferran's precious garden.

The air did little to calm her, but she could pretend it did. At least the air was slightly less stank. Barli narrowed her eyes as she glanced through the slits again. She wished she could see the rest of the Asylum. This view was just teasing—she could see all of these people she couldn't speak with, people she never would have the chance to know. And she wanted to know. She didn't really want to know them, but she did wish she could at least have the chance. The opportunity to do something was nearly as important as doing the thing itself.

She stared up at the sky, bright even as the day was passing. Barli's head twisted away till she was looking at Ferran's precious garden. It seemed he cared more about these small green sticks than her life. What sort of messed up person was that?

He did belong in this place.

Barli hands grasped at the dirt where some of the plants had come loose, whether from the last time Barli had fallen and crushed them, or some other unfortunate time. She wove her fingers through the dirt, playing with it until it pulled beneath her fingers. She wondered vaguely if there was anything poisonous in this garden, but disregarded the thought quickly. Who would be stupid enough to let something like that grow here? Surely, the Priests would have disallowed such a thing. Barli wouldn't know what was poison and what wasn't either way. But Farren was just as much a victim as her. The Priests had built this place, put Farren here, isolated from everything, so that all he had was a few plants. How could she destroy them?

She lingered in the garden as long as she could, but ultimately her weariness drove her back inside to Farren, the most interesting aspect of the locked ward. Barli stood at the counter, watching him work. As usual, he was ignoring her.

"I really didn't mean to."

He glanced up at her, as though surprised to see her still there. "Not meaning to do something doesn't change what's been done."

"So? Of course not! But what does that matter? Look, I don't mean everything I do, 'cause it's an accident!"

"What is an accident?"

"Ah…" What? "Like if you dropped something you were cooking, it's not because you meant to, it's just an unfortunate thing that happened."

Ferran's eyes narrowed. "How did it happen then?" he asked.

Barli blinked. "Well, I was—I was trying to climb the wall, only there's not many footholds so it wasn't exactly easy."

"You fell?"

Something about his tone irritated her. "So what if I did? I'd like to see you do better!"

Farren set down the knife. "How high did you get?"

"I—ah—not far," she admitted. "There's nothing to hold on to."

"Are other walls different?"

Barli gaped at him. "Have you—have you never seen a stone wall?" she asked.

Ferran's eyes narrowed as he looked up at her. "No," he said. "The only things I've ever seen is what can be observed from this ward."

Barli's eyes widened and she stepped back. "Wh…you've never been out? Ever?"

Farren shook his head. "What did you think all this security was for? The setup is convenient for the Priests' other tasks, but primarily it's for me."

She stood in quiet shock as he turned back to his work at hand, utterly unconcerned. She knew they kept him separate but…never? He'd never been outside these confines? Astounding. "Wh…" How did someone survive that sort of existence? She couldn't help but look him over again, unerring and deep pity winding around her heart.

"I've tried climbing it before. I've never gotten anywhere. I don't think I have the strength for it. Or the practice. Maybe I'm doing it wrong."

"It's not an easy wall to climb. Believe me—I've climbed plenty," Barli said. They were settling slowly into a conversation, albeit a strange one. She couldn't help it—she could see why he might be so peculiar. His life was… improbable—and enough to make anyone perpetually cranky. "Anyway, like I said I really didn't mean anything."

"I understand now," Farren said. He tested the fire and placed a pot into its depths, wiping his brow. He looked away. "All the same, I don't want to get to know you. What I said is all still true."

Barli tilted her head. "Well, what I said it still true, too. Don't you want the chance for something more?"

He stepped away from the kitchen. "When I was younger and new people would come, I was always so excited. I would look forward to seeing them. And—they'd play with me sometimes. Back then, people even touched me, sometimes. They had to." He sighed. "And I would get so excited to be around them. They would say they were coming back, but they didn't." He wasn't looking at her. "I used to cry, when I was younger, for hours, and no one would come."

Barli shivered a little. It seemed horrid. "I wouldn't do that."

"And I don't cry anymore, so it doesn't matter anyway." He glanced sideways at her. "I know you won't come back. You're flighty already. They'll have a hard time keeping you under control. I can tell. And they will kill you, you know, if you leave without permission. They'll send the Black Sins."

Barli felt as though the temperature in the room suddenly dropped. The Black Sins. She stared at the fire, not feeling its heat. "You're so casual about it!"

"I've known many people who have been dealt with by the Black Sins. I have never known any of them well, nor do I intend to."

She swallowed. "Aren't you scared of them?"

"Why?" Farren asked. "I don't think death would be so bad." He gestured to her wrist. "And clearly you've felt that way too, at least once."

"What do you know about that?" Barli snapped, holding her wrist to her side. How dare he!

Farren wandered over to the bookcase, picking up one of the tomes she had let fall earlier in one of her many irritated musings...or mini rages, whichever term you preferred. "Ginsun tells me everything he knows."

And what did he know? She'd never told him anything. "Well, he doesn't know as much as he thinks," she replied snappishly. That boy was probably always underfoot. Maybe he did know the situation. But he couldn't know how she felt about it. She hadn't told anyone what she'd been thinking. None of them would have understood either. None of them understood her.

He shrugged. "Maybe not." Farren was not good at

human interaction—whether he was lying or bothered or didn't quite believe her, she could read it all in his face. It was a simple matter, since he had never had to conceal his emotions from anyone.

Barli bit back a snarl. "I don't want to die," she said. "I never did."

Farren gave her a curious look. "Then why," he asked, "did you try to kill yourself?"

Chapter Three

BARLI DIDN'T COME OUT of her room for two days. She wasn't sure why Ferran's comment had struck her so much, but that had been the end of her conversation and any conversation they'd had since. Ginsun came knocking on her door, but she ignored him. She heard Walunata too, and they played outside of her door.

There was nothing to do in her room but think, and though such a pastime did not suit her, she endured it all the same.

Even during the nights, when there was no one to see, when it was only Farren she might risk coming across, and even then it was unlikely, she stayed in her room. She was planning on doing the same, despite her noisy stomach, until she heard a strange sound. She couldn't say exactly what it was, but it sounded like some sort of pain. Someone was hurting.

She ignored it a while longer, and she thought the sound became fainter with her negligence. There. Someone else would take care of it—what were the chances she could do anything about it anyway, trapped as she was in the locked ward?

There was a hesitant knock on her door.

What? At this hour? Could it be a Priest? Everyone else had left the ward by now. It should have just been her and Farren—and there was no way Farren was at her door.

She sat up slowly, staring at her closed door. Perhaps she had imagined it.

No. There it was again.

She opened the door slowly. It *was* Farren—after all he'd said about not wanting to get to know people what was he doing at her door? "Wh-what do you want?" He didn't look hurt. He hadn't been crying.

"Come on," he said. "I need your help."

Her help? She followed him as he walked quickly back through the corridor and out into the garden, following the source of the pitiful sound. "What..."

There. It was a black smidgen, mewling softly. A...a kitten? Cats roamed the islands freely, but they weren't exactly common. Barli knelt beside the creature. It had a cut on its side and was breathing piteously between its pained cries.

She craned her neck toward Farren. He was standing awkwardly to the side, looking as though he was not sure what to do with his hands. "Do you have anything for wounds?"

Farren held up his hands. "I-I don't know."

Barli sighed. "Stay with her, okay?" She got up and

went rifling through the kitchen's drawers—but there was little to work with. Her gaze stopped at her wrist. There were some bandages. She grabbed some of the food from that night's meal and headed back into the garden. Farren was sitting on the ground, not touching the creature but still quite close. He had his hand held over it, nearly touching the kitten, but not quite.

She settled beside him. He moved away as though on instinct. She rolled her eyes and slowly unwound the bandages from around her wrist. She refolded them so they were clean, trying to ignore the stinging pain as she pulled them away from her wrist. Once she had repositioned them, she wrapped them around the kitten's side, pulling the wrap tight and affixing it with a clip. The kitten mewled in protest, but she was too weak to make a physical effort.

"What happened?" she asked, taking some of the food and feeding the small cat from her palm.

Farren had watched her with quiet interest. "I don't know. I just followed the sound."

He'd cared more than she had. Barli picked the kitten up and pulled her into her arms, cradling the small creature. "Aren't you going to touch her? She's soft."

Ferran's hands ground into his leg and he shook his head. "I don't know…I shouldn't."

She gave him a curious look. "I hadn't heard animals could catch it," she said. "Plants don't—is that why you love them so much?"

Farren shifted. "I…I'm not sure," he said. "I don't think they can."

"So why then?"

His hair fell in front of his face. "What if I hurt it?"

"Her," Barli said. "And as long as you're careful, you won't."

He reached his hand out slowly, careful to avoid actually touching her. Barli heard a soft sigh as his fingers came against the warm breathing body of the feline. His hand ran over the small kitten.

"Here," she said gently. He was afraid to touch her, and the exchange was awkward, but eventually the injured kitten was settled in Ferran's arms. Barli studied her arm, which was healing well. It would leave a scar, of course, but it wasn't trying to bleed at the slightest irritation anymore.

"I can feel it," Farren said softly. There was a catch in his voice that had her looking up again. Barli swallowed, alarmed to see his eyes had taken on a certain gleam—and that look in his eyes, it was more than just the collection of liquid. It was like a little bit of his utter blackness had become broken.

"What?" she asked softly.

Farren shifted slightly. "A heartbeat that's not my own."

Barli swallowed and looked away. "You just found her out here, all alone?"

He nodded. "What do you think happened?"

"I don't know." She looked up at the rough wall. "But it looks like she was abandoned." Poor thing. There were few things worse than being abandoned.

She watched him with the kitten for a while, shivering slightly. The night was beginning to chill her. But she couldn't seem to look away from the gentle peace that had settled over Farren. It was a peace she couldn't remember the last time she had felt.

Barli's stomach grumbled.

"There's food in there for you too, you know."

She hunched her shoulders. "What do you care?" she asked.

Farren bent closer to the kitten. "I don't understand why you've been ignoring everyone. It won't help you get out of here."

She sighed. "I don't want to die," she repeated quietly. She stood up. The chill was getting to her. Barli sighed. "You should take her inside too. It'll keep her warmer."

"I—no, you should take her," Farren protested. "I don't know how to take care of a living thing."

"You do okay with these plants, don't you?"

"I…it isn't the same," he said.

"Just keep her warm and fed," Barli said. "And we can look at those wounds tomorrow. But they didn't seem too deep. She's probably more tired than anything else."

It was impossible not to feel bad for Farren. Barli didn't think she'd ever met anyone so in need of pity, as much as she might dislike the sensation or the way it made her reconsider every stupid comment he'd made. But maybe she was too quick to judge—that was what people always said.

"Do you think so?" he asked softly.

She nodded. "Besides, no one goes in your room, so they won't come across anything strange. I'm guessing the Priests wouldn't want you to have any pets."

Farren's arms tightened slightly around the young feline as he got to his feet. "You're right," he replied. He hurried back inside, disappearing into his room.

Barli stood outside his door for a few more seconds before wandering back to the kitchen. The bit of food she'd given the kitten had reawakened her own need. Barli piled up a plate and relaxed onto the couch, digging in with the need of someone who had not eaten for days. Somehow the kitten had brought her appetite back.

She had just finished eating when Farren burst out of his room again.

"Barli!"

She was surprised he remembered, after all he'd said about not having a name—at least not one that made sense. "What is it?"

"I just…" He was still holding the cat. "It was…I'm glad you are eating."

She blinked at him for several seconds, unsure about this odd alteration from Ferran's usual state of odd disinterest. He had said he did not want to be close to anyone. Even saying this must have been quite unusual for him. "Um…really? I thought you didn't care."

"I—" Farren glanced down at the kitten before turning away. "I guess I do."

He started walking back to his room when Barli smiled slightly, realizing what was bothering him, what seemed so strange about it. "Thank you," she called after him, "those are the words you're looking for."

Slowly, he turned back to her, looking slightly troubled. "Thank you," he repeated, but shook his head. "I don't think so."

"Why?"

"Ginsun says that when Parlsey gives him tastes, or she says it when they manage to do something right. I…it is not so simple a thing, what you have done." He looked down at the exhausted feline. "Thank you is too simple and does not mean enough."

Barli couldn't think of anything more to say, as Farren went back to his room, shutting the door soundly behind him. She curled up on the couch, slowly letting the dreariness take hold. She managed to rouse herself before she really fell asleep, returning to her quarters where she spent the rest of the night.

She was going to get out of here—eventually. And she would cut the time she was stuck in here down as much as possible. Farren seemed to know a lot about what the Priests were looking for. If she stayed on his good side, he might even help her. If she could see Visea again… Her heart leapt at the possibility.

Yes, making Farren happy was definitely a good plan.

She wondered if others had used him too. Perhaps that was why he was so cold. Others, too, must have had this same thought. They would have wanted to get close to him too, so he would help them. But by helping them, he was losing whatever friends he'd thought he'd made.

So. She couldn't do that, could she?

What? Did she care? It was simple. Once it was over, she wouldn't see him again, and it would be of no concern one way or another. Besides, she hadn't promised to be his friend. She would just give him a bit of what he was missing and maybe that would be enough.

Barli spent the morning out in the garden, and the afternoon trouncing Ginsun at marbles. He was pleased to see her still, even though she beat him terribly. Parsley commented on her good mood, but Barli mostly ignored her. She might have made a commitment to get out of here, but that didn't mean she was changing herself entirely. But she liked marbles, and she certainly liked messing with Ginsun. And the food Parsley made wasn't bad.

That evening, after her door had been unlocked, Barli wandered out into the main corridor. Her fingers weren't quite as frisky today as they had been, though she still felt unsettled. She could feel it building inside of her. Soon, it would become too much. But for the moment she could handle it. Still, if nothing took her down, she would wind up setting whatever progress she was trying to make back again.

Eventually, Farren came out of his room. There was the familiar black bundle curled in his arms. Barli smiled a little. "How is she?"

He shifted. "She seems okay." He didn't really know, did he?

"Let me see," she said.

Farren reluctantly let the feline down onto the couch. She was stronger today and mewed gently, lifting her head to track him as he stepped away. Barli knelt beside the kitten and undid the bandages again. The wound was clear and looked better than it had the day before. She smiled softly. "She should be fine," Barli said.

He nodded quietly, letting her nuzzle her head against his finger. "I…"

She hid her smile. He was trying to say thank you again, wasn't he? "If you feel grateful," she said, "you could do something for me."

He gathered the cat back into his arms. "What?" he asked suspiciously.

She swallowed. She still wasn't sure she felt quite right about this, but if he knew going in what he was getting into…he couldn't be too mad, right? "Tell me how to get out of here."

Farren stared down at the kitten, then back at her. His gaze flipped between the two a few times, before he settled on the feline. "It always takes time, but I can tell you what they like to see," he agreed. The kitten got up and paced on the couch, looking down with anxiety, unwilling to fall so far.

Barli's face flushed slightly. He was going to help her. He was really going to help her. And she'd done little enough for him. "What?"

He glanced sideways. "For someone like you, they want to see purpose and desire. Something besides just a desire to get out, though. Playing with Ginsun is good—but if you always beat him, they won't think you'd do well with more people. Too competitive a spirit is dangerous. They want to see you interacting with the others peacefully. Helping of your own accord. They want you to make bonds so that you are unlikely to run away."

"Are they so demanding for everyone?" She found that hard to believe.

Farren shook his head. "It depends on why you're here, and why they think they need to keep you locked away in the first place. It's particularly tricky for you because they aren't sure what to be worried about."

Barli stiffened her shoulders. "What do they know anyway?"

"Quite a lot, actually." Farren let the kitten bat at his finger. "They have experience. And they aren't ignorant. They've studied the demon's effects all their lives." Farren sighed. "They have reasons for what they do."

Barli's jaw tightened. "Maybe," she said. She wasn't sure what she thought anymore, now that she'd been here. Maybe she deserved it. But it was hard to believe that Ginsun was dangerous or evil. He was a kid and he seemed like a completely normal one to her, aside from his clubbed foot.

Before, she'd assumed that there was something more, something darker in them. She'd been told the physical distortions were a symptom of the evil inside that should exist in other areas as well—making him prone to harming others. But Ginsun…she couldn't see that happening.

Farren glanced at her. "You don't want to say *that* either."

"Will you tell?" she asked again, withholding a sigh.

Farren shook his head. "But you can't trust anyone else."

Barli nodded slowly. "Well, thanks, I guess."

"Whatever," he murmured.

"Do you think…I mean how long will it take?" she asked.

"Why do you want out so badly?"

She swallowed. "I just…I—" What could she say? She hated being cooped up? As if Farren wouldn't understand that. And he had so much less experience. But wouldn't that make him want it less? He didn't know what he was missing. He couldn't understand how much it meant. So in two ways, that was a bad explanation. What did she say?

He was still staring at her.

Barli sighed. "I get this itch inside me sometimes and I can't get rid of it. I need to do things, move…this is all too small for that. I like to run and tumble and climb…there's no space here. My legs have nowhere to go."

Farren frowned. He did not look convinced.

"And," she said, "there are people I know I…want to see again."

Farren swallowed. "I see," he said slowly. "And it can't wait a little longer?"

"Why should I be here longer than necessary? You can't argue a life away from here would be better than this!"

Ferran's hand dropped, much to the kitten's dislike. "I suppose I wouldn't know."

"Have you eaten?" she asked abruptly, standing up and moving to the kitchen where the leftovers were always stationed.

He shook his head, sitting down on the couch now that she had vacated it. Had he been waiting for her to move this whole time? She took out a plate and loaded it with Parsley's concoctions.

"What do you want?" she asked, picking up another plate.

"I can get my own—"

"It's not a problem."

The kitten climbed into his lap, settling down. He sighed. "Just give me a little of everything," he said.

She handed the plate to him, which he took awkwardly, keeping their hands as far from each other as possible. He shifted uncertainly as she sat on the other end of the couch. For a moment she thought he would jump up and leave, but it seemed the contented kitten was just enough to hold him in place.

She wasn't sure what to talk to him about now. She couldn't ask him about the Asylum—he knew things, but he hadn't seen them himself. It would have been cruel to force him to dwell on that, wouldn't it? Or was she being overly sensitive? She didn't know how to handle him. He was so unlike anyone else she had ever known.

What could she talk about? Her life? Stupid. And besides, he wouldn't know half of the things she was talking about. How did she explain boats to Farren, who had never even seen a body of water?

Farren ate slowly. "What do you know about these?" he asked.

"Cats?" Barli tilted her head. She kept forgetting he could only know what other people had told him. He had no real experiences of the outside. It was difficult to relate to him, more than just because he was so quiet and unfriendly. "Ah…they're scavengers. Survivors. They're excellent climbers and can jump pretty high too."

Farren set his plate aside, most of it only half eaten, and curled his fingers into the kitten's fur. Barli lingered a while, doing dishes until there was nothing left to do, and she returned to her room for the night, toying with Ferran's advice and the best means through which to show it.

The kitten improved over the next few days, until when Farren was out of his room, the kitten was too, and wandered around the locked ward with wide-eyed curiosity. Often it followed Farren, and was content to curl up in his lap, whenever he sat down. A week passed and it was Ferran's turn to cook again.

Spending a whole day with only Farren had its advantages and drawbacks. She didn't have to watch herself or her words in front of Farren. He had said he wouldn't tell on her, whatever she said or did that might be contrary to the Priest's wishes. It gave her a certain freedom. At the same time, she never knew quite what to say to him. What did you talk about with someone who had never really been outside? Who never touched another living person? What could he know? What could they have in common?

She worked in silence beside him. Farren sometimes gave her instruction, but beside that he said little.

"Is she okay?" Barli asked, eyeing the kitten as it clawed at the bookcase.

He nodded. "She doesn't like being cooped up though. It's so small in there."

For a grown boy too. But Barli didn't say that. She was sure it would only irritate Farren, and it wasn't as though he could do anything about the situation. They would take the kitten away from him, if they knew she existed. It was only because they left Farren so completely alone that he was able to keep her existence a secret.

Farren didn't seem to need her, so she went to play with the kitten, who tripped over her own feet as she struggled to find her place. "Have you named her yet?"

"Maigi," he said. "I named her Maigi."

"I like it." Barli stood up.

"They'll let you out soon," Farren informed her. "Walunata told me."

Barli froze for a second. "H-how do you know?" she asked. "How does she know?"

"She knows many things. She's a favorite of the Priests." Farren explained. "She hears things from them. They don't think anything of it."

Barli wondered if anyone thought anything of any of them. The children were always more clever than anyone gave them credit for. Did the adults play games too? How many people in this place were under the Priest's thumb? How often were their thoughts about their treatment tendered? How many were unsatisfied?

"How soon then?"

"A few days, as long as nothing goes poorly."

What would go poorly? Did he think she would do something? Why would he think that? Had she given some sign of it?

"You'll have to speak with one of them. I'd try to hide your dislike."

She stuck her tongue out. "I can have manners," she said. "I'm not awful, am I?"

He shook his head. "There are people out there who

like it, you know. They don't mind…maybe you don't think it's right. I don't think anyone does, all the time. But what other solution is there? Do you understand?"

"People," she said, "like you."

He gave her a long look and nodded. "They've kept lots of people safe like this. You don't doubt them, do you? It's just upsetting sometimes. I understand."

Barli opened her mouth slightly, then closed it again, trying to understand what he wanted from her. "When I was younger, I thought they were all right. They told us everyone in the Asylum was dangerous. Evil. I believed them—everyone I saw always seemed so shifty, but maybe it was just the marks on their face that made them seem that way…"

Ferran's dark eyes were staring at her. His heavy brand marks stood out on his face, though she'd mostly gotten used to them. Her stomach curled.

"Do you think we're all evil here? Ginsun and Walunata and…everyone else?" she asked Farren.

"Of course," he said. "It's something that festers, under the surface. And even if they don't seem so, we're all still dangerous to others."

Contagious. That was what the Priests said—contact was dangerous. The demon could pass—even multiply, maybe. "What evidence do you have of that?" she asked.

"You haven't been here long enough. You haven't seen enough." His voice was quiet.

Barli's throat tightened. What did she say about that? She wanted to push more—but would it be wise? "And you have? You have reason to believe that?"

He gave her a jagged nod. "It's all lingering beneath the surface, to come out sometime when it's not expected. It's clever. The demon makes you doubt too, that's part of the game."

Maybe. But…what if they were all wrong about this?

No. That was stupid—could she even hear herself? She was implying that everyone else was wrong, they'd been fooled their whole lives, lived this way when they didn't need to. Crazy. Of course she was crazy. She was the odd one, not everyone else. Surely, if it had been a sane thought, she would have seen it before—someone smarter than her would have seen it before.

"Right," she said. "I…I get these thoughts in my head sometimes. They sort of sweep me away."

"The demon," he said. "What sort of things do you think?"

She didn't want to get into that. Instead, she turned away. "Can you feel it, inside you?"

Barli held her hand to her chest, where her heart was beating. Was there some other faint beat there? The pulse of a demon?

"Sometimes I think so."

Barli watched the cat a while longer before disappearing back to her room for the night.

It was midmorning. Barli was playing marbles with Walunata and Ginsun when the most unusual circumstance occurred: the door opened. Not Farren's door, which for a moment Barli thought it must have been—that at least was more plausible than anything else—but the main door. The door to the rest of the ward. Her whole body breathed tension.

The Priest was not the same one that had visited her on her first day here. He had a small mustache, dark hair plastered to his head as though it had been dunked in water, clinging to his forehead. His robes were the same, however, and the look on his face—a slight sneer, a dislike and disgust in his eyes. The way he walked, she could tell he was not happy to be here: the depths of the Asylum.

Barli took her cues from the others. The children stopped their game of marbles, immediately lying down on the ground on their stomachs. Barli leaned forward slowly, mimicking their quick actions.

The Priest stopped before them. "Girl, get up."

Barli paused for a moment before making sure Walunata wasn't the subject of his interest. When she didn't move and she caught his eye on her, she stood up slowly. What did she do with her hands? Should she make fists? Or, no, would that be seen as aggressive? But they felt strange just hanging limply at her side. Shouldn't they be ready to protect her? Just in case?

Her knees shook a little, knowing how quickly this decision could be made—and if it was done poorly, that would be the end of her. She was not often off put, but the threat of death was one that tended to sway her.

He sighed. "Come," he said. "Stay three paces behind me."

Barli followed hesitantly after him. She felt a shiver run through her body as she walked through the doorway. How long had it been since Farren had passed through these doors? Had he even been able to stand on his own feet, or had they carried him, as nothing more than a babe?

They continued down a short hallway then down a stairway. Barli followed quietly. There were fewer doors here, instead a number of archways gave a clear view into what the interior rooms held to one side. They passed food storage rooms, one that looked like it held looms, and another where smoke crept up and out of the room and fires smoked, another where she caught sight of several weapons hanging on the wall. The other side was open, giving breeze and view into the lower courtyard they were quickly descending toward.

She looked out on the other side, down into the courtyard. There were several people milling about, some sitting on the well at the center of the yard. There was a cluster of others in the corner of the yard. They looked like they were working out. A few small children laughed as they tore through the yard. She counted at least ten strangers, none of them in Priest's robes.

He led her into a small room with several desks and one larger desk at the front of the room. He sat down behind it, gesturing for her to pull up a chair. "Sit down, Sin."

She did.

"How are you settling in?" he asked. "I've heard good reports."

From who? Parsley? The children? There was no way they had talked to Farren. "I…it's fine," she said, her heart beating harder in her chest. "It's quiet."

His eyebrows narrowed slightly. "And your wound is healing?"

She nodded. What had Farren said she needed to do? How was she supposed to seem? "Thank you, sir."

He gave her a quizzical glance. "For what?" he asked.

She swallowed. "It's safer here for me, isn't it? So…thank you. I don't want to hurt anyone."

"No one?"

What did he mean? "Of course not."

"You do not have to lie, child. We understand Sins are not like normal humans. We cannot punish you for your desires—only where they are misapplied."

"You mean, when they hurt other people."

"The people without demons, yes. Are you not familiar with your situation? Have you not heard what we do here, in all this time? As a child?" he pressed.

Was he angry? She couldn't tell. He was being so confusing. She didn't want to die. What was he expecting? What did he want her to say? "I was raised on a ship, Priest. I never had much time for learning, about the gods or anything beyond numbers."

He gave her a long stare. "But you've heard of the Sins, I assume."

The Black Sins? "Of course. Everyone has."

"Do you understand what they do?"

Her fingers clutched the bottom part of the chair. "I…no," she admitted. She knew they were dangerous and feared, like wild rabid dogs held on the Priest's leash. That was how her father had described it, once. The Black Sins were one of the Priest's most valuable tools. "They kill people."

"The right people. The deserving. The ones we can't control, otherwise. The ones who won't come here, to us. Or the ones who run away. Their job is important, you understand."

Barli sat quietly.

"We've reviewed your case, and it's possible you might have what we want. You have certain qualities that have made successful members in the past."

They…wanted her to be one of them? A killer?

Barli swallowed. "I…"

"There is a spot that has opened in their ranks. In three months, there will be a competition. I would encourage you to participate, and if deemed worthy, you will become the newest Black Sin."

Barli couldn't even manage a swallow now.

He studied her quietly. "You will be free to move about the compound. Competition will be fierce—after all, the Sins not only do us a great service, but they have a privilege and freedom our other members could only imagine."

She could hardly breathe. Her lungs didn't want to take oxygen in.

He sat patiently, watching her face. She tried not to think about what he might be reading from it. She wasn't sure how she was supposed to feel—she wasn't even sure how she actually *did* feel.

"I…you want me?"

The Priest inclined his head slightly. "That's what I said," he said tightly.

"W-where will I stay?" she asked.

He tipped his head. "If you want a chance at this station, you will need to practice. But we're quite full in the normal locations, so you'll keep your room for the time being. You'll be locked in at night still."

But she would be able to be outside? How could she say no to a thing like that? She took a deep breath. "Thank you, Priest."

"Manners will serve you well, Sin." He stood up. "Don't get into your nature, and you just might see the outside of this place: a rare gift for someone like you." He walked to the edge of the room. Barli did not trust her legs just yet.

"W—Priest?"

"What is it?" His tone was already full of dismissal. She was nothing to him—only a threat that couldn't afford to go up against him now, not with the promise laid out before her.

"You said there was a competition?" Barli asked.

He nodded. "You will compete for the position, along with several other candidates from different Asylums."

"Can anyone compete?" she asked.

"Of course not. They must have permission from the Priests."

So…she was an exception. What had she done to gain their interest? Barli took a deep breath and watched the Priest leave. She sat a while longer, trying to gather her thoughts.

She had a chance—a chance never given, not to anyone who came to this place—a chance at something like freedom. It was something Farren could not even begin to grasp the meaning of.

Barli finally got to her feet, trying to ignore the uncomfortable feeling pressing at her chest. She could have a chance at a real life again, at freedom, at seeing her family and Visea again. All she had to do was agree to murder evil people. Oh, and beat out all the competition to do the same.

Chapter Four

SHE WALKED OUT OF the room and into the corridor, gazing out into the courtyard, and up into the sunlight. Her eyes scrunched against the brightness of the day. Barli knew a few things, and she was tough. There had been dangers in her life before, but nothing that had meant she had to learn how to kill. If she wanted a chance at winning, she would have to work hard.

But not today. Everything was too new. Shaking slightly, she stepped out onto the lawn. The grass tickled her bare feet and she wriggled her toes against the bright green. It was funny. Bright colors often seemed unnatural, but here at her feet was a perfect example of how nature made things just as brilliant.

"Barli!"

She turned in surprise. Ginsun waved at her. "The light's nice, isn't it?"

The sun was warm. Somehow it had never seemed as vibrant when four walls pinned her in. "Hot, almost."

"So, what did he want with you? I thought they were

going to let you out, but they don't usually talk to anyone unless they're teaching."

Barli looked down at him, curious. Ginsun knew a lot of things, yet he hadn't known this? "I…I don't know," she lied.

Ginsun gave her an angry look before scampering off.

She sighed, ignoring him. She wasn't sure what to think, wasn't sure what she wanted…but if she had this space to explore, shouldn't she do so?

Barli spent the rest of the afternoon exploring the compound carefully. She didn't push in on any doors, aware they could well be private rooms or lead to places she wasn't supposed to go. She didn't want to get in trouble the first day she was given wider freedom.

She wouldn't push her boundaries.

Barli discovered a few more rooms, but most of them held closed doors. The other people gave her looks, but they did not talk to her and Barli ignored them for the most part. She wondered how many of them had been in the locked ward before—besides for dinner. And how many had been here from such a young age it had never even been necessary? Barli thought about the children. They didn't know another life to miss. Perhaps that would have been better, easier. She felt strange and awkward in this place, but as much as she didn't belong, these people didn't either—much as they might pretend they did.

A young man was eyeing her. He looked to be in his twenties.

"What?" she asked sharply.

"You're new."

Duh. "So?"

"What's your name?"

"Barli." His face seemed strangely flat, as though it had grown pressed against the womb wall. "What's yours?"

"Xinpaku," he said, "if you're in the business of names."

"You're the one who asked."

"You were talking to Gaberow. What did he want with you?"

Gaberow? "Oh, the Priest? He told me about the competition."

He appraised her. "You're young. Strong." The marks on his face were old and healed, leaving her curious as to his nature. His limbs, from what she could tell, were in working order. Was his issue a matter of the mind then?

"Are you my competition then?"

He smiled wanly. "Perhaps. But I doubt I'll make real competition."

"Why?" He was young. Strong. Fit. Was he trying to psych her out?

He gave her a long look. "I'm certain you will see for yourself. Even if by some miracle I managed to win this competition…" A dark expression settled over his face. "Sometimes I wonder if I won't just…ah, never mind. But, I do know many things. I've grown up here and seeing as you haven't, I'd be willing to offer you a helping hand."

She didn't trust him. "No, thanks," she said. No one who offered help right out of the gate meant it as a free offer of help. They were all looking for something—favors down the road, you owing them, and them hanging it over your head. It was no deal she wanted to be involved with.

"Are you sure?"

"Yes."

He smiled a little. "Prickly too. You'd fit right in with their ilk."

"Who?"

"The Black Sins, of course. They're either religious fanatics or uncharismatic vultures. Either way, they don't care for anyone but themselves."

Her eyes flashed and she barely managed to keep herself from punching him. At least Farren was better company than this! She turned on her heel and hurried back up the stairs, finding her way back to the locked ward, still unlocked.

It felt weird to open the door and come in, to return to the solitary nature of the rooms. But this was what she wanted, strange enough. She had never liked to be alone, but all of the sudden, she desperately needed it. She ignored Parsley and Walunata and headed straight for her room, lying down on her bed and staring at the ceiling as the sun gently set.

As usual, Barli didn't leave her room until sometime past when everyone should have been gone. She didn't want to talk to the two young kids anymore, and she certainly didn't want to see Xinpaku. He might have been the biggest jerk she'd met.

Once she was certain they were all gone, she slipped back out of her room to get something to eat. While she was eating, Farren appeared, the black kitten running between and around his ankles.

He did not notice her at first, and he walked with ease

that she was unaccustomed to seeing. For once, he did not seem to stutter in his every movement. Instead, he sauntered with an easy grace, for the first time seeming almost unconcerned. The moment he saw her, he stopped. His shoulders tensed and his whole body seemed to create sharp lines.

"B—what are you doing here?" he asked. "I thought they let you out."

He'd almost seemed relieved by it too. Barli licked her fork. "They did. But I'm still staying here at night."

"Why didn't you eat with everyone else?"

"Why are you…angry?"

He narrowed his eyes. "I'm not," he said.

She snorted. "You can't fool me." She put some food in her hand and lured the kitten to her, picking up the poor thing. They had taken the bandages away and although she seemed to be in discomfort on occasion, there was nothing else Barli could think to do for her. "Your master doesn't like me, Maigi."

His lips parted before he made a strange sound in the back of his throat and turned away, rummaging through the kitchen drawers. "She doesn't like being cooped up."

"Haven't we talked about this before?" She tilted her head. "Once she learns to climb, you can let her out in the garden and she'll be able to see the world." Unlike him.

Farren didn't respond to that. He simply got his food and left.

Barli stared after him, at least until Maigi nipped at her hand, drawing her attention away. "Not like I wanted company anyway," she muttered under her breath. She played with the kitten until they were both weary. Finally, she picked the feline up and carried her back to Ferran's room, knocking gently on the door.

"What do you want?"

"Maigi's tired," she said. She took a step back as the door opened. Farren was not wearing a shirt. There were no muscles, no definition. His skin was exceedingly pale. He was utterly unimpressive. She held the bundle out to him, but instead of taking it he pushed the door wider.

"Set her down on the bed," he said.

Ferran's room did not have many defining factors, despite the fact that he had lived in it for what she assumed was almost his entire life. There was a drawer, partially open, that seemed to be full of something. He had a desk, unlike her, and it had a few papers spread out on it, though they didn't appear to be covered in writing. The walls were still plain. They did not tell the story of a life. She tried not to look around too much as she set the kitten down on carefully pooled blankets. She realized he had used all his bed sheets for this purpose—and to create a strange slide-like structure she could see claw marks on.

She set Maigi down, nestling her into the bedding. The kitten purred slightly and yawned as it settled. "Does no one ever come in here?"

"Never," he said.

Farren held his arm out. "Now, get out."

She held up her hands, getting a better view of the papers on his desk as she did so. Her eyes widened slowly, but given the warning tone of Ferran's voice, she didn't want to push things. She left quickly, hearing the door snap shut quickly behind her.

Farren. She didn't understand him—and honestly she didn't think she wanted to. He had grown apart from humanity for so long she wasn't sure he was human.

But on his desk...

She stared at the ceiling a long time before falling asleep.

It wasn't a hard decision. Of course, she was going to try to beat the competition. Otherwise, she might never get out of here. So what if it meant she had to kill a few people? Anyway, if she managed to get out of here, she could run away if she wanted. There would be no reason they had to hold sway over her. Besides, the Black Sins were only dispatched for the truly heinous demon-touched. There was nothing wrong with killing their likes.

Barli started the morning off with a brisk workout, focused on her arms. She had fallen out of shape in her time here, and it irritated her that she had let herself go this way. At the same time, she'd had nothing to work for. It was hard to motivate yourself when there was nothing to spark that motivation. Barli had always enjoyed running, but the rest of her had been made hardy from weeks on the sea, climbing up masts, tying knots, and weighing anchor.

After doing as many pushups as she could, she lay on the floor until she could hear Ginsun wandering loudly through the halls. Barli scowled. She knew what she had to do today.

She just hoped she didn't run into Xinpaku.

Barli passed through the kitchen where Parsley was busy making her meal. It was a strange feeling, opening the door that had for so long been locked, and stepping out into the strange new freedom.

And then she reminded herself that she was not free, and this was only a sham of freedom. It only felt that way to her because the freedom she'd had was so restricted. Now it felt amazing to have so much more, when really, compared to the world, it was nothing.

Barli sighed into the morning air. The day seemed crisper than many had been lately. She found herself drawn into the storage room. There was plenty of junk in here: coils of rope, dusty nets, an anvil, several piles of holey linen, and heavy rugs.

Once she had determined there was little of interest, she continued down the hallway to the room where she'd glimpsed the assortment of weapons. Barli stepped inside, the breath in her lungs freezing up. No wonder they kept people in a locked ward when they first got there—access to this world might well have caused her to go on a little murder spree. She wasn't proud—sometimes she went out of control. That was why she was here. And angry, afraid, alone, and reeling in the loss of her normal life…standing in the doorway, Barli was suddenly very uncertain. Perhaps things would have gone the other way. She tiptoed inside, looking at the rack of weapons. Her fingertips trailed against cold blades and hefted handles.

Some of these were weapons she'd never handled in her life. The others she had not held in a long time, aside from knives. She found herself gripping her wrist where the wound had scarred over to a bright puffy red.

She took a long knife in her hand, recognizing its shape and form for what it was—a gutting knife. She flipped it in her hand, remembering exactly how to slice a fish open and take out its guts. How difficult could it be to do the same to a human?

There were mats laid out on the main floor. She pulled a larger sword from the wall and held it in her hand. The massive weapon was heavier than she'd anticipated and she had to hold it in two hands as she swung it experimentally.

A weapon like this…perhaps it was not for her. It was not the most suitable weapon for an assassin anyway, which was more or less what the Black Sins were. Righteous assassins. And she would attempt to join their ranks.

She whirled it up over her head. The weight made her arms ache and she groaned under its intense heft.

"You're too slight for a thing like that."

She actually *did* have muscles. They just weren't the right type. Barli turned, swinging the sword as she did so. A ringing sound filled the room as the force of her blade was stopped short. Her eyes locked with Xinpaku. He seemed more amused than anything as he stepped back, twirling his own long blade in hand. She hadn't even seen him slip in. She hadn't heard him pick up a blade.

He was impressive—scary impressive.

"I can make it work, if I wanted to." She set it down, reaching for the knife again. She tossed it into the air, watching its three revolutions before she caught it easily.

Barli lifted her eyebrow, staring him down with a confidence she didn't feel.

Xinpaku smiled wider. "Even so," he said.

"What are you doing here?" she asked roughly.

He threw his own blade, catching it deftly. He was not new to these weapons. "Just checking in on our latest member."

Her eyes narrowed, irritated. "You never really said one way or the other. Are you my competition?"

"I believe I did inform you on that nature. At the moment, I haven't quite decided."

"Why?" Why wouldn't he attempt it? What wasn't he sure about? Why had he said maybe?

He gave her a long glance. "Many are open here. They do not have a care or a sense of secrecy. They see no reason for it." He swapped which hand held the sword, displaying his ambidextrous prowess. "I am not one of them."

So what was it he was hiding? What did he hold so close he wouldn't tell a bunch of other Sins about? Or was it just her who wasn't allowed to know? Was it because he clearly seemed to dislike her?

She would ask Ginsun about it.

"I haven't retracted my offer, in either case. I'm certain you could find someone else to tell you about the nature, but few that know how to use these." He spread his hand, gesturing to the wide wall upon which set the wide array of weaponry.

"Why would you help me?" she asked. "Do you just want to get to know what I can do? Or do you think it would be too boring otherwise?"

Xinpaku hung the sword back on the wall. "Why do you want to be one of them?" he asked.

She wasn't sure what to say. The truth was not particularly...it wouldn't have come out well. But she didn't want to say it was for any of the reasons he'd listed in their first conversation.

He was staring at her, dark eyes like little pits, deep and intelligent despite his situation. And he was skilled with blades, for whatever reason. She wasn't sure she wanted to know why.

"Does it matter?"

"Of course it does." He scowled. "And if you can't understand that, perhaps it's best I don't aid you." Xinpaku lunged toward her suddenly and she tried to move back, but he had slipped his leg behind her and she tumbled backward, falling as he lunged forward in an easy, practiced motion to let his fingers graze her neck.

She shrunk away, pulse quickening.

"Remember this. Think about it. Because, easily, I could have killed you." He removed his hand and straightened up. "I won't bother you anymore. But, if you decide you want it, and if you can tell me your reasoning, I will teach you." He wiped his hands. "If you practice on your own, you have a chance of not dying. I can tell you with utter certainty, however, that you will not win. There are others who have spent their whole lives training for this chance and they will not give it up easily." He looked up, but when Barli followed his gaze she saw nothing. And with a long breath, he left.

Barli got up slowly, letting her breath return. That was,

she realized, the first time anyone had touched her there in a long time. She put her hand to her neck, massaging it gently.

In fact, she thought Ginsun and Walunata were the only ones who had touched her at all since she'd gotten here—a hand pulling hers off to some other location. That was it. That was all the touch she'd experienced.

The sudden realization brought sudden tears to her eyes. Sitting on the ground, she let her right hand caress her left shoulder, closing her eyes to pretend for a moment that it was someone else—her mother or even better, Visea.

Visea. That was all she wanted. She wanted to touch her again, hear her voice, feel her caress. Working as a candle maker, she had exceptionally soft skin. Barli took a deep breath, remembering how it had felt against her own.

"Barli!"

Her eyes snapped open. "Walunata, what do you want?"

The young girl's hair was in two long braids today, skittering down her back as she stood in front of her. "Do you want to play?" she asked.

"Play what?"

Walunata shrugged. "I don't know. Sticks?"

Barli shook her head. "Sorry. I have work to do."

Because she was going to be touched again. She was going to get out of here and find Visea and be touched. So, of course, she had no time to spare, going about playing silly games with Walunata.

"You don't even have a job!" Walunata whined.

"What're you doing in here anyway?" she asked, glancing around reproachfully.

Barli knew she had to work on her own fitness before she could really be effective in this room. But she also knew Xinpaku knew what he was talking about. Whoever else she had to face, would be tough competition. And they would have a leg up on her, since she had only just gotten here, after living a completely different life.

She had to find a way to work that to her advantage. It was the only advantage she had.

Walunata stuck her tongue out. "You're no fun," she informed her.

She sighed. "Hey, Walunata, what do you know about the Black Sins competition?"

Her eyes widened. "T-the Black Sins tests?" She tugged on one of her braids. "There hasn't been one for years. Four, maybe? I don't remember the last one." She stared at Barli, seeming to take in her presence in the room all over again, reconsidering. "Is that what they wanted you for?" she asked quietly. "To be one of them?"

She nodded slowly. "What do you know about it?"

Walunata swallowed. "N-not much. Only that a lot of the competitors die."

"What is it? A fight?"

She shook her head after a pause. "A—only a little. There are duels, but the biggest test is a test mission they watch you for, to see how you do it. Whoever does the best, impresses them the most, gets the most points or whatever…they're the ones who win."

"So why do people die?" she asked, her heart beating harder. It was a risk. But how could she not take it?

Walunata shrugged. "That's just what I heard. You should ask Xinpaku or Ployame."

Xinpaku was out. "Who's Ployame?" Barli asked.

Walunata shaded her eyes as Barli followed her outside. She scanned the yard and pointed out a woman with exceptionally long black hair that swept past her curved butt.

"Is she competing?" Barli asked.

Walunata shook her head. "I think you're probably the only one from here."

"So…how many people are there? From how many others?" How many did she have to beat?

But the girl shrugged again. "I don't know."

"Are you going to try, when you're older?"

She shook her head. "I like it here. Why would I want to leave?"

Barli was still staring as the girl walked away.

Why would she want to leave? Did she really feel that way? But, then, with the marks on her face, she supposed it would make sense. She couldn't have ever received a very good reception from normal people. And so why would she want to leave a place that accepted her?

But it would be different for her, wouldn't it? She'd lived outside. She knew what it was like, how it could be. And wouldn't people she used to know be able to look past the scars on her face? Wouldn't they know she was no different than she'd once been?

Barli couldn't waste more time like this. If they were

scared, she'd just make them see she was the same. If she could become a Black Sin, she could do anything. She crossed the yard to the woman Walunata had mentioned.

What Barli hadn't noticed from a distance was that Ployame had no ears—or, rather, no ear on the left side. And her face was strange, droopy, as though she had no cheekbones at all.

More than likely, she had grown up here.

It was strange how a look could tell you all that.

Still, her eyes were sharp as she focused in on Barli. "You're the new girl."

"Yes…"

"Why were you not at dinner last night?"

Was she…expected to have been? Barli frowned. "I was tired."

Ployame's gaze slid away from her. "You're sweet to put up with the youngsters. I suppose you haven't gotten tired of them yet."

What did she know about it? "I suppose not." She still wasn't sure what exactly was wrong with Walunata, but she wasn't about to ask. Her parents had managed to instill some level of manners in her. "Walunata said you could tell me about the competition."

"Gaberow…that's his interest in you." Ployame lifted her chin as she cast her eye over Barli.

The Priest—Xinpaku had said his name too. Barli shifted from one foot to the other, waiting.

"What has he told you?"

She shook her head. "Nothing."

"Of course not," she said, and Barli picked up on the

disgust in her voice. "Well, the basics are this: there are several simple skill challenges…which mostly acts as a means to gauge who is the most dangerous. And there's the final challenge, to see if you can manage the real tasks that will be demanded of you."

"Walunata said people die."

"Only the best get to go on, and if you're dead, you're not competition," Ployame informed her.

"What are you saying?"

"The competitors have been known to murder each other."

Falls. "T-that's allowed?"

"Technically, no, but if it can't be proven, they won't worry about it." She gave Barli an appraising look. "Have you committed yet?"

"No."

"If you're good enough to be a threat, you will be a target. So I would think carefully before you make a choice."

No offers to help from her, then. So why had Walunata sent her to her? How did Ployame know so much about it? "Are you…"

Ployame resumed her previous task, which seemed to be scrubbing out huge filthy vases that were so large half a body could be easily submerged within—possibly a whole one, if a real attempt was made.

Barli took a step back.

"You should come to dinner tonight," she said. "We're a small community, but all outcasts are welcome enough, so long as they don't hurt any of us."

"Right," Barli said.

Ployame tossed a bucket of water into the vase and sloshed it around before pouring it out into a stone drain, along with a healthy amount of sludge.

Barli found her way back into the locked ward and out into the small garden plaza. The plants seemed to be doing well. She couldn't even see the spot where she'd fallen anymore. Farren had fixed it.

She stared up at the sky, watching the sun sink lower. Did she really want to do this? Could she? It was dangerous—if she wanted to win. And obviously she had to win, otherwise there was no point at all.

Visea. This was all to see Visea again. To escape this hellhole and get back with the person who meant the most in the world to her. If only she hadn't been so stupid for that one second…if only she'd managed to hold it together just a little bit longer, she would have never ended up here. She could be in Visea's soft arms right now.

Those other people, the ones who had been here so long, they couldn't possibly have the same determination as her. They didn't know what they were missing. They didn't even know to miss the things she did. She was stronger for it. She had motivation they couldn't understand.

Barli knelt down, studying one of the small flowers. They were pretty, but so fragile and small. They were nothing. A few flowers was all the beauty that existed in this place. This couldn't be the most beautiful thing she saw the rest of her life. She refused.

It didn't matter if it was dangerous. If she was the best, she would survive. And she would be the best. It was that simple.

She did not waste another minute. There was enough space between the wall and the garden to lay down in, and she proceeded to start a dizzying set of crunches, pushing herself until she heard the sound of more people in the locked ward.

She slipped the door open, running her fingers through her ragged hair before she joined the throng of people.

The food line was a distracting mess of misfits. Some issues were obvious—if Barli had to guess, clubbed feet or arms was the most likely cause of incarceration in the Asylum. All of them would have been here since the beginning of their lives. There were some other strange deformities, and Barli was careful not to stare. A few looked normal on the outside, but she knew that didn't mean anything. Then again, maybe it did mean nothing at all. After all, she didn't belong here. Not really. Maybe she got a little wild sometimes, but that didn't mean she belonged here.

As one of them spotted her, she saw his finger raise and the chatter that had been at a fairly constant low murmur seemed to die away as they all turned toward her.

So many eyes. There weren't more than twenty of them, but it still felt like too many. She didn't think so many people have ever looked at her at once in her whole life. The attention had her squirming.

"Welcome," an older man said with a slur to his words. "Welcome to our family."

The others smiled at her, raising their hands in greeting.

"Welcome, Barli!" Ginsun exclaimed. He grinned at her.

What was she supposed to say? What was she supposed to do? Thought seemed to leave her mind behind. "Ahh…"

Ginsun rolled his eyes. "Don't be shy," he scolded her.

"I am not shy!" she protested. She tried to ignore the eyes and took her place at the back of the line, where she was certain she belonged.

Slowly, chatter returned and the eyes moved away from her. The middle-aged man in front of her gave her a quiet nod.

Barli ignored everyone as she took her food, thinking she would skip this mealtime ritual as often as she could. The moment the plate was in her hand, she slunk back down the hallway and disappeared into the safety of her room.

Twenty people was far too many, she reflected as she ate.

When had that become true? When had twenty become overwhelming? Or was it only because they had noticed her?

She didn't like this place. She didn't like what it was doing to her. More and more it was making her wonder who she even was. And that was an uncomfortable question to be asking.

She spent the next two days working out, mostly in either her room or the upper courtyard where no one else would bother her. She kept her ears open for any information about Xinpaku, but heard nothing. Other names filtered through her ears, but she didn't care about them and immediately forgot and dismissed them.

Barli was meaning to go outside on the third day and possibly take some supplies from the weapons room so she could practice lifting heavier weights and get used to the length of the blades she might use. A sword was too long, and she was an assassin. Or she would be, anyway. Daggers were just knives made for cutting people and she knew knives.

When she got to the door, however, it was locked. For a moment, she wondered what she had done wrong, until she heard soft mews.

"I guess you got trapped in here with me. Sorry."

Barli turned around. "It's fine," she said, "I don't need to go out anyway." Still, she sighed.

"What do they have you doing, anyway?"

"What do you mean?"

Farren gave her a strange look. "Everyone gets a job—going to market, cooking, smoking, packaging, sewing…what are you doing?"

"I…" They really were expecting her to do this, then. Maybe she hadn't said anything or given some verbal "yes", but…it was as though they'd known she would say yes. They hadn't even bothered to give her another path. "They want me to be the next Black Sin."

Farren was quiet for a long time. She couldn't tell what he was thinking, only that the pervasive darkness about him had not abated in the slightest. "I suppose you'll get your wish, then."

"If I make it," she agreed.

He nodded quietly, poking around the kitchen. She wandered closer, watching him idly.

"Hey. What do you know about Xinpaku?"

"Why do you ask?"

Barli brought her hand to her neck, remembering where his fingers had touched her right below her jaw. She hadn't spoken to him since that incident. "No reason."

They went back to ignoring each other. She found herself looking over the bookshelf, but once again nothing caught her eye. Like she needed to know more about demons when she supposedly had one inside her. She proceeded to work her core. Every time she sat up, she could see Farren working.

"Farren?"

"What?" he replied immediately.

"Why aren't you competing?"

There was a moment of quiet and then she heard a crash as something went shattering to the ground. She bolted upright. "Farren? You okay?"

A yelp of pain informed her he was not.

"Farren?" She couldn't see him until she was at the counter. Shards of glass were splintered across the floor and Ferran's hand was bleeding, fast enough that it was already dripping off his elbow onto the floor.

"Falls," she muttered. She tossed him a rag. "Stay there till we can get this glass out of the way."

He pressed the cloth to the palm of his hand and nodded mutely.

Barli found the wicker broom and carefully swept the

glass dust into a pile. Not quite trusting the broom, she folded her blanket and set it on the ground to ensure a safe crossing. "Are you okay?"

Farren stood up slowly, ignoring the hand she offered. "Fine. I just…" His hand was still bleeding.

Barli was once again unsure where to find bandages. There was no way they were reusing the bandage from her arm again. Farren stood there awkwardly while she attempted to find something capable of providing medical assistance. When she struck out, she threw herself onto the couch. "Is there nothing in here?"

"They don't need to try to keep anyone locked in here alive," Farren said quietly. He had been keeping steady pressure on the wound the whole time she'd been fruitlessly searching and as he took the rag away, it seemed the blood had at least clotted.

"Bastards," Barli growled. She stripped a rag into smaller segments. "Here, let me wrap that up. At least it'll be protected then."

He kept his hand close to his chest. "I can do it."

Ungrateful. "Fine." She threw the strips at him and then watched with growing amusement as he attempted to secure the make-shift bandage. It was funny for the first ten minutes, and then she was just annoyed, waiting for him to ask for her help. When he didn't, she rolled her eyes and went out to the courtyard, taking Maigi with her.

Maigi was growing quickly, despite the awkwardness of her situation. She was easily twice as big as she had been when they'd first found her. She moved through Ferran's garden like it was a forest, pouncing on one of the little flowers Barli had been admiring the other day.

She resumed her workout in the warm air, though Maigi did her best to interfere. "Silly thing," she murmured as she pushed her away for the umpteenth time.

When she went back inside two hours later, the glass had been swept up and Farren was staring at the kitchen. There were ingredients out, but he didn't seem to be making anything. Her eyes caught sight of the bandages, discarded on the couch. She grabbed them. "Farren, give me your hand," she said, reaching out to grab the wounded limb.

He jumped back, nearly slamming himself into the wall. "D-don't," he said, "stop."

Touch. It was such a simple thing. She was asking hardly anything of him. Touches were constantly exchanged. What was wrong with him? What sort of pride did he have that he couldn't let her help bandage his wound?

"You're being ridiculous," she said, grabbing him anyway.

He was entirely still for several seconds. She could feel the tension in his body, but ignored it, taking the strands she had torn before and readying them in her free hand to force the makeshift bandages into conformity with his injured hand. His breath was soft and shallow. She touched the fabric to his hand.

At that moment he seemed to come back to life. His arm fought against her, but she was used to reeling in fish and he had never done hard labor in his life. He was weak. It wasn't even a challenge to hold him in her grasp.

The wound unglued partially from the strain, and new

droplets of blood burbled to the surface. She raised her head slowly. Farren was looking at her in shock, body trembling even as his efforts to pull her away stilled. No doubt he realized the pointlessness of his actions. His supremely dark eyes were focused on the junction of their skin.

"Let go," Farren hissed. He lifted his eyes to her. He was angry. His eyes were crinkled just slightly at the edges, a sign she was beginning to recognize.

"Just relax," Barli found herself saying. She froze a little when she realized what she sounded like. She released him immediately.

"I'm sorry," she said softly.

He stared at her, still quivering a little, pressed up against the wall. She stepped back and saw him relax slightly.

"I'm sorry," she repeated. She took another step back, her lips pursed and an uncustomary, uncomfortable feeling clinging to her insides. She backed away from him. The darkness in his eyes did not abate.

She left.

Chapter Five

BACK IN HER ROOM, she sat on the bed, swaying gently back and forth.

It was just a touch, but it was a touch he hadn't wanted. Why, she wasn't sure. But the fact remained she had crossed over some sort of line, pushing him where he hadn't wanted to go.

But she just didn't want his stupid cut to get infected! He was an idiot not to let her do this one simple thing for him… She was trying to *help* him. What was his problem?

She fumed quietly. She was torn between going back out there and forcing him to submit to her administrations. What else was he going to do—bleed all over their food? But if he was so against it, even just as little a touch as was required…shouldn't she let him suffer instead?

Barli sighed and formed fists off and on until she heard clamoring from beyond. Was it dinner already? She certainly wanted the company of some normal people after dealing with Ferran's oddities all day.

She poked her head out of her room, but she did not

see bodies filling the hall like she normally did. The sound of conversation was also strangely muted she realized.

When she got to the main room, it was empty. There were loud poundings on the door, and she could see several disgruntled faces pressed up against the small window, looking through it. She recognized Ginsun's face, and one half of a close couple she had seen together on previous occasions. The two men were almost inseparable. Barli had seen it herself, though she tried not to look at it too often. It tended to make her jealous.

Barli frowned. Why was the door still locked? She was sure it was well past time for dinner. She glanced toward the kitchen. Nothing was set up. There was no food waiting to be passed out. Nothing seemed to have changed since the last time Barli had been in the kitchen. She frowned. Farren was…where was he, anyway?

She sighed. The food was, at best, half cooked. Barli didn't know how to cook. She wasn't sure she could remedy this problem. Barli walked over to the door. Ginsun gave her an indignant look.

"Why can't we come in?" he yelled through the door.

"I don't know! But there's no food anyway," she yelled back.

"Why not?" There was general disgruntled murmuring from through the door as her message no doubt got passed back.

Barli shrugged. "Farren didn't finish making it." Like she wanted to get into *that* conversation.

There were mutters and confused looks. "Do something!" Ginsun whined.

What was she supposed to do? This wasn't her responsibility. Barli stuck her tongue out, wondering how they knew not to unlock the doors. Did they have eyes into this place? How did the doors get locked in the first place? She had never seen anyone actually in the act of locking or unlocking a door, she realized. They had to have some system, to know whether it was safe or not.

Barli stepped back, wandering back into the kitchen. Maybe…no, she didn't know the first thing about what Farren was making. Where was he anyway? If the door was locked, was he locked up too?

She *so* did not want to deal with him anymore today. He was clearly insane, which she supposed wasn't surprising. But that didn't mean she wanted to hang out with him. Barli sighed, wandering down his hallway and knocking hesitantly on his door. Only a soft and curious mewling answered her.

Barli wasn't willing to test the door—like she needed Farren to be any more upset with her. He had little enough. She shouldn't invade what little space he had. She was tired of all of this. She stood outside his door a little longer before she went back to the hallway.

Some of the people seemed to have given up and left. The murmurs were even quieter and Ginsun's face could no longer be seen pushing in at the door. In fact, there were no faces up against the glass anymore, though she could still see figures farther back, crowding the hallway. She spotted a spare piece of paper that seemed to have been slid through the crack in the door. Barli picked it up and pried it open.

Barli, I don't know what's happened with Farren. This is

a most unusual circumstance. It was a very slow process before they allowed Farren to do even this much. He would not risk this privilege without reason. If he's sick, place a note to tell me what's wrong. They would never heal him.

Parsley.

She let out a frustrated sigh as she crumpled the note. So Farren wasn't allowed to do anything! And he'd let them down one night. It couldn't be so large a concern, could it? Everyone was no doubt irritated only because they were hungry. Would the Priests find another source of food?

Muttering under her breath, she walked back to Ferran's door and knocked again. "Hey. Everyone's wondering what's wrong with you. And they were expecting some food."

The silence was repressive and after standing there a moment longer she gave up and returned to her room. He wasn't sick, so there wasn't anything Parsley could do for him anyway—except maybe actually bind up his wounded hand. But Ferran's door was always locked when the older woman was allowed in, so Barli supposed she probably couldn't even do that.

Ridiculous. She let out a scream of frustration. She needed to see *somebody*. Being stuck with Farren alone all day was bad enough—now she could not even see anyone for dinner either. It was all his fault. If he hadn't freaked out so badly about her trying to help, if he'd not dropped that glass dish in the first place... She'd never seen him be clumsy before. What had they been talking about before that? She couldn't remember—only that is was something that made him uncomfortable, which did not narrow it down much.

Farren! Why should Parsley even care about him? Useless and strange, scrawny and awkward…there was nothing desirable about him. No, pity was likely the only reason for his continued existence—that and the not particularly well-meaning care of the Priests.

Fuming, it took her a long time to fall asleep that night.

Barli dreamed about Farren. She wasn't sure why—she only knew she disliked the direction it was taking. Farren was running from her, though she was not actively chasing him. She watched as the world seemed to shatter into glass. She dodged falling shards, surging toward him to pull him out of the wall of a large sharpened piece that might have pierced him in half.

Now he was pulling away from her, as though she hadn't just saved his life. The fear in his eyes seemed to grow and strike her still in her heart so that she froze to the spot, enveloped in Ferran's fear, making her only more fearful due to her lack of understanding. Whatever was he so terrified of?

She watched as Ferran's form shifted, and he melded into a form Barli had dreamed of far more often. But the flashing, freezing fear did not fade, even as his flat chest grew to heavy curves. Tired and tangled hair was replaced with ebullient shine, a rarer brown as opposed to black with almost a red hue. Her eyes were larger, wider, her nose softer and flat. And her lips…

Fear. Shock. Betrayal.

She swallowed as Visea, no longer Farren, pulled even further back from Barli. "How could you?" she asked softly, her voice like the trickling of a fountain, just the way Barli remembered it.

She felt the words like knives, slicing her up for some perceived wrong that Barli wished she could forget had ever happened. Over and over again, she wished it.

Her eyes opened into darkness, breathing quickly. It was still early morning and the darkness from her window informed her even if it had been day, it was to be a stormy, cloudy sort. Miserable. Cloying. Trapped. The clouds were as oppressive as the darkness, and all throughout her head she heard Visea's words repeated again and again.

"How could you?"

She could feel her heartbeat in her chest, and it did not recede.

Panic. Heat. Hurry.

Barli's insides squeezed. She sat up quickly, swinging her legs from the bed. She knew this feeling. She knew it too well.

She lay down again. She couldn't give in. Whatever words were pouring through her head didn't matter. They didn't change anything. That look on Visea's face… She had to get it out of her head.

What did she think about? The only other things that came to mind were not much better. Farren, looking just as horrified at her. It didn't matter whether that look was justified or not. It was the same way Visea had looked at her. Now she was on Visea again.

Visea. Beautiful. Wonderful. Haunting. And betrayed—betrayed by her, Barli the Sin.

She jumped to her feet.

The room was too small. The walls were closing in on her.

She fled the confines. Her heart was pressing against her chest. Her lungs refused air. She felt the dizziness that always accompanied her moments of oddity. No. She wasn't going to fall again. She wasn't.

Her fingers found the rough uneven scar on her wrist, remembering how it had occurred.

She hurried into the hallway, not bothering to close the door behind her. It swung on its well-oiled hinges, banging against the interior wall. Barli hurried to the main room, breathing hard despite the little physicality she'd been partial to recently. Her breath was still lost from her dream. The dream.

She couldn't shake it. She needed to. She needed to force herself beyond it somehow. She needed to escape it— to forget that vision, or more importantly, the way it felt inside now. That was what she needed to shut down.

This room was too small. Even though she knew it was futile, she tried the door that would have led out of the locked ward. It was, of course, locked. Even though she had suspected as much, she felt a wave of panic hit her.

Visea. Dojim. Farren.

Victims.

She rushed down the other hallway and pushed out on the courtyard door, exploding into the early dawn's cold air, looking up at the heavy oppressive sky. Sometimes feeling the wind helped. Sometimes the feeling managed to sweep a little bit of the wildness away.

She could already tell it wasn't enough. Tonight the wind could not hold back the tide.

She walked with hurried and uneasy steps, trying to get a better view of the night, hoping maybe she could catch a glimpse of moon from between the thick clouds.

Her foot caught on something soft but firm and she suddenly found herself plummeting. Her hands reached out and she caught herself roughly, feeling the scrape of the ground against the heels of her palms.

A disgruntled and pained sound issued from just below her as she managed to pick herself up as quickly as possible.

"Ahhh," Farren hissed.

"What are you *doing* out here?" Barli asked.

It was dark with the sky so overcast, and Barli could barely see the expression on his face, but it wasn't hard to guess he was angry once again. That was a common expression, though she thought bored disinterest was probably the most common.

"I was sleeping."

"Out here?"

He glared at her, answer implicit.

She looked away, nearly as irritated with him now as she had been earlier. But somehow it seemed worse now. No, it was because she couldn't be frustrated at *him*, instead it was a tense continued darkness that lingered from her dream, and the words that echoed still through her head. She shivered, looking up at the overcast sky.

It wasn't enough. She wasn't sure it would ever be enough.

Barli's breath sped up again, feeling dizzy and sick.

She wanted it to stop. She needed it to stop. The voice in her head kept coming, pressing on her heart, her head, and her lungs.

She tried to breathe deep but it wasn't working. The sky wasn't working. Her hands itched. Her body itched with a scratch that was far more than skin deep. Her nails dug into her arms, pulling at the feeling, trying to free it. She couldn't get deep enough.

"Parsley was worried about you," she managed to say, her jaw tight and teeth gritted. Farren. Why did she care?

She didn't have the patience to stay any longer. She had to get rid of the way her insides were being crushed and pulled. She had to do something. Fast.

Barli's squeezed insides were going to kill her. She could hear Visea's voice in her head, could feel the heat of her eyes, not turned this time in delight or pleasure. Barli's stomach curled just thinking about it.

She turned around when she remembered there was a kitchen inside. And kitchens, she knew, had utensils. Her legs seemed to work without any input from her.

She found herself standing in front of the counter. Several unattended stacks of only partially prepared food. Barli wondered if any of it tasted good, unbaked and slowly rotting.

Her insides crawled. She was, without a doubt, a terrible person. She belonged here. She was mad, like so many others. But hers was a special sort. She was almost envious of those other people here, who had something on the surface they could point to and claim precisely what was wrong with them. Sometimes she wasn't even sure. She might have been imagining everything.

She wasn't imagining it now. She couldn't take it. Every second it felt like her insides were dissolving inside her body. Barli fumbled around in the drawers, her fingers shaking slightly.

Her hand closed on one of the knives and she pulled it out of the drawer, holding it up in the darkness. All the lights were off and only a faint gleam of the cloudy moon shining through the window gave witness to her act of madness.

Barli's stomach was churning. She wanted to throw up, but couldn't quite bring herself to do so. Barli's breath caught in her throat, feeling the rough though healed edges of her last wound.

Dying?

No. Not dying. She only wanted to put the fish hooks that were finding their way deeper and deeper and put them to sleep so they wouldn't hurt anymore. Just for a while. Just until she could run until her lungs burst. There was no space for that relief here. Her feet did not have far enough to go. There was no way to catch the wind and force it through her body, chill herself in its cold rapture for a moment's relief. Because, often, just a moment was enough. She just needed to break out of the cycle for a moment and it would fall away, until it rose up again in an hour or a day or a week or a month or several months.

Just a moment.

Her heart beat faster and faster, pressing at her chest nearly as much as the discomfort of her squeezing insides threatened to overwhelm her in the sheering madness.

The blade bit into her flesh. She let the blade pass deeper through the soft of her stomach. It bit deeper than she'd meant it to, but not deep enough to be damaging.

She gasped a little at the pain and the clarity. It was a moment's reprieve. Barli smiled slightly. She glanced down at the blood spreading across her belly, bleeding onto her shirt.

She stood there, breathing in the silence and stillness. Her mind was finally resting. The pain rippling all throughout her insides had vanished, replaced with the utterly physical pain of the knife wound. She could see it. She knew it was there.

It was real, unlike everything else she felt.

Clarity. It was beautiful.

She reveled in it a while longer before she returned to her bedroom, all at once drained from the nervous biting energy that had fueled her just a moment before. Barli took off her shirt and used some of the leftover bandages she'd made to wrap her stomach. She pulled it tight so it stung, reveling in the pain until she fell asleep.

Chapter Six

THE NEXT MORNING FARREN was still outside, and they'd locked the door to the outside. Barli tried to find some way of concealing the blood on her shirt, but with only one, it was impossible.

Her head was clear and her eyes were bright and she headed to the practice room where she began her workout. Several of them tore at her recent wound. She could feel more blood welling up, staining itself thicker against her bandages.

She left off with ab work for the day and picked up several of the smaller daggers, practicing her palming skills. Barli had never been particularly good at it, but people on ships got bored and ended up practicing all kinds of tricks. No one ever fought—but there had been contests to see who could get their knife out first. Barli had tried it a few times, to moderate success. Barli made sure she could slide the knives from beneath her sleeve. She didn't have boots to wear anymore—they had taken those away from her—so she could not practice another good hiding space.

Barli didn't speak to anyone the whole day, but she was okay with that. In this state of sweet relief, she felt peace descend on her and she didn't need to have people filling her up with their stress and jumpiness. She knew from experience it only built the cycle back up faster.

That evening, dinner was prepared as usual, but Barli stayed in her room while the rest of the Asylum ate. She wasn't sure what would happen if anyone spotted her soiled clothing, but she preferred them not to know. It would lead to questions she didn't want to answer. It would possibly also lead to a return to lock down. She had risked going to the practice room today, but being in close quarters with so many watching her felt dangerous.

It wasn't long after she heard the voices disappear she started at an insistent knocking on her door. She'd thought everyone had gone, but she must have been wrong.

She pulled her rough blanket up over her stomach, thinking it was probably Ginsun. Barli pulled her knees up. "What is it?" she called out.

There was a long hesitation. "Can I come in?"

Not Ginsun. She frowned. "I…guess."

The door opened slowly, almost hesitantly. He looked more tired than usual.

"What is it?" Barli asked hesitantly. Her fingers tightened around her sheet. Maybe she wasn't over the episode—not with him standing right there, reminding her of her dream.

He opened the door a little wider and she saw something grasped in his hand. As she recognized the bladed edge, a thrill of fear when through her and she scrambled backward. She had never been afraid of Farren before, but she could see a little red on the edge of the knife.

"Farren..." Yes, he'd been upset about how she'd grabbed him the other day, but was this...was he really reacting like this? How wrong had she been? Did she deserve this?

He held it up in two fingers. She couldn't read his expression. It wasn't anger. It wasn't indifference. Those were the only two she really knew. "What is this?" he asked.

She relaxed slightly when she realized what he was asking. Still, her face flushed as she tried to figure out what to say. What did he want to hear? And why was he here, standing in her door, over this?

Barli shivered. "Nothing," she said. Her face still felt hot.

He stared at her for a long time, not saying anything. She noticed his injured hand was still unbound, exposed to the air.

Well. It wasn't as though he had anywhere to go that might get it infected. Barli got to her feet. She wanted him to leave. The best solution she had was to leave herself. She moved toward him, and, just as she'd anticipated, he moved quickly back. He would not allow her to get too close. Why had she been scared of him? He wouldn't touch her.

Barli walked down the hallway, passing Farren as he was pressed up against the wall. She tried to ignore his eyes on her as she pulled out a plate and collected her food. She didn't want to deal with him tonight, just like she had wanted to preserve her peace a little longer through the rest of the day. She was functional. She wanted to stay that way.

"Did you go out wearing that?"

What was he still doing watching her? Barli glanced over her shoulder. "So?"

"Didn't anyone *see* you?"

She still couldn't suss out his tone. "I guess not." She'd been keeping her distance. Barli took her plate and flopped down on the couch.

He glanced at the food but didn't take any. Wasn't he starving? They'd had no food for nearly two full days. It had been hard for Barli to resist coming out for dinner earlier.

Barli glanced at him a little longer before going back to her food. She shoveled it into her mouth. "I'm sorry," she said, once she had finished.

She heard shuffling behind her. She stood up and deposited her tray. When she turned around again, Barli's brain skipped a beat. Farren had, for some inexplicable reason, removed his shirt. As she stared, he tossed it onto the couch. "What..."

"Take it off," he said.

"What the—wh—no!" Was he crazy? Was he serious?

Farren blinked. "You're going to get in trouble," he said. "They'll keep you locked up, even longer than the first time. And there's no way they'll let you into the competition after that."

Barli swallowed down a cry at that. Not being able to run had been bad enough last night. It had made her even more certain that she had to get out of this place. Even if she could move freely through the compound, it wasn't enough space. It wasn't enough. Besides, any time she went wild, all they would do would be to put her in tighter and tighter spots until she wouldn't be able to breathe at all. "I don't...I don't have anything else."

He nodded to his shirt. "So switch with me."

She stared at him for several seconds before slowly pulling her shirt over her head. They were about the same size. She stood half naked in front of him as she let the shirt slip from between her fingers. She moved like a snail for his unmarred offering, laboriously pulling it on.

Farren was nothing to look at, Barli thought. Midsized and, with his eternally messy hair, his stark, and unsettling black eyes...his skin was too sallow to be attractive. Once she was far enough from her discarded shirt, he picked it up and pulled it over his body.

"Won't they notice you don't have a cut?"

"They won't come close enough to know."

Barli folded her arms over her stomach. She sniffed at the shirt, full of Ferran's scent—which was more or less a mess of mashed food, sweat, and dirt. Barli had heard the old tepid water being sloshed around late at night. She knew, with no other means to do so, Farren could only wash himself in whatever water was still available after the cooking was done. The same likely went for his clothes.

"Oh," she said.

Farren looked strange wearing her blood. "Don't do it again," he said. "I don't have any spares."

She opened her mouth to say something more, to try to explain, but nothing came out. A few seconds later, Farren was gone, disappeared back into his own room.

Once he was gone, Barli took his shirt off and filled a tub with mostly clean water. She scrubbed it clean as best she could and hung it to dry in her room. Once she was alone, she unwound the rough bandages from her stomach, wincing as she pulled the fabric away from the wound.

It wasn't deep, and she hadn't meant it to be. Once she had assured herself it was fine, she rewrapped her stomach and went to bed.

"Barli!" Ginsun shouted.

She got up from the floor as Ginsun ran over to her, stumbling a little from the difficulties his foot presented. "Hey, hey," she said quickly, putting her hand up so he didn't run right over her.

"One of the Priests want to see you," he said.

Barli tugged on Ferran's newly washed shirt, making sure it was covering any sign of the bandages she still had tugged tightly across her middle. "Where?"

Ginsun gave her a funny look. "Come on," he said, taking her hand and leading her down the stairs. He stopped outside one of the many doors. "Well? They don't like waiting," he said.

Barli gave him a strained glance as she hesitantly lifted her hand and knocked, hearing a crisp command for entry before she opened the door. She stepped numbly into the room. This one was different than any of the others she'd been in. The walls were a light blue color, and posters with stylized writing were plastered all over. There was a nicer, fancier door on the other side of the room.

The Priest she'd seen before was standing upright, his hand resting on a low table that took up a good portion of the room. There was a piece of paper on the table, and his fingers brushed gently over it.

"Sin. Have a seat."

She did, staring up at him while intermittently trying to read the paper that part of his hand was obscuring.

He seemed lost in his own thought, staring out at one of the many posters. She tried not to fidget too much as she waited. Finally, he turned toward her. "This is the official information for the Black Sin competition. If you sign it, you recognize the competition is dangerous. And if you win, you will be afforded special privileges, in return for assisting the Priests in keeping people safe from the demons."

He looked almost bored. "There will be no preliminary competitions."

"What?"

"Generally, there is a preliminary competition at each Asylum. The top two contenders go on. However, since you are the only one entering, it is unnecessary. Although if you want to improve your chances, it would be wise to take bouts with some of the others."

He slid the paper toward her, along with a pen. "The competition will take place in two months. Hopefully this will be adequate time to prepare. We have reason to believe the skills required will come naturally to you." The Priest tapped the paper, pushing her to sign it before she'd even read it.

Not that it mattered, she realized. Barli knew they could kill her whenever they wanted. So it was particularly strange they were even having her sign anything at all. She scribbled her name out without another thought. It wasn't as though she had rights anyway. They were just pretending.

Barli pushed the paper back toward him.

"After that, the competition will be centered on Shalka Island. There will be a few warm-ups. After that, you will receive a target and will be charged with its elimination. If you do well enough, you will be selected as a new Black Sin."

Barli swallowed. "W-why is this happening now?" she asked.

"There is a vacancy," he said. But there was something else, something he bit back that Barli saw in his eyes before he turned away, waving his hand, dismissing her. He opened the door across the way, and she caught sight of a full hallway, more people in Priest's uniforms, and beyond some great doorway of rich wood and double doors.

The door closed sharply and she realized at some point he'd snatched the paper away. She'd never know what it said.

Barli took a deep breath and went back to the practice room. It was real now. She was entered now. She had just signed up to be a murderer.

When Barli took dinner, she was cornered by Ginsun. "So? Did you say yes?"

"Do you know everything around here?" she asked.

He shrugged. "Pretty much."

She spotted Xinpaku in the crowd and her eyes narrowed thoughtfully. The Priest had said that she was the only entrant from here. That meant he officially was not involved. "If you know so much, why isn't Xinpaku entering? Or Ployame, for that matter?" she asked as she spotted the back of Ployame's head in the crowd.

Ginsun shoveled salad into his mouth. "Well," he said around a mouthful of lettuce. "Xin's got a thing where he sorta goes…he gets sick, I guess. A lot."

Was it his affliction—the reason he was here? She knew better than to pry. She supposed that answer was enough—though she'd probably still try if she were in Xinpaku's shoes. So what if he got sick? She had some sort of sickness too, that came and went. But she could handle it. She could work through it. She always had.

"Ployame?" If she'd tried once already…was it because she'd lost?

Ginsun paused. "I don't know." He tipped his head. "When she came back Parsley said she stayed in her room for months. She hardly ate." Ginsun took a long sip of water, smacking his lips.

What happened? Did someone try to kill her? Barli knew Ginsun didn't know the answer, but she still wanted to ask. Could she go up to Ployame and ask? Or was it possible Farren knew? He was already mad at her half the time—but she didn't want Ployame as an enemy. She was way too dangerous to approach about something that seemed to have had a quite devastating effect on her.

She glanced over at Farren's hallway, though she'd noticed he was in the courtyard again today. The days were growing more and more overcast. It wouldn't be long before it started raining again. During the rain season, it was nearly constant, pouring down in floods that took over unslanted streets and raised the docks more than a foot.

Barli put a hand to her stomach, though the wounds were healing quickly. It itched more than anything, and she wanted to pull the scabs off. Her mother's warning voice echoed in her head; "Don't pick at your skin, it'll scar."

Her fingers traced her face. She had far worse scars now. There was no going back from scars like the Sin brands.

Two days later, Barli caught Farren out of the courtyard for once. She stood in the hallway, watching him collect his meal and sit down on the floor as he twisted the fork slightly and drew it through the mash. She also caught sight of his mangled hand. It was exceedingly red and puffier than it should be.

Barli rolled her eyes as she walked into the room. Stubborn fool. She cut herself and she knew how to take care of herself way better than Farren. He was an idiot. She turned to the stack of dirty plates and got to work.

Farren came up after a while and added his plate to her slowly diminishing pile.

"That cut's infected," she said.

He didn't say anything.

"Did you even eat anything?" she asked, glancing at his plate. There were fork marks dragged through the food, but each heap was still suspiciously high.

"Come on, Farren. Wash it out. You've got to, if you won't let me. And put something over it!" She stopped what she was doing and lifted up her shirt. She had no need for bandages around her middle anymore. It was healing well, little more than a slightly puckered red line now. Ferran's hand almost looked worse. "This is what a properly dressed cut looks like."

Farren looked at his hand. Now that he was closer, she had a far better look, and it quite confirmed her suspicions. Falls, how had he survived so long?

Barli rolled her eyes. "Have you lost the ability to talk? What have you been doing out in the courtyard so much?" It was cold today and he didn't have much besides that shirt—and Barli knew it wasn't particularly warm. She'd been shivering before she started working out.

He shrugged.

She scowled and bit back the desire to grab his palm and force it into the water. "Farren, I'm not going to hurt you. You know that, right?"

He took a step back from her—her words were making him tense. Apparently he did think she would hurt him.

"Farren."

"No one touches me," he said.

"I know but—"

"No one. Touches. Me." He stared at her, the dark black of his eyes boring into her, making her chest hurt. "The demon passes that way."

"We've got demons already!" she said.

"If you hadn't already realized, most rules don't apply the same to me." Farren traced the puffy cut on his hand. "Literally no one has touched me that I can remember. Except you."

No one…at all? She shivered a little. "It's just a touch."

But it wasn't. Even she could understand that. She remembered Xinpaku's fingers at her throat. It was strange—almost haunting.

Farren shook his head. "They've always told me I have so much in me—that I could make it worse for anyone I got too close to. I don't want to mess anyone up."

They must have drilled it pretty deep in his head. What exactly was so dangerous about him? He didn't even display any outward signs of the demon's touch. It couldn't be too bad, could it?

"I'm not scared," she said. She held her hand out. "I'll risk it, if you'll let me."

Farren glanced at her extended hand, his weight shifting from one foot to the next. "I shouldn't."

"It's my choice, isn't it?"

His hand crept forward slowly, edging back and forth but slowly still moving closer and closer. Barli held still, breathing through her nose, approaching him like she might a wild animal.

"Are you sure?" he breathed.

She nodded. And, finally, finally, his gentle fingers touched her palm. They were quiet, standing still for what felt like hours. She subtly moved her hand until she could envelop his hand with hers.

"D-do you feel any different?"

"I feel fine. But you—you feel warm." And sweaty. She was glad they weren't really holding hands or they would have slipped apart from a whole puddle of sweat.

He swallowed. "Sorry." He withdrew his hand.

"Farren, you really need to wash that out."

Farren stared at it, but finally nodded. She stepped away, watching as he pulled at the still pus-filled center of the wound, hissing slightly as he pulled out the old leaking filling. The tender wound filled with fresh blood. He dipped it into the water, his soft hands prodding it gently as though it didn't hurt at all, though Barli knew it must have. He brought it out of the water and watched it begin to drip down his arm again.

"Will you let me wrap it this time?"

His Adam's apple bobbed, but he nodded mutely.

"Good." She fetched a bandage from her room—seeing the state of things, she'd collected what she could and kept them balled up. She doubted her stomach would be the last injury the locked ward saw.

Farren closed his eyes as he held out his hand. He flinched as she touched him, pulling the fabric across his wound, moving in and around his hand until it was tight.

"There. That wasn't so bad, was it?"

He stepped away, looking at his wrapped hand. "I…" He swallowed and turned away.

"Are you trying to thank me again?"

He disappeared back into his room without another word.

Barli grinned.

Chapter Seven

SHE WORKED MOSTLY IN the locked ward for about a week. Once her stomach was perfectly fine, she wandered back to the practice room and started working with weapons again. The swords were still heavy and she couldn't wield then for long before her arms felt like they were going to fall off. But she didn't want to be walking down the streets with a massive thing like that. With her size, it'd probably drag on the ground. Besides, it wasn't an assassin's weapon. So she stuck to her daggers, practicing throwing them at varied ranges and easing them in and out of her clothing. She practiced stabbing from a variety of positions, but with nothing to sink the blade into, she couldn't be sure how effective it was. With a weapon as small as a knife, she would need to find the right points to finish her victim off quickly.

Was she really going to kill someone?

Barli tried not to think about that snag. She was sure whoever they were going to send her after deserved it.

Otherwise they would only bring them to the Asylum like normal. Otherwise, it would have just been wrong.

When she took a break for water, she saw Xinpaku watching her. She had noticed him over the past several days. Sometimes he would stand in the doorway for a few minutes. He always left whenever she caught sight of him.

"Xinpaku?" she prompted quietly as she took a long sip of water.

He tilted his head politely, extending his chiseled jaw. "Can I help you, miss?"

She swallowed. "I-I wanted to take you up on your offer."

"You're going."

Barli nodded. It hadn't really seemed like she had much of a choice in it anyway. They hadn't even given her another job. She wondered what it was about her that made them think she'd be so good at this. Was it just because of her arm? They couldn't know that much more about her, could they? "Will you help me?"

He crossed his arms. "I do not do things part way. If I help you, you will do what I say. You will not complain. If you do, I will stop helping in any way."

Barli swallowed before finally nodding. "Okay. I want to win."

Xinpaku narrowed his eyes. "Very well." He looked her over critically. "Follow me," he instructed, taking her back to the practice room.

Barli soon discovered that Xinpaku was a tough taskmaster.

The first day and she could barely drag herself into bed. He had her running up and down the stairs, making endless passes at him that he blocked or moved smoothly out of the way for. Barli was sore and tired and insanely hungry for whatever Parsley had managed to cook up. The days passed in a blur, and soon she wasn't sure how long she had left before it was time for the competition.

"I can hear you from a mile away!" Xinpaku complained as he caught her for the umpteenth time. "What about sneaking do you not understand?"

Barli was still catching her breath from the runs he'd had her doing earlier. "How did you learn all this stuff anyway?"

His eyes narrowed. "It doesn't matter. Do it again!"

And she obeyed. She kept her breath shallower this time, her footfalls light. He still slammed her against the wall the moment she was within reach. Barli's shoulders ached as she got back into position.

"Better," he said.

"Is this all necessary?" she asked.

Xinpaku folded his arms. "Do you think it is easy, girl, to end someone's life? Do you think that person, if they are anything like you, would be willing to be put down? They will fight you, if you give them the time, and they will fight you with everything they have, because soon enough they won't have anything left at all."

She swallowed.

"If you're going to be successful, you are not just going to take out one person. You are going to take out one after another after another. The only way a normal person could manage that would be to believe their existence depended just as strongly on these people's elimination. Can you live like that?"

Her nostrils flared. She had to admit, she hadn't given much thought to the continuation of the job, once she possibly won. "Never," she said.

"Then what are you doing?" Xinpaku asked.

Barli bit her lip. "Maybe I'm not a normal person."

"You don't like seeing people hurting."

"Who does?"

Xinpaku held his hands up abruptly. "That's it. I'm done for today. Do a hundred more crunches and up and down the stairs until you can't do it without stumbling. Understand?"

"Y-yeah," she said, finding the abrupt dismissal bizarre. He passed her briskly, disappearing into the door she now realized led off into the men's room, where Ginsun and most of the other men in the Asylum slept.

She shook her head. She was tired of trying to figure all these things out—everyone around here was keeping secrets, had strange reactions to perfectly normal things, and seemed to get ticked off for no reason in particular. She had never met such a large population of infuriating and messed up individuals in her life—but she supposed it wasn't surprising. They were here for a reason, weren't they?

Barli took a few minutes to catch her breath before she got on her back and began the work assigned to her. With the early leave of Xinpaku's training, she finished before dinner, and dragged herself back to the locked ward where she promptly fell asleep.

A few hours later she woke up, legs still hanging off the bed. She groaned, rubbing her eyes as she rolled off the bed and slipped into the kitchen. Her stomach was growling like crazy—no doubt that was why she'd woken up at all.

Her whole body aching, she gathered her bowl—it was stew today—and sat down to enjoy it. Xinpaku had been keeping her so busy she hadn't even realized it should have been Ferran's day to cook. But she'd been let outside like normal. In fact, she was sure more than one week had passed—and yet no days had she woken to a locked door.

When she finished eating, she loitered outside Ferran's door for a few minutes before knocking briefly.

She was surprised how quickly the door clicked open—though, as usual, it was only just an inch. Barli was so surprised she almost forgot what she was going to talk to him about. "I…how's your hand?"

He held it up. The skin had healed over and it was finally looking normal. "Good." Maigi appeared at his feet, curling her tail between his legs and mewing slightly. She didn't look like a baby anymore—she was looking full-grown.

She knelt down, putting her hand out to the cat. "She looks good."

Farren shrugged. "I don't know what they're supposed to look like. But I don't know if I can hide her too much longer."

"I thought you said no one ever got close."

"Yeah, but she scratches and whines sometimes. I'm surprised Ginsun hasn't found out yet—and once he does it's all over." Ferran's face fell.

"There's no way they'd let you keep her?"

He bent his head. "I don't think so. They don't let anyone have pets."

"Falls," Barli muttered.

"You look tired," he said.

"I've been working hard." Barli sighed, rubbing her shoulders. "Xinpaku's making me work till I'm exhausted."

"Oh," Farren nodded. "That's coming up soon, isn't it?"

Was it? She shrugged. "I guess. I'm trying not to think about it."

He gave her a strange look. "How's that working out then?"

"Mostly okay, actually. I like working hard. It's what I always do, when my mind gets full of things. I make it move till my mind can't even think anymore."

"Is that possible?"

She gave him a half smile. "Of course."

"I don't…think I've ever done that."

Barli couldn't see into his room—she couldn't tell if he still had stacks of papers everywhere—the only thing it seemed they saw fit to provide for her. She thought back to Ferran's reactions—to the kitten, to her hand. "There's a lot of things you've never done." Like really been outside, or tucked into a hug, or tasted the sea.

There were so many things a person should experience in his or her life.

She took a deep breath, petting the kitten.

"Hey, Barli…"

"Yeah?"

"Would you…touch me again?"

She blinked, wanting to turn her head away for a second, before she remembered that this was Farren and he didn't mean things the same way some other guy would. "Sure."

Barli took his hand. The door swung open wider as he took a step forward. She pulled him out of his room. His face was twisted, like he couldn't quite decide whether he liked it or not. He was still fighting himself, probably, trying to decide if it was worth all the risk.

She put a hand on his shoulder. "Come here. Closer."

"I...no." He took a step back, shaking her hand from his shoulder. But he didn't let go of her hand. "This is enough."

Barli shook her head. He really was an oddball. "You should really try some new things," she said.

Farren didn't reply.

"You don't have to talk to me anymore," he said. "I told you, anyway, you'd be just like everyone else."

"I would, I just...I've been so exhausted. And—you're not cooking anymore, so..." Barli squeezed his hand. "But I am, you know, I'm going to leave so..."

He let go. "Yeah. It's not—I shouldn't be doing this." Farren backed away. "I don't know why I'm doing this. It's—it's because you didn't just go away. Exactly. You didn't move out, like you were supposed to."

Barli tilted her head and sighed. "I'm sorry. But you know you'd still be feeling miserable if it wasn't for me."

"I wouldn't have gotten cut in the first place."

"What? You never have accidents?"

Farren walked past her, out into the courtyard. Barli

followed him slowly, shivering as she stepped into the outdoors. The walls protected them from the wind, but it didn't change the fact that the days of summer were swiftly passing.

"Farren." She rolled her eyes.

He looked up at the sky. "I don't get it. You have all this passion. For life. Is it really that good?"

Barli gave him another strange glance. Always with the strange glances—or maybe the pitiful ones, sometimes. She rarely knew what to say to him or anyone in here. She wanted to get back to normal people, where she didn't have bizarre conversation like this one, that had her head turning over itself again and again. "Yes," she said clearly. "You just haven't seen enough of it to know."

He sat down, running his hands through the soft dirt.

Barli sat down next to him. "Your hair looks terrible."

"Walunata tried to explain what braiding was," he said. "I don't think I got it right."

Barli shook her head, suppressing a laugh. "Here. Let me do it."

He hesitated before finally relaxing, pulling at his hair till the half-done messes were unmade. "Okay."

She reworked his hair, pulling at what felt like a decade of knots. Did he even have a hairbrush?

"This is the sort of thing," he muttered as she yanked as gently as she could on his hair, dividing it into parts and weaving his hair together. Braids weren't the classic look for a guy, but she didn't think it mattered in here. Farren wasn't seeing anyone anyway. He'd probably never even heard of a haircut.

"What's this sort of thing?"

"Stuff I can't get used to."

She yanked on his head.

"Ouch! What're you doing?"

"Making sure you don't want to get used to it."

Farren scooted away. "I'm not kidding, Barli. Even if you don't win this competition, someone's going to leave and they'll move you down with everyone else and I won't see you again."

"It's not like it's my fault!" Barli said. "What do you expect me to do?"

"I should have never found Maigi. Then we'd still be saying nothing to each other."

"Falls! It's not bad to get close to someone for a little bit. Besides, you love her. And she's not going away."

"Yes, she is. I shouldn't have gotten attached to her either. They're going to find her and take her away and it'll be just like before, only worse, because I know just that much more what I'm missing."

"I'll just have to show you things you can do without anyone."

He rubbed his forehead. "Why are you doing this?"

"You don't want me to anyway, what do you care?"

Farren hunched his shoulders. "Because you're confusing me, that's why! I never know what you're going to do, when you're going to show up. You come barging into my room, then you don't, then you're running around like a lunatic, then I almost think you're okay, then you're going to go kill some people but first you'll do my hair and you say you want to live but you're the one who took a knife to the chest."

She'd never heard so many words come out his mouth before. "I already told you why I did that. Not that I should have to—it's not like we're friends or anything."

"Do you care about anyone but yourself?"

"Do you?"

"I don't have anyone else to care about but myself."

"Well, neither do I. Not anymore, anyway."

Farren glanced at her. "But you want to get out. Because you have people. Outside of here. People you care about."

Barli didn't have a reply to that.

Chapter Eight

"BARLI! ARE YOU EVEN paying attention, girl?"

She got off the floor, where Xinpaku had knocked her once again. "Sorry, sir."

"I don't think you're getting the immediacy of the situation. Your competition will not be easy."

"I *know*." And she still didn't know why Xinpaku wasn't entering. Ginsun made it sound like his being sick was common, but in all the time they'd been training, he'd never even seemed faint. Barli could hardly ever beat him. She wondered if others were as good.

Barli rolled her neck. "I just don't know what the point is. As long as I'm not obvious about it, they won't know I'm going to kill them."

"The point of these last exercises hasn't been about approaching your target. It's about taking down anyone you might run into after you kill your target, or anyone who might come after you because you're a Sin – especially because you'd be a Black Sin."

"People would kill me, for that?"

"Absolutely." He regarded her from behind his deep eyes. They were softer than Farren's, and far lighter too. His brows, however, were thick. "You have not been among the people since you've been marked."

"I know how they're—we're treated." She wasn't naïve. She'd seen them before. She'd seen how people treated them. She knew how she'd treated them too. They were looked upon with disgust—worse than urchins, homeless beggars, or drunken vagrants. Barli knew she'd said unkind enough things herself, before she was one of them. They all looked so terrible, after all. They were monsters and so many of them wore it in their bodies, in more than just their face.

"I don't think you do, sweetheart. You do not walk in the dark parts of the world, the only places open and willing to even do business with our kind. We do not generally move in the nicer places. We are not allowed there, except to use the streets. They are more scared, because we are a rarity, and put off by our visage too much to cause trouble. It is the places you have never had to go before, girl, you will find need of these skills."

"You've been out there? After coming here?"

"I don't find that you are taking this seriously enough."

What? "I am!" She just had Farren on her mind, the neglected miserable kid trapped in a single room He'd gotten under her skin, especially since the last time she'd seen him, still wearing his hair in those stupid braids, despite the fact that half his hair was no longer in them.

He shook his head. "You don't understand. They will

tear you apart on those streets, especially with your small frame and that pretty face."

She glowered. There was no way anyone would call her face pretty any longer. Barli hunched her shoulders. "That's not going to happen."

He grabbed her shoulders and threw her to the ground. "You're letting me get far too close before you mount a defense."

"Well, I know you're not actually going to hurt me."

He slammed his hand into the soft of her belly.

"Falls!" She kicked out at him as she tried to take a breath in again. Barli scrambled back to her feet, holding her hands up defensively as they circled each other.

"Don't make assumptions. They will only get you into trouble."

"What? I'm not supposed to be able to trust you?"

"Never," he said.

She glared at him. "I hate you."

Xinpaku prowled. "You will meet men—and women— in your work, even the first time you go out, even if it's for nothing at all. They will not be afraid. Some don't believe in the demon, or maybe they're all demons themselves. Not all the scum of the earth is bottled up here. If you don't defend yourself, they can be ruthless."

"I get it. I'm not stupid, okay!" Maybe she hadn't been in the roughest places, but it wasn't as though she'd grown up anywhere near rich.

Barli pulled away, coming against the board of weapons. She reached out and grasped one of her favorite knives. "I'll be fine, thanks for your concern."

Xinpaku gave her a thin smile. "You should try pitting yourself against another partner, someone who moves differently and isn't as predictable."

"Who?"

His eyes shimmered. "I might have a few ideas." He held up his hands. "Enough then."

"No way. I'm not letting down my guard. That's when you always get me."

"You're finally getting it." Xinpaku smiled.

Barli bared her teeth back at him. "Thanks."

Xinpaku smirked. For the first time, she realized that he looked tired. He had been calling the ends of their sessions after briefer and briefer periods of time. Sometimes it seemed like he would jerk randomly, but she figured now it was only something he did to try to distract her.

"Can I ask you a question? Again?"

He raised an eyebrow.

Why was she doing this? "Never mind." It was rude to ask and he'd already made it clear he didn't want to say.

Barli put the knife back, keeping her focus on Xinpaku even while her back was to him, but he didn't make any moves of her.

They went back to working, or rather Xinpaku took the opportunity to sit down and watch her as she went through the movements. He corrected her every once in a while, but he had mellowed lately. She assumed it was because she was doing better now and there was less to correct. But he always seemed to have at least one thing to say.

"You know what you need?"

"What?"

"A quick escape."

"I can beat them—anyone," Barli said with self-assured confidence. Xinpaku never seemed to believe her. She wondered what his obsession with it was.

"You can't beat a hundred—or even ten at a time. Barli, if you want to survive out there, you need to know when to run too. And how."

Barli rolled her eyes. "I grew up on a ship," she said. "I know how to climb."

He leaned forward, rubbing his short beard. "How long has it been?"

"What?"

"Since you climbed."

Barli shrugged. "I guess, a little bit before I got here."

"So…three months at least. Those muscles have probably died some. You should practice that too. Yes. Why don't you focus on that for a while? I'll let you know when you'll go up against someone else. And remember to watch yourself."

It wasn't a bad idea, so Barli collected the ropes and nets from the storage room and brought them back to the locked ward. Even if she didn't get what Xinpaku's paranoia was about, she did miss being up in the rigging.

It took her three evenings to get enough of the rigging done that it no longer fit in her room. She took it out into the main room, trying to figure out where she should test it out when Farren wandered into the room.

Farren.

She'd been avoiding him, or maybe he'd been avoiding her, or maybe a little bit of both, she wasn't sure. All she knew was she had hardly seen him since the day she had braided his hair, and he had told her she had someone.

And she did. She had people. She just wasn't sure if they would want her anymore.

She ran her hands over her ruined face. She could see the scars mirrored on Ferran's face—and then of course his other larger ones that obscured even more of his face. She looked away, giving him his peace.

He filled up his plate and she thought he had walked back to his room, but several minutes later she heard his voice. "What is that?"

She blinked, looking back at him. He had finally taken the braids out and his hair hung loosely, tangled and abused, down past his shoulders. "Rope."

He glared. "I'm not a complete idiot," he said. "What are you making? What is it for?"

"Xinpaku wants me to practice climbing. It's too big for my room now." She didn't ask how he'd been. It would have been a stupid question.

"Oh."

A sudden thought came to her. "Uh, actually, can you help me with this?"

He paused for a moment before stepping closer. Like everything he did, he seemed to have to hesitate first. What he was thinking in those moments, she had no idea. Barli had never been so thoughtful in her entire life. That was partially why she was in trouble here now. "What am I supposed to do?"

She surveyed the mass of nets and line she'd assembled. "Well, I need a few more ties first. Here," she said, and showed him how to knot the thicker rope against the heavy nets, weaving them together. Once she had it affixed the way she wanted, she hefted the pile over one shoulder. "Help me lift this."

Farren, understandably, was not very strong and he didn't take that much weight from her shoulders—but it was enough that she managed to slog forward slowly, until they were standing out in the brisk night air in the courtyard. The sun was beginning to depart, and she worked quickly in its dying light to set her gear to her satisfaction.

She took the corners and laid them out, widening out the impressive netting. She looked up at the higher stonework, so far out of reach. Climbing. If she was a real climber, she would have been able to scale even an impossible wall like this. She'd given up entirely too easily—because of Farren and his stupid plants.

Farren watched her silently for a long time, as she stumbled around the edges of the netting and murmured under her breath, trying to figure out what her next move was.

"Is that it? What's it for?"

"Don't bother me, Farren!" she replied.

He left.

Barli went inside too, once the sun was down and she was too cold to think straight and too dark to plan. How did she get it up there, like she wanted? She went to bed puzzling it over.

The next day she worked on rigging it up—she'd finally settled on an idea. She took more hooks and assorted fishing equipment from the main storage room. No one had asked about the supplies, so she figured they were not missing anything.

Ginsun came out to watch her, asking enough questions to make her head spin. The worst of them was what the Priests would think. But she explained tightly that she was preparing for the competition and Xinpaku had told her to, so obviously the Priests would be okay with it, and it seemed to sate him.

She attached the hooks to the ropes and tossed them until they dragged on the higher roof segments. She pulled the ropes taut and worked on affixing enough other rigs to hold solid weight and the rest of the mess of nets.

She tested it, climbing up a few feet before coming back down. She figured it wasn't likely a good idea to climb too high during the day when there were watchful eyes like Ginsun and pretty much everyone else in the Asylum to note her ascent. Barli figured it was generally frowned upon to get into a position that might allow one to rappel down the other side of the Asylum and escape into the world. Sins on the loose—the Asylum would lose any of its credibility. Common people would be terrified of the notion of a Sin on the loose.

She spent the rest of the day practicing. She could feel

eyes on her, and Walunata launched herself at her sometime past noon. Xinpaku hadn't been joking—he was really making her watch her back…though she doubted anyone but him would be a real challenge. Maybe one or two of the others too. She wondered who he could convince. Walunata and Ginsun would be easy targets—but she was generally alert of their presence, since they liked to jump into her all the time anyway.

Barli had looked around after tickling Walunata to the ground and her cries of mercy were expended, but there had been no sight of Xinpaku. In fact, she'd hardly seen him since he'd walked out of their session.

Barli skirted the dinner-goers at the evening meal, taking her food quickly and eating with her back to the wall. She didn't trust that Xinpaku's influence and warnings wouldn't expand to dinner too. She thought she saw one of the younger guys giving her a heavy glance.

Ooh. She'd never thought about one of them going after her. They didn't seem overly strong, but they were men and larger than her. She wondered why they wouldn't jump at this chance: why didn't she have any competition? Why was everyone who had been here so set against getting out? Did they love it here so much?

She stayed in the kitchen area after everyone left. She heard the locks flick shut when everyone but her was gone. She started in surprise realizing this was the first time she'd actually been around to see what happened. It seemed as though the doors had the ability to be locked by some remote switch, once everything was settled the way it was supposed to be.

Barli curled up on the couch and waited a few hours, until the sun outside was beginning to darken. She knocked on Ferran's door.

"What?" he asked suspiciously.

"Do you want to see it?" she asked. "What I've been working on?"

He eyed her uncertainly but stepped out of his room, closing the door softly.

"They watch us sometimes, don't they?" she asked as they walked outside.

He nodded. "There's slits in pretty much every room. Limited vision, but enough to know if I'm where I'm supposed to be. Slivers. If you look through, sometimes you can see a robe passing. But it's hard to make anything out for sure."

"Outside?"

Farren shook his head. "I don't think so. The first time I stayed outside there was a whole panic—they thought I'd somehow escaped, or something. They had a major lockdown—you haven't seen what that's like. They dressed up in this thick gear and swept every—" He stopped abruptly as they entered the courtyard, eyes going wide as he looked at the impressive setup Barli had done. "What the…what's all this for?"

She smirked at him. "Climbing."

His eyes widened. "Y-you're going to-to climb up there?"

She nodded. "And you are too."

"What?"

"Yeah, come on." She took his hand, holding on till he

got past his inevitable original flinch at any sort of contact. He followed reluctantly as she led him to the base of the nets. "You ever climbed before?"

He shook his head.

She hadn't expected anything else. "Watch me then." She stepped forward, slitting the balls of her feet into the webbing. Her fingers wound around the thinner rope as she tested her weight before hoisting herself higher. "It's just like climbing stairs…more vertically."

Barli moved on, taking another step, forcing herself higher and higher. She kept climbing until she was at the shingled roofing. She hoisted herself up and took a seat, staring out over the Asylum's yard and then beyond, where she could see the rest of the world laid out in the setting sunlight.

It was beautiful, but she couldn't focus on that. This… "This isn't Hevon'i."

Farren was looking at the ropes with trepidation. "Of course not. You can't have thought you were still on the same island. They always move the new Sins." He put his hands into the ropes, tugging on it hesitantly. "Are you sure about this? It's going to hold?"

"You don't weigh more than me." If he did, it was just barely. Barli could feel her heart pounding in her head. What an idiot! Of course, this wasn't the same island! She swallowed down the flash of despair that came over her. "Come on up here, it's great!"

Farren made slow progress. He was nowhere near as strong or fit as her—especially now that she'd been training up. She could see him straining to make any progress, but he was determined. She wondered how often he had tried to climb this wall, or done other things to try to escape from his prison. He wasn't quite as content as the others. But he certainly believed the party line.

"Come on, just a little farther!"

She grabbed his hand once it was within reach and hauled him up until he was sitting beside her on the roof.

"There. Isn't it..." She trailed off, still upset about the fact that she hadn't even known what island she was on. It did underline her problem—even if she could slip off the roof and down into the streets, she wouldn't be able to reach Visea unless she could get passage on a ship of some sort.

She glanced over at Farren and Visea vanished from her mind.

Farren was staring at the golds and oranges and pinks, but he was also looking wider—out across a city he'd never seen, to mountains he'd never climbed, to waters he'd never swam in. Farren's breaths were shallow. She saw a shine in his eyes—but more than that, his black hollow eyes had a glimmer in them. It wasn't from liquid tears. The glimmer was like a spark of life, the beginnings of a person who had been trodden down and forced not to live for years and years.

It was that moment that Barli knew it wasn't just her she had to get out of here. She had to find a way to take Farren too.

Farren didn't say anything, but Farren wasn't one known for words.

They sat in silence and watched the sun set. Without a buffer for the wind, the cold set in quickly once the sun's rays had vanished. Even though they were shivering, they stayed on the roof, uneven and prickly shingles scraping against their thighs.

Finally, when her fingers were beginning to freeze together and she was wondering whether she'd even be able to keep a hold when she climbed back down, she touched his shoulder, shocking him out of his quiet reverence.

"We should go back down," she said softly. "You can come back up tomorrow, Farren. It's too cold to stay out here."

He glanced at her, the hardness of his gaze reasserting itself. Farren nodded quietly. His fingers fumbled on the ropes and he nearly lost his grip once and Barli realized that it was at least fifteen feet and there could be some serious harm if one of them did fall. Off the other side it would have been even worse—maybe as much as forty feet. That was enough to kill a person.

"Careful!" she warned.

He didn't say anything further, only stumbled back a few steps, catching his balance, and walked away. By the time she had followed him inside, he was in his room.

Barli couldn't get the look on his face—of quiet wonder and a heartbreaking longing out of her mind. She fell asleep thinking about his eyes.

Chapter Nine

THE NEXT MORNING BARLI found the courtyard locked. She wasn't really surprised. She'd known the minute Farren had gotten up there this would happen. There went her climbing equipment.

Barli sparred with the hanging bag until she got tired, then turned her attention to people watching. It was only a few more days and she would be leaving. She hadn't asked where they were going, and she doubted the Priests would tell her anyway. There was a small chance they were going back to her home island—it was one of the larger ones. If she could slip out of the competition…if she could see Visea…

No. She couldn't do that—she couldn't jeopardize her win. Because if she couldn't win—if she got caught—everything would be that much more difficult.

She shook her head slightly, staring out over the people working below. The Asylum residence, in their normal day's work, were placid and unhurried. It felt weird, not having a job. Did Xinpaku have a job? How had he gotten away with taking out all that time teaching her? And where was he, anyway? She didn't see him below. Barli sighed.

What was she supposed to do? She couldn't...no. It didn't matter—first things first. She had to win—that was the only solution. She had to win.

A hand grabbed her roughly by the shoulder. She felt a flick at her throat, then her wrist, and last her stomach.

"Dead three times," Xinpaku breathed in her ear.

She shoved him back, turning on him quickly as she elbowed him. Xinpaku fought her a little, but he went slack suddenly and she made the best of it, pinning him down. Sudden jerks crept across his body for a few seconds before he stilled.

"You..."

"I told you to watch your back," he said—but he wasn't smiling.

"And I thought you were leaving me alone."

Xinpaku grinned. "I have a test for you."

She lifted her eyebrow. "Really?"

He nodded. "Your goal is to take out Ployame."

"What?"

"Pretend she's your target," he said.

Barli frowned. "Is she expecting it?"

Xinpaku folded his arms. "You'll find out."

Barli sighed. "Hey—why does no one else want to leave? Isn't there anyone else who wants to compete? Juulon or Brikan? Or-or..." She didn't know all of their names.

His expression was dark. "Most people don't like change. Once they adjust to this place, it's not so bad. And they like the way it is here—these are people who are freaks in the rest of the world but are perfectly normal here. No one feels judged or unsafe. So…it might seem like a prison to you, but to some of us, it's a sanctuary."

"I…do you feel that way too?"

He hesitated, his head swinging away from her. "Yes."

She didn't believe him.

"Go on, now. Let's see how fast you can finish this." His eyes flicked up toward the roof. "And tell Farren to be careful, won't you?"

She squinted, narrowing her eyes to see a faint little spot of black against the mostly dark brown shingling. "Like I could stop him."

"I worry about him, so isolated from everyone else."

Barli eyed him. "Yeah? So what have you done about it?"

"I can't do anything about him. What do you say to the Priests?" He shook his head. "There's plenty of us who would like to see a different life for him, but there's nothing to be done. We don't have any say the way we are. Sins."

Barli bit her lip. "It's not right."

He stood up. "Ployame. Don't forget."

"Is it timed? The test?"

"They give you three days. But you have to search the town for your target. I'll give you…one."

Barli rolled her eyes as Xinpaku stood up, sweeping away with a grace he did not always seem to quite manage. "One day," he called over his shoulder as he walked away.

Barli stared at the little spot that was Farren and hoped no one else had noticed the black smudge on the roof. She shivered a little. The days were getting colder—and the sky today was heavy. She expected it would rain before long. She also expected Farren would stay up there through it all…

She turned her attention towards Ployame, who was cleaning those huge vases again, buried halfway inside. She surveyed the yard, still full of people, constantly moving. And she wasn't a usual fixture in the yard. Her presence would definitely be noticed. This fake mission might almost be harder—especially if Xinpaku had tipped her off. What if she knew already?

She went back to the weapons room, flipping and placing daggers. Obviously, she didn't need to actually kill her, but a blade to flesh would certainly demonstrate to Xinpaku that she could actually do what she wanted. It would prove to Xinpaku that she was ready.

She stuck a few weapons into her clothes. For the first time, she realized she could get into a lot of trouble if she got caught. Barli realized if they saw her taking weapons like this in certain places, they might pull the plug on even getting into competition.

Barli wasn't sure she could get away with it out in the open yard. Someone would think something was strange—and if she wanted to really simulate street conditions, it wasn't as though she could escape after killing someone out in the open like that.

She frowned. When was the best time? If Ployame worked out in the open most of the day and it would seem strange for her to approach, when wouldn't it be strange? Barli bit her cheek. Everyone was at dinner—and if she was actually going to kill Ployame, she could probably sneak her body into one of the empty rooms that no one ever went into. Since they only ate once a day, dinner was always a major affair and after a hard day of work, nearly everyone was fully invested in eating. Distractions marked the best time to cause a smaller one, unnoticed.

Barli watched Ployame's muscled shoulders as she cleaned the huge jars. She really was strong. It would be smartest to sneak up on her, in whatever way she could. She tried to decide which approach to use, how to sneak the blade between the flesh of her body.

She looked up as the sky opened up, unleashing the first drops of what looked to become a real storm. Hmm. That might throw a wrench into her plans. She hadn't been here long enough to see what people did on rainy days...though she assumed everyone still ate dinner.

As the rain began to come down harder, the people in the yard disappeared into the sleeping rooms. Barli watched Ployame turn the vase over so the rainwater would collect inside. Ducking, she disappeared like the rest into one of the first floor rooms. Barli hadn't investigated them all, wary as she was of provoking someone like Farren by cutting in on them unaware.

She shivered as she heard a roll echoing down from the sky. It always seemed so angry to her, she never liked to stay out in such weather. Being on a ship was even worse during a storm, when gray was the only color to be seen.

Barli tipped her head up to the sky, waiting to catch the flash of lightning. She breathed a sigh when it took several seconds to light up. The storm was pretty far away already.

Barli hurried back through the passageway to take

refuge back in the locked ward. Ginsun and Parsley were making dinner, and neither of them had any word for her as she swept by them to vanish into her room, where she tossed daggers as she listened to the storm and tried to convince herself, as she always did, that it would pass.

It was her first storm away from her family. Storms like these could last days. Barli liked to curl up beside her mother for hours, and they would tell stories and sing songs until their voices were hoarse.

She had no one to curl up with now. She could hear the rain splattering against the roof. She shivered, pulling what was left of her miserable blankets around her and over her head as fat rolling raindrops slipped down the sides of the wall outside. Barli almost felt as though they were inside; the roof had somehow failed her, and she would be left to the mercy of the storm.

Barli waited until she heard the sounds of chatter in the hallway. She tucked her knives away and slipped into the main room, observing the line carefully. She saw Ployame halfway through the line. Barli slid along the wall.

She didn't get into line—she could get food later, if she wanted. She kept her eyes shifting, looking for Xinpaku as well, but for whatever reason he couldn't be seen in the line.

Didn't that mark at least two days in a row? Barli frowned, turning her attention back to Ployame. She was almost to the head of the line. Barli glanced around at the others, narrowing her eyes. No one was really looking at her. After that first day, they had mostly left her alone. Barli didn't feel close to any of them. They were nice, she supposed, but they were all so much older than her—except for Ginsun and Walunata, of course.

She couldn't wait to get out of here.

Barli marked Ployame's step as she walked away from the food table. She had to act quickly now, before she was converged upon by her usual company—some of the young women who were still way too old for Barli to feel as though she had anything in common with them.

Ployame stood, eating her food, plate balanced on one hand. Barli slipped closer, hugging the wall. No one seemed to notice her. She saw one of Ployame's friends getting close to the front of the line.

Barli stepped up beside her, the echoes of the storm still playing out in her head. Or was it? Was it still going on, outside? She wouldn't be surprised. She couldn't hear the storm over the chatter, but sometimes the storms went on for days.

She slipped one of her daggers from her clothing, flipping it once in her hand. Barli stepped up beside Ployame, ready to tap the flat of her blade against Ployame's exposed throat.

Barli gasped as her wrist was grabbed. A second later her feet were knocked out from under her. Barli slammed onto the ground and Ployame stood over her.

"I'm not so sure about your chances, girl." One of the other women laughed a little.

Barli's face flushed and she groaned as Ployame let her up. "Xinpaku warned you?" she asked, glancing around at the growing circle of women who were staring down at her.

"A few weeks ago. I'd forgotten until I saw you paying too much attention."

"I was just looking!"

"More than you usually do." Ployame smiled softly. "You did almost have me. But…you gave it too long."

Barli swallowed and nodded. "Any other advice?" she asked.

Ployame glanced sideways at her. "Come here," she said, and took her down the hallway a little ways so they were away from the others. "I was in the competition before, when I was younger. I wanted to get out and see the world. I was almost like you."

"But you've been here your whole life."

She nodded. "Not quite. My parents were not the usual type. They kept me for several years, until they couldn't hide it anymore. I was six when I came here, so I remember a few things about the rest of the world—enough to long for it. But I've had dreams of going beyond, seeing things I've never seen. But I wasn't willing to do what it took."

"What do you mean?"

"I could have won—I was ranking well, and I could see my target. They were perfectly alone. It would have been easy. I went up to them. I had blades, like you. But you know, the thing about daggers is, they're up close and personal. You can't not feel it. You can't avoid the force. You can't get away from the feeling of the blade sinking into flesh, taking the life out of someone. It's something that…well, I was standing there, and even with all that potential freedom laid out in front of me, I couldn't take that last step. I couldn't do that deed. It's not as easy as it looks—do you understand what I'm saying, Barli?"

"You're saying you couldn't do it."

"I'm saying it's not so simple as a flick of a wrist. I couldn't do it, but I haven't, for a second, found any sort of regret in the fact that I did not kill that man. And if that means I'll never see the world, it's alright with me."

Barli dropped her gaze. "I can't stay here. I had... everything."

Ployame regarded her quietly. "It's not so simple. Be careful, whatever you do. And think hard about it." She swept her long hair behind her back. "After I was sure I couldn't do it, I ran."

Barli's eyes widened. "Really?"

Ployame nodded. "I tried to make it for a little while. But with these..." She drew her hand across her face where her brand was bright against her skin. Her slacking face was as good as the brands, however. It was a sign in of itself. "It's not easy. I couldn't take it. I was trying to live in a...not a decent place, eating trash and whatever I could try to catch with my bare hands.

"Listen to me, Barli. Everyone needs people. You can't do it alone. I've heard there's some people who go off like hermits but they're—they're not normal, so much more different than any of us. They can't have a demon, because they aren't *human*. Human people need other people. They need them in case something happens, sure. But they need them for other reason too, ones that aren't as tangible. And your people now, they're us. This brand separates us from other people, and maybe it's not right or fair, but it doesn't change the fact that it makes it so we're all each other's got.

"So if you're thinking of running, you should reconsider."

"I-I'm not...not...I mean, I thought about it, but..." Barli shook her head. "So I guess I'll just end up back here in a little while, like nothing ever happened at all."

"I know no one here is like the people you grew up with. But if you let them, Barli, they can be a new family. And, of course, you can try again the next time...if they don't kill you first."

She nodded quietly. "Thanks," she said awkwardly. "I...I'm just going to go back to my room." She got off the floor, dusting herself off and trying to ignore the embarrassment she felt that she'd been caught so easily.

Barli could hear the storm still raging from her room. Her heart seemed to thud in heavy beats like the raindrops splattering on the roof. Outside, the metal drains clanged as they banged against the ground.

She knew Ployame meant things nicely. She knew she meant well but...it didn't matter what she said. Barli didn't have anything in common with these people. She'd grown up in a different world, and she didn't want to get used to this one. Barli didn't want to stay here. If she wasn't getting out of here one way, she would do it another way. She wasn't about to give up, but she wasn't going to wait around for another chance.

Barli looked at the daggers, spinning them through her fingers. She nearly dropped one as the thunder roared outside. It was still storming—and badly. She took a deep breath, remembering that Farren was still out there.

She waited anxiously by the hallway until the dinnergoers were gone. Once she felt the silence and saw the lights blown out, she hurried to the far door. She stepped out into a torrential rainstorm. "Farren!"

She blinked up into the heavy darkness, the oppressive rain pouring down on the Asylum. The courtyard's drain was working overtime. She blinked up at the roof, to her old slightly bloodied shirt and Ferran's thick black hair. It was hanging considerably closer to his body now, wet and tangled.

"Farren!"

He didn't move.

"Farren!" She rolled her eyes, coming to the ropes, slick and thick. "Farren they're gone now. Come inside!"

The thunder rolled again—and far too fast lightning flashed.

She didn't like storms. "Farren!" She was beginning to get angry. It was freezing cold out here. In spring and summer, the storms were warm. Today was not one of those days.

Barli reached the roof. "Farren, can't you hear me?"

Finally, he turned toward her.

"Come on." She took his hand, which was freezing cold and helped him stumbling down from the high perch. "Why didn't you get down?" she asked, once they had made it back inside. Barli twisted her hair and felt it get considerably lighter. She squeezed out the rest of her clothes, though she was still completely drenched.

Farren was shivering. "I couldn't have gotten in anyway. Why not see more of it?"

She rolled her eyes. "You shouldn't have stayed out there today."

He glared. "What do you care?"

"Well I don't want you to die! Or drown..." Barli sighed. "Besides, without a doubt I'll be stuck back in here before too long."

"What do you mean?"

She shrugged. "Xinpaku gave me a test thing, but I completely failed." And after talking to Ployame...well, she wasn't sure she shared the same concerns. When it came down to it, she was certain she could kill—if she was good enough to get there.

Farren stared at her. "What are you saying then? You'll come back here? And you're okay with that?"

"It's not..." Barli swallowed. "I'm not sure what else to do yet. But there's no way I'm giving up."

He was still shivering, but Barli was tired of babying him. Maybe he hadn't had a mother to tell him to change out of wet clothes, but she wasn't about to take that place for him. He wouldn't listen anyway.

"Why?"

She blinked. "Well...there'd be no point then."

"You know, you don't have to get close t-to kill someone."

Never mind. She couldn't handle it. She'd feel guilty if he died. "Get out of those things," she said, pushing his door open and rooting around for something, anything warm and dry for him to wear. "You're going to get sick."

He stood mutely until she was driven to strip him herself. He wasn't resisting. He just seemed distant and uncaring. Barli rolled her eyes. It was just as well he was locked up in here. He'd be perfectly useless in the real world, end up killing himself before the day was out. She could see him just walking into the ocean and drowning because he didn't realize he wouldn't be able to breathe.

He didn't have much by way of spare clothes, so she wrapped him mostly in a bed cloth.

"There is an overhang out there, you know."

He just shivered as she propelled him to the bed, sitting down next to him. The storm was still flashing outside and as much as she hated to admit it, she really did not want to be alone.

Barli sighed. "How stupid are you?"

"I wanted to feel the rain," he said quietly. "I never get to feel anything. I just…wanted to feel it. And then I couldn't really feel anything anymore. And maybe that was okay too."

He bowed his head. "I'm not stupid, contrary to what most people think. But there's no point for me, to be anything but. If I'm stupid, it's easier. Because I know there are so many things I can never know or experience and there's so little here that I care about."

"What…"

"I'd rather feel the rain."

"Than not catch hypothermia?"

Farren nodded.

Barli let out a long sigh. "Listen. I don't know how it's

going to happen, but I'm not going to let myself die in this place. And I'm not going to let you, either."

"You're crazy."

"So I've been told." Barli's fingers rubbed over the thick scar on her wrist. "Maybe that craziness makes it possible."

"You'd have more power and opportunity if you were one of them," Farren said. "Even then…it's not as though you'd come back for me."

"You don't believe people will do what they say, do you?"

"I haven't seen much p-proof of it."

Barli bit her lip. "Well. I won't promise you, then. But I have a strong inclination toward doing something, if I can figure it out with everything else. When I get back from this stupid waste of time…maybe we can get down from the roof, throw it down the other side…"

"They'd catch us. Especially me. I'm not stupid, but that doesn't mean I can do anything. It's…embarrassing."

"What would you do, then?"

"I'd win that competition."

She lifted her eyebrow. "How would you do that?"

"Poison." Farren's voice was surprisingly firm.

"Where would I get that?" she asked, laughing a little.

His stark black eyes were completely serious. "The courtyard garden."

"That stuff's poisonous?"

He nodded. "Some of it is."

Farren was full of surprises, wasn't he? "Wow."

"I can show you, what to do with it, if you want. There's a few different types. But if you think you have a better shot with it, then I…" He trailed off, looking upset in addition to soggy.

"Yeah," she said. "Show me. Sometime when it's not storming." She was still dripping on the ground. "I'm getting changed." She stood up, trying to ignore the many drawings stacked up in Farren's room. "*I* don't want to get sick."

Farren curled up on his bed, Maigi jumping up to lick his face. The black cat settled in front of him, her tail twitching.

"And you don't go getting sick either—you've got stuff to show me."

Farren smiled a little, and it seemed strange on his face, like his muscles weren't quite sure what they were doing.

Barli went back to her room and stripped, shivering. There wasn't much to put on in exchange, but she did her best. Flashes of intermittent lightning crowded her sky and with each burst of light she was reminded of before.

Finally, she couldn't take it anymore. She knocked quietly on Ferran's door, popping it open slowly when she heard a soft response. "Hey," she whispered, "can we stay together?"

He sat up, looking strangely at her.

"I…don't like storms."

Farren's eyes widened. "You're scared?"

"Shut up," she said.

"Well, you shouldn't sleep in here, or you'll get locked in for the day."

Barli bit her lip. "The couch?"

Farren smiled again, and it seemed slightly less strange. "Fine."

They relocated to the couch. Farren was tense for a long time when Barli snuggled up against him, but he didn't push her away. And eventually he relaxed enough to fall asleep. Barli stayed up most of the night, even with Farren's body pressed up against hers. She held her breath after every roar.

Chapter Ten

FARREN WAS GONE IN the morning. She wasn't sure when she'd fallen asleep, but at some point she had finally dozed off and he had disappeared back to his room. Barli yawned, shivering slightly as she brushed sleep from her eyes just in time to have Ginsun leap onto the couch beside her.

"I hate rain," he announced.

Barli nodded resolutely. "I agree."

But she didn't join him in conversation as he continued on and on about why he hated the rain. When she didn't rise to the occasion, he left her alone. He couldn't know him going on and on just reminded her of how comforting her mother had always been…and how she would comfort her no longer.

Would Visea be able to look past the marks on her face? She had to, didn't she? After all, they were the same. Not in every way, but in ways that counted.

She worked out the rest of the day. Xinpaku didn't come looking for her, and he wasn't at dinner. Barli could hear rain pattering throughout the day. At least Farren had the sense not to go outside yet another day.

After dinner, she waited in the kitchen for Farren. As soon as she saw him, Barli couldn't help but break into conversation. "I was thinking, what sort of poisons do you have? 'Cause if they were the kind you could eat, like I wouldn't have to get anywhere near my target. It'd make me great. And if I won—I could definitely win, right? I could tell them that I need your help, you know, to make things work. Other Sins have helpers too, don't they?"

"No. I mean, yes, they do, but, no, it's not going to work like that."

"Why not?"

Farren's brow furrowed. "They don't do it just for kicks, keeping me locked up. They'd never let me out. They don't even let me out in here. Don't you understand? You can't save me. It's not that easy."

"I will figure it out."

"That sounds like another false promise."

"I will *try* to figure it out. Maybe. There, are you happy?"

There was the barest of smiles on his face. "Maybe." He headed outside to the still-drenched courtyard. He knelt down beside the main planter, churning the dirt until he had secured a few different plants, from the roots down. Barli marked them with interest, scooping Maigi away from them.

"So these are poisonous?" She cradled Maigi in her arms and scooted away from the offending vegetation.

Farren smirked. "It's not dangerous like this, Barli."

"Oh. So…what do you have to do to it?" she asked.

Farren separated the plants into three different bunches and brought them into the kitchen where he began chopping up one of the piles, and heating a pot of water where he tossed a few others.

"It depends on the plant. They have different poisons, and different ways of bringing them out. That's yew. It's supposed to be a pretty sudden death—not a ton of symptoms. Over there, calfoil. It slows the heart down, too much and it stops it entirely. On this it's the berries. They give you hallucinations that'll lead to a coma and eventually death. I figure you want ones that'll kill them, right?"

She nodded mutely. "How did you learn all this?"

"It's all in one of those books," he said, gesturing to the shelf. He simmered the calfoil, stirring the pot. "This should distill down into a paste you could put on weapons. And I can make draughts of the others too, you can add it or actually parts of the plants to food if you want."

"It…you've given this a lot of thought, haven't you?"

Farren shrugged. "No one comes to check on me. Some of those plants are medicinal. There's a book on health there too, which you've clearly never read. I don't get enough sunlight or a host of other things. I used to be a lot sicker because of it, but Parsley got me some of the plants I asked for and I take them as supplements." Farren picked up some of the calfoil, twirling it through his fingers. "And I've taken some of the other things sometimes."

Barli raised her eyebrows. "Some of these?"

Farren looked sideways at her. "Sometimes."

Barli's stomach twisted, wondering exactly what that

meant. Ultimately, she decided she didn't want to know. His business was his business—but he was certainly right. He was far less stupid than she'd thought. Barli would never have had the patience to read all those books, much less to get anything out of them.

"Thanks," she said quietly.

He shrugged. "Hey, can I ask you a favor?"

"Sure," she said immediately. "What?"

"Take Maigi with you."

"What? But..."

Farren hunched his shoulders. "They do look in on me, every once in a while. And since that day, they've been looking to have another examination."

"What day?"

He held up his hand. "When I didn't make dinner."

Oh, right. She'd noticed that day had vanished. "They won't let you anymore?"

"No." Farren rolled the berries through a thin cloth, smashing them into a pale paste. "Don't touch that!" he warned her, and she pulled her hand away from the berries he wasn't working with. "The oil isn't good for your skin. Contact is enough to get some side effects."

"You touched them."

"I've also gained some immunity," he replied, "but you'll notice I'm not caressing them."

She folded her arms and stood back, watching him work. "So...Maigi. You think they'll find her? But they haven't yet."

"I told you. I have these...examinations a few times a year. A couple Priests come up and look me over, ask some questions, decide if they should kill me. Standard stuff. But they will see her, if she's here. And if you come back, you can bring her back and if not…well, it's better that way anyway."

Barli sighed. "Fine. It'll be temporary anyway."

"Exactly," he said.

The next few days Barli kept working as usual, though she took an afternoon to school Ginsun in marbles again. At night, Farren showed her the poisons he'd created and she tried to come up with a better plan. After having been gone several days, Xinpaku finally showed back up, the day before she left.

"Ployame told you, didn't she?" Barli asked with a dejected sigh.

He nodded. "If you wish it, a chance may come again. The two of us trained for years."

Years? She swallowed. "Why aren't you going then? Could you—could you not do it?"

He shook his head. "Before I came here, I was a guard. For years out there I honed my skills, did my job. I've killed many times, Barli. It wasn't really until I stopped I thought about what I'd…they were never good people. And I don't feel guilty. I never had to kill anyone—I wasn't ordered to. But there were men who would threaten children, and many other things…it wasn't a demon. When I looked into their eyes, it was just a human. And humans, simple humans, have no excuse for such things. So, no, I had no qualms about missions, where capture is as common as kill and there's an understanding behind it."

"So why then?"

Xinpaku looked away. "I am too weak for it now. I have bouts of sickness, in addition to increasing spasms. The demon gets stronger. Besides, I am content enough here. I have no one outside to welcome me, and to walk alone is worse than not walking at all."

Barli was not sure she agreed, but she nodded politely. "I suppose you're right."

The sweep of deep brown robes called her attention away and Xinpaku immediately stiffened and stood back.

"Sin. You have been granted leave for an important competition. Reassemble with whatever you wish to bring with you to the blue room."

"Yes, Priest," Barli said quickly, bowing her head deferentially. The Priest was gone in another flash.

"Luck, Barli," Xinpaku murmured as he dipped his head quickly before scurrying down the stairs.

She headed to her bedroom, heart pounding. She was leaving. She was going to leave these damn walls! She'd been avoiding thinking about it, not because she was scared, but because she was sure it would feel so good. And if her insanity caught up to her, she might forget the reasons why she wasn't going to take off the first chance she got.

Farren had made her take Maigi to her room for the last night, so he wouldn't get shut up with him. They'd given her a small bag to take her things in. She thought most of it was supposed to be for weapons, and the one change of clothes she'd been afforded, but she tucked Maigi into the small satchel, making sure the jars of poison were well sealed. Farren would not be pleased if she killed his cat.

Barli shouldered her bag carefully, willing the feline to stay quiet until they were out of the Asylum. If she mewed after that, Barli could at least loose her in the city. Actually, that was probably the best plan. A lot more things could go wrong for the young feline if she waited till they were aboard the ship.

Ginsun and Walunata were waiting outside her door when she stepped outside. Both of them surged forward to hug her fiercely. "Are you coming back, Barli?" Walunata asked.

She was surprised to see tears in her eyes. How had she come to mean that much to Walunata? She certainly didn't feel the same way. "Oh, um…I don't know, Walunata."

"Sins have home bases, right, Ginny?" she asked Ginsun.

He shrugged and nodded at the same time. "I've heard that. After all, we're all families in here. Barli wouldn't leave us like that, right?"

Falls. She hated children. "I don't know what will happen. Now, really, I have to go." And if they weren't careful with their grips they'd jostle the poor kitten until she shrieked. Farren wouldn't easily forgive her for that. He was closer with the feline than anyone else.

"Bye, Barli."

"Good luck!"

She headed out of the locked ward and down the stairs, sheltering her bag under her arm. Barli didn't want Farren's poisons spilling.

The blue room was empty and eerily quiet. Just beyond, at the door across the room, she could hear gentle murmurs and the sound of several dozen footsteps. Barli frowned. She knew there were classes at the Asylum sometimes. She'd been to only a few, spending most of her time aboard the Shining Flotsam, less shining and more flotsam as she'd known it.

She waited quietly, moving around the room to read some of the posters plastered on the wall. They were rhymes and phrases she recognized from stories. They were all about the breaking of the demon, how it hid itself in the innocent people, creating evil and abominations.

Barli swallowed hard. Evil. That was what was at the heart of the Priesthood and the Asylum. Some piece of the demon was in her, in all of them, making the world that much a fouler place.

"Admiring the student's work?" a voice said in her ear. "They've learned their lessons well."

She was impressed. Some of the drawings were quite good—good enough to terrify. "They made these?"

"Indeed," the young man said smoothly. He was in his late twenties and bore a thin mustache with his carefully cropped hair. A small black mole lingered just to the left of his corresponding eye. "Now, are you ready to go?" His tone was even, as though he was unconcerned, but his eyes—a reddish brown color—danced with subtle excitement.

Barli gave him a long look before she remembered she wasn't supposed to do such things with normal people anymore. "Yes," she said.

The man waited by the door for a few seconds, he too

seemed to be listening. "Very well. I am Vorain and will be accompanying you on this journey."

Vorain. It was impossible to gauge anything about him, except that he was a Priest. Any contextual or clothing oriented clues were lost in his typical Priest robes. There was no individuality in them. "I'm Barli."

He smiled slowly. "No. You have no name here. You are simply 'Sin' or 'Contestant' or 'girl.' Is there a moniker you prefer?"

Right. Her face burned. She felt the weight of the mark on her face. "No."

Vorain nodded briefly. "Let us go then." He led her out of the room. He did not touch her, but instructed her to stay within three steps of him as he headed out into a short hallway that opened up into a grander hall, with great wood doors on the far side. He cautioned her as they walked. "Do not run. If you do, the Black Sins will be after you in a heartbeat. You will behave yourself, or you will lose your chance, any chance you will ever have."

"I understand," she said as they stepped out of the door.

It wasn't quite as wondrous as she'd thought it might be. Rain had begun to fall, and judging from the heavy sky it was not about to let up anytime soon. The streets were mostly empty, and anyone that was in the vicinity was quickly leaving, ducking under rooftops to get out of the downpour.

She took a deep breath. It wasn't as magical as she'd imagined, but it was still… Her stomach tumbled and she couldn't help but smile. No walls. Space to run. Barli spread her hands as she stepped off the stoop into the rain. Unlike

Farren, she had no appreciation for being spat on by the sky. But rain was not enough to stop her from leaving the place she'd been bound for months.

Vorain made a sharp clucking noise as he too stepped forward, pulling his cloak up over his head. He followed her into the street, a quick unerring stride about him as he led her on.

Barli was hard pressed to keep pace with him. She had not seen this Island before, had not walked these streets, and every step brought new dreary sights to bear. After a few sharp clicks from the Priest, she stopped dawdling quite so much, making sure to keep within the designated paces Vorain had set. "What's this place called?" she asked.

Vorain's shoulders hunched. "The city is called Brokerstown. But it is irrelevant. We are not staying here."

"But I'll come back."

He hesitated for a long moment before nodding. "Unless for some reason you require handlers elsewhere, your base will be here. If you win."

Barli could hear his unimpressed tone. Her eyes narrowed slightly, but she suspected he was right. She didn't look like much, and she hadn't been training for long either. "Who's the youngest Black Sin?"

"You are full of questions," Vorain commented dryly. He made a sharp turn and Barli could smell the salt in the air. They were close. She couldn't hear the waves break with the rain coming down, but the considerably saltier taste in her mouth and the unmistakable stench of fish flared in her nostrils, leaving no doubt in her mind. "Thus far the youngest Black Sin has been ten."

"Ten!"

"But she was a special child," Vorain said. He flashed her what was almost a smile—definitely the friendliest gesture she'd seen from any of the Priests.

"Was?" Barli blinked as a teen glanced at her face, paled slightly, and hurried away. Disgust. She could read it in his body language.

"Well, she's not a child any longer. I think she's in her twenties? Ah, I don't recall." Vorain shrugged. "Keep up!" he had to remind her again.

Barli forced her feet to keep going, shaking away the unsettling feeling she had in her stomach. As they moved into more populous areas, Barli noticed the people avoiding them. It wasn't that they didn't want to be near people—it was that they didn't want to be near *her*. They would spot her, walking in a line just behind Vorain, and they would part like tidewaters before them.

She found herself bowing her head. It wasn't purposeful, but it was better that way. It hid the marks on her face a little better, but more than that, it meant she didn't have to see the people's fear and unease as they stepped away. She only needed to focus on Vorain's feet. That was all she needed to follow. She noticed a light blue hem on his brown robes and wondered if there was a reason it was there that it was colored.

Barli realized what it looked like—it looked like she was ashamed. She took a deep breath and brought her head back up. She refused to bow over like she was less than them…even if she was.

Vorain had to remind her once more to keep up, but

she caught a glimpse of his face and he looked just slightly regretful. She also spotted a long thin blade at his side, affixed to a thick leather belt wrapped thrice around his waist. A few bags hung from the warped leather. She realized he wasn't carrying anything, which surprised her.

The cobbled leaning buildings gave way to more sky and rain as they opened up into the port section. Over the years, Barli had realized that almost all port towns were the same, and their ports were even more similar than another part of town. It made it easier to navigate for sailors who never spent too much time in any one place. There were even often inns and taverns on the same corresponding corners.

Barli thought she might have made land here, once a long time ago. There were only a few docks that shipped slaves, and Barli could see them standing in line up against one of the docks. There was an overhang they were huddled under, and Barli noted with a hint of jealousy that they were more warmly dressed than her.

As a strict rule, slaves were not accepted in the Islands. The idea of owning another human was repugnant to most of them, but it was commonly accepted as a way of settling debts when a person had nothing but their life to offer. Slaves could fetch high prices, particularly if they were skilled in something, as most individuals from the Islands were. The Islands also risked overpopulation with every new generation, and trading slaves to Meinweit helped keep them in balance with the ecosystem.

She supposed she was lucky she was a Sin rather than a slave—not that her family would have ended up in a situation like that. Her father was careful not to make deals he couldn't complete.

"Come. And keep your questions to yourself for now. They will not want to speak with you, and you should not speak with them."

Right. She'd forgotten that was one of the rules. It seemed like forever since she'd been in society—and now her class was all messed up. She didn't know how to respond. Barli nodded and found herself dropping her head again—against the rain and the desire to speak. The more she looked, the more she would want to talk.

As Vorain stepped up to a ship, she looked the vessel over. It was a short-range ship, with ample cargo space and very little space above decks. It could be manned easily by three and likely did not take on many passengers.

A middle-aged woman stepped off the walk. "Are you my crew?" she asked. She had a high nasally voice and spoke with the authority and volume of one struggling to be heard above the wind.

"Indeed," Vorain said politely. "May we come aboard?"

"I was only waiting for you to cast off," she replied, extending her hand. She did not spare Barli a single glance, but afforded Vorain rather little more courtesy. She kicked the board off and unwound the ship from the dock, pulling ropes from their moorings. "Calikun!" she called. "Let's cast off!" She directed her guests to the center of the deck before rushing off to preform her own duties.

The rocking motion of the boat under her feet felt like coming home. It still took her a moment to reign in her balance, but after that she felt as steady as she ever had on dry land.

She walked to the bow, despite the fact that it was still raining. She had forgotten the spray from the ocean, how it felt. Barli hated rain—but the spray up from the ocean was somehow so different. Barli knelt on the deck, her bag hitting the deck and she suddenly realized she hadn't unloaded her pack yet. The Priest had been paying too much attention to her to this point. She glanced back at him, relieved to find he still seemed to be finding his sea legs. She unbuttoned the pack and slipped Maigi out. She mewed once before quieting, looking with wide green eyes at the strange circumstance she suddenly found herself in. Her gaze turned back to Barli, who sheltered the cat from the Priest's view as she urged her to jump to the dock.

"Go on," she urged.

Maigi growled lowly.

They were pulling away from the dock. "You'll like it out here, I promise," she said. Soon they would be too far. She swallowed and picked up Maigi, fighting her writhing until she tossed the poor startled feline back onto the dock.

She landed on all four feet, keening loudly as she paced the dock, staring after Barli as the ship pulled farther away.

"A little unsteady?" the woman asked, striding over to her.

Barli rebuttoned her pack quickly and stood up, shaking her head and biting back her words. "I grew up on the sea," she said.

"Oh," the woman withdrew slightly. "I didn't realize…" She was looking more closely at Barli now. Barli turned away, hiding her branded face. It was impossible not to feel shame.

Barli watched as the Island slowly became smaller and smaller. She frowned, looking for the Asylum in the mess of scattered buildings. The town ran up to the foothills where the buildings petered off into mild forest.

She ducked her head as she turned back to the woman. "Where are we going?" she asked.

The woman's face tightened further and she stepped away. "You can stay up here or go below deck: just don't touch anything."

So her questions were to remain unanswered, were they? Barli swallowed hard. The rain was growing harder and as much as she wanted to watch over the sea, she resolved there would be time enough for that once the storm let up.

The below decks were cramped and crowded, full of okra and something with a tangy scent that was held in crates. A few hammocks hung low, swinging. Vorain was sitting on the bottom step, head on his knees, arms round his stomach.

Barli smirked. "I didn't think anyone form the Islands could possibly be seasick."

Vorain's gaze, as he turned it on her, was far less amused. His orange-brown eyes had a harder note to them, but when he opened his mouth to reprimand her, he gulped quickly and closed it again.

"Isn't it funny some things are too egregious to account for random variance?" she said, crossing her arms and leaning against one of the support beams.

The Priest was breathing through his nose. "Are you referring to yourself?"

Barli's smirk faded. "You'll breathe better in the open air."

He stood shakily, taking a step up. He made a quick gesture of thanks.

She squinted at him. "How do you not know that? Have you never been on a ship before?"

Vorain shook his head.

Impressive. "Well, I'd hope for your sake then this voyage isn't too long." The captain hadn't said anything about sleeping arrangements, though there were clearly some beneath. Still, she assumed the trip wouldn't be more than two days. This was a hopper, not made for long journeys.

Barli swallowed. What island could they be going to? She wished she remembered her lessons in geography better, but it had never seemed too important before.

She took a deep breath, looking behind her to make sure Vorain had left. He had. Barli unbuttoned her bag, checking the jars Farren had prepared. None were broken yet.

Barli flung herself into one of the hammocks and lulled by the gentle rocking of the familiar sea, she found her eyes closing. It was the most restful she'd felt in a long time. She couldn't help but fall asleep.

Something hit her and her eyes burst open.

It took her a moment to reorient herself. She had

gotten used to waking up in the Asylum. Now, of course, she had to reorient herself again. It felt very much like waking up in a time long past, back on her father's ship. But the smell was wrong, and Barli couldn't hear the even rhythm of the paddles beating on the water.

She swung out of her hammock, jumping to her feet.

"The Priest is looking for you," the captain said. Her hair was pulled back and her tan skin was slightly red.

Barli nodded. "Has he gotten his sea legs?" she asked.

The woman's gaze shifted away and she did not reply. It was as if Barli could only understand human speech—it coming from her was too much to handle. She hurried back to the surface.

Barli took a few minutes to settle herself before following the captain up the stairs. The storm had blown over and there was a pleasant blue sky stretching out in every direction. She shaded her eyes, pulling her thin clothing tighter around her as a cold wind blew over the ocean.

She glanced around the ship and saw the Priest by the bow, leaning against the rigging. Barli took quick steps up to him. "Priest? The captain said you wanted me?"

He glanced toward her and nodded to the shore. The island was small, but even from a distance she could tell it was densely populated. "We'll be at our destination soon enough."

Her mind flipped through the Islands. "Jeeku?"

Vorain nodded. He still looked a little green around the edges, but his eyes were clearer.

"Are you feeling better?"

"Somewhat." He was staring at the Island harder than Barli.

A though suddenly occurred to her. "You've never been on a boat before…so you've never been on a different island?"

"That is correct."

How could…Barli was impressed. "And they decided *you* should accompany me?"

Vorain held up his hand. "Remember yourself," he said.

She took a deep breath and dropped her head. She had to remember who she was now. It just wasn't natural to her. "I'm sorry."

"It's alright. I…don't mind as much. I'm more forgiving. You must be more circumspect with the others. I gather it must be more difficult for you, being so short in the system. We usually don't send anyone out into the world until at least a year has passed…often more. And for this competition? Far longer than that."

"I'm still…not sure how to respond. It's not natural."

Vorain nodded. "I understand—but you have to try harder. Other people will dictate it for you, from the way they react." They would see the mark on her face, like the captain, like all those people in the streets. "But with the other priests, when you see them, they will not be kind if you if you are so bold."

Barli bit her lip. "Why don't you mind?" she asked slowly.

He pressed his fingers together. "I…am younger, I suppose. I've spent too much time around Sins. I don't have the same inhibitions."

"Why did they choose you, if you've never even…"

"Never been anywhere else?" Vorain ran a hand through his slightly damp hair. "It was because I wasn't afraid."

The Priests were afraid of her? Barli bit the inside of her cheek to keep her mouth shut, trying to keep what Vorain had warned at the forefront of her mind. Jeeku was coming slowly into view until she could see a few other vessels out on the water, undeterred by the storm's pass.

Barli watched with him as they drew closer. The captain issued orders that Calikun quickly followed. Barli had to contain herself to keep from jumping up at the barking, to help steer the ship into port. The motions would have been familiar, and she played them out in her head as she watched Calikun do the work instead. She was convinced she could have done a better job, but it hardly mattered. She wasn't allowed to do those things anymore. She had a new life.

When they were docking, Barli grabbed her bag from the hold and stepped off in perfect order behind Vorain. She kept her head down as they walked through the crowded streets. She could feel the uneasy manner of people as they spread out around them, making way for the man of the cloth and the deadly demon in his wake. Barli almost felt as though he should have had her on a leash. Maybe people would have been less afraid that way, if they knew she couldn't leave his company.

It helped, she thought, that she didn't know this place well. She might have been here once or twice before, but she didn't know the people here. There wouldn't be familiar faces to watch turn away from her, leave her where they never would have before. There was no Visea to be tempted to see. There was still nothing for her.

It was strange to realize, when she'd been trying to get out, wishing so hard to be free from the walls that had kept her hemmed in, that even though there were no walls now, even though she wasn't trapped, she didn't feel any better. There was nothing for her here, just as there had been nothing for her in the Asylum. There was no point to anything, not without people she cared about…people who no longer cared about her.

Barli pulled her bag tighter against her shoulder. The brands on her face made her head feel heavy. Or was it just the way people were reacting to her? It just seemed so, so heavy.

She was impressed with Vorain—for having never been to another place, he seemed to be taking everything in stride. He referred to a map he had pulled out of one of his pouches, turning it every once in a while. But he hardly stopped moving, even when he was consulting it, and before long she could see the resolute peaks of a classic Asylum building. They were all adorned the same way, though the shapes and sizes could vary depending on their location. Their manner was all the same—large worked stones that petered into little more than pebbles glued together by thick mortar past the second story, and two towers equidistant from each other on either side of a large main arch that stretched into the wide door of the prayer space that was central to each installment.

This Asylum was bigger than Barli had seen before. It

was at least three times the size of the one she'd been staying in. She realized after several seconds had passed and she hadn't heard a cluck from Vorain to keep up that Vorain had also been struck dumb by the sheer enormity of the locale.

"Wow," she heard him murmur under his breath. He took a deep breath and let out a soft whistle. Then he squared his shoulders and stepped forward, giving a quick unnecessary cluck as Barli stepped up behind him, the double doors swinging open as they stepped up the first step.

An older man in the deep brown Priest robes met them at the door. "Here for the competition?"

Vorain dipped his head. "Ketsup Vorain."

The man had a full thick white beard and very little hair on the rest of his head. His eyes were pits of black, reminiscent of Farren. "Very well. Come along—this way." He ushered them inside. "Dimushi will show you where to go, Sin. Vorain, we'll be meeting in the conference room."

Dimushi was a girl slightly younger than Barli, dressed in the Priest's robes, though with more blue on it than Barli had seen previously. She had soft brown hair, curled around her face and framing her peculiar blue eyes. She was definitely not from the Islands…or her parents weren't, at least.

"Please, with me," she said quietly. She did not touch Barli—but that was only to be expected—as she took her through a side door of the main prayer chamber and down the hallway. They turned a corner. She slid a heavy key from her pocket and placed it into the lock of a thick heavy metal door. Barli swallowed as she heard the ping of the lock releasing and a low whine as she pulled the door open. Barli could see her arm muscles clench as it opened wide enough to slip inside. The door swung shut slowly behind her as they stepped in together. Barli eyed the keys she slipped back into her pocket.

In this new section, the light was dimmer. No windows shed any light on the interior and the torches provided only limited glow. There were doors evenly spaced on either side all the way down the hall. Somehow it was ten times worse than the locked ward in Hevon'i.

Dimushi counted five doors down and then swung the door open. "You'll be staying here," she said. "Lipa, you've got a roommate!" Dimushi said cheerily.

"Roommate?" Barli asked.

The girl nodded. "We've found fatalities decrease when everyone has their own room, but with this many contestants there's not really another method. Besides, you'll all be locked together anyway."

Barli blinked as she stepped into the doorway. A tall muscular woman was looking out a small window. Her hair was cut short, exposing her neck. She turned toward Dimushi as Barli took a small step inside.

Her gaze narrowed. "New blood? Young. Whole." She tugged at her ear. Barli saw the woman had only stubs for fingers on her left hand. "What's your story, sweetheart?"

Barli's jaw clenched and she hoped the woman stayed well out of her way—and out of her things.

"Well. Don't kill each other. We'll bring food along

later. The competition tasks start tomorrow." Dimushi smiled softly and the door snapped shut gently behind her.

Barli swallowed and walked to the made bed, setting her bag down gently.

Lipa folded her arms. "You haven't been here before. Where you from, anyway?"

"Hevon'i."

"Ah. I suppose it makes sense. They haven't anyone better to send."

Barli swallowed. It was true, but…her tone pricked at her insides. There was nothing *wrong* with the people who hadn't come along. Ployame had her reasons, and so did Xinpaku. It wasn't their fault they weren't here: it was their choice. She could understand it, even if she would have made different choices.

"What's your name, girl?"

"Barli."

Lipa turned back to the window. "Well. Maybe I'll see you again next time."

Barli watched her uncertainly for several seconds before she sank down onto the bed, pulling her knees up. She stared at Lipa, wondering what her comment meant, before deciding she didn't care. She just had to put up with this situation for a week. Then, no doubt she would be back in Hevon'i.

They didn't talk for the remainder of the evening, even when Dimushi came by later and dropped off food for the two of them.

It grew later and Barli felt a slight pressure building up inside her. She didn't want Lipa to think she was crazy, but she couldn't stand just sitting still. The competition, whatever it was, would be coming soon. And she didn't do well with sitting around, locked in a small cage.

She sat on her hands, trying to keep her fingers from itching all the places on her body that were squirming now. Why was she so uneasy? Why did she have to get unsettled now of all times?

Barli kept glancing away and then back at Lipa. She looked hard and tempered, as though she had spent considerable time lifting weights—and who knew what else?

She felt her insides crawling. She wasn't good enough. She couldn't do this. She'd known that already, but it didn't matter. Reality had caught up to her. Even with Farren's assistance, Barli wasn't sure how she was supposed to measure up to those people who had spent their lives training toward this singular possibility to be the best of what little status there was for Sins.

Barli glanced over at Lipa. She was obviously stronger, and Barli was a little unnerved by the fact that she was here despite the fact that she only had one functioning hand. But she couldn't take this silence anymore. She couldn't take the stillness. If it went on much longer, she'd end up pulling a knife out of her bag and use it before her time.

That would be bad for everyone involved.

"So...you've been here before?"

Lipa's gaze narrowed slightly. "This is my third competition," she said. "I'm one of the old hats."

She'd done this three times before? And she hadn't been good enough? Barli swallowed nervously. "Oh." Her fingers squeezed together and she wanted to claw at her insides. "Are we…can we leave this room?"

"If it's not locked, you're free to." Lipa's gaze returned to the window. "But these people aren't here to make friends. Any alliances you think you can create…might just end up being your grave."

"I'm not planning on making any alliances," she said, jumping to her feet. Her breaths were shallow and uneasy. She couldn't take air in quick enough and she wished for the burn in her body to match it. She popped into the hallway. It was dark and a couple of the torches had gone out so the passage was even dimmer than it had been when she'd entered. The lack of windows made it completely impossible to see the passage of time. But at least there was more space, and no one else was there to see her.

Barli's fingers stretched and pulled, her feet trembling on the thick stonework. She walked, legs shaking, to the far end of the cell. Her breath was catching, still too shallow to be comfortable. The door on the far side of the hall was not barred, but when she checked the knob it was definitely locked—and it was a thick lock.

She started walking back the other way. Timid steps began to fall harder and harder and she found herself moving faster and faster. The heavy door was getting closer and closer but she couldn't stop. She couldn't stop.

Her feet fell out from under her and her ill-advised charge was brought to a sudden halt. Barli's arms barely managed to shoot out in time to catch her. She heard a soft laugh issuing from behind her.

Chapter Eleven

WHAT'RE YOU DOING, GIRLY?"

Barli scrambled into a crouch, her fingers twitching, searching for blades she'd left in her temporary quarters. "I-I…" The panic hadn't left. The need to move, to do, lingered. It pulsed through her insides like a pump slowly sucking her dry.

There was a boy she guessed was about seventeen leaning against the wall. When, exactly, he'd appeared she wasn't sure. He had extremely short-cropped hair and narrow, thin eyebrows. His cheeks were hollow, as though someone had sucked the breath as well as life out of him.

"I'm here fo-for the competition."

"That's not what I meant. Why are you here at all?"

She fought the strangling feeling of her insides being pushed together. She knew it would go away if she did something. Something big enough would make it recede for a little while.

Barli closed her eyes and took a deep breath. Even if he'd just tripped her, he didn't appear to be armed. She didn't think he was about to lay her in the grave. "That's a personal question."

He smiled and his teeth appeared almost sharp. "Maybe I want to get personal." His grin widened slightly.

She stood up, aware that he was quite close and no one else seemed to be around. "Where did you come from?" she asked.

"Well, weren't you knocking on that door over there for a reason?"

She looked back toward the far end of the hall. He would have had to move quickly to catch her if he'd come from there since she'd turned around. And…how had he come from there?

Barli stepped backward. "I…I wanted to…it's too small here." She swallowed, and as nervous as she was, she realized what she'd missed when she first looked at him: the marks on his face. The standard marks were there, but it drew on to his cheek and her eyes widened as she recognized the additional brand.

He was one of them. He was a Black Sin.

"How did…why did you…what are you doing here?"

He shrugged. "You knocked. I answered."

Once her shock faded, her itching insides had her feeling worse and worse. Barli took a deep breath. At least if he was already a Black Sin he had no reason to want her dead. She wasn't his competition. She stumbled forward until her fingers slid between the bars, pressing up against the cold iron.

"I don't like being cooped up either," he said.

Barli pressed her face against the wrought iron. Her tongue could almost taste the bitter metal.

"You got some demon powers I don't know about?"

She swallowed. "I need to run."

"You want to go outside?"

She sighed. "More than anything."

Suddenly she felt a hand on her shoulder and Barli started upright, whirling around. "Wh—"

"If you want to come outside, follow me," he said. He rolled well-made shoulders, his grin wolfish. She wondered how many people he had killed. He sauntered toward the far end and the door he'd come from.

She hesitated. "Are you…serious?"

"Sins can lie. In fact, Kazini does hardly anything but. I, however, don't care much for lying, except when it amuses me." He took a ring of keys from around his neck and slotted one of them into the lock until it released. Pushing the door open, she stared into the space beyond, but she couldn't see much beyond a turn in the thick stone. "Are you coming?"

Her insides were going to crush her if she didn't. She was going to do something with those knives in her bag and she was sure to regret it later. "Yes." She stepped past him, swaying a little as she waited for him to relock the door. "Where are we going?"

"Outside," he said, completely unconcerned. He led her down the passageway for about half a minute before he stopped at another door, slitting yet another key into the lock before pushing it open.

Sunlight flooded the passage. Barli had to screw her

eyes up against the brightness. It was getting dark, but it was still considerably lighter than the passage, where torches hung every dozen feet or so.

"A-are you sure this is okay?" He hadn't just meant outside to the courtyard. This was…this was truly outside. Outside and free.

"You're with me. If you get out of hand, I'll kill you. So, yeah," he said, "the Priests don't care. They aren't stupid enough to question me." He tucked the chain of keys back under his shirt. It made a slight jingling sound as he walked.

Barli took a breath. She was outside again. It had been so much easier than she'd thought it would be. But being outside wasn't enough. She watched as the teen stretched his legs. "How old are you?"

For the first time, she felt afraid. "Can we just…I need to run."

He smiled again, and his teeth caught her as still more dangerously sharp. He didn't say anything further, slipping away from the building into an easy jog. Barli kept his pace. Although she hadn't had the room to really run in months Xinpaku's insistence on her rushing up and down the stairs had her in relatively good shape.

It felt good to feel the wind, but it wasn't biting her in the face yet and her lungs would not burn for a long time at this rate. She glanced at him and sped up, smiling a little when he stepped up to match her pace.

The Asylum was on the edge of town, the way it was most places, and he took her further away from town. She was relieved she wouldn't have to see any normal people. She wondered what it would be like to be in the company of a Black Sin. Would they keep a still wider berth? Would she be the one less feared?

They headed uphill. The mountains were sparse here, and hard rock covered more of it than tree. What grass there was poking up between rocky bits was pale compared to the generally lush greens of the Islands.

She pushed harder, running until her lungs felt ready to burst and her side hurt from stitches. But she thought it might be enough. Barli finally had to stop, and it irritated her to see that her companion did not seem winded in the slightest.

She bent over, breathing hard. Her throat burned but it was better than the pains that faded less easily and that seemed unreal.

"So…what's your name, girly?"

"Barli."

He grinned. "You run pretty good for a lock-up, Barli." He took a few deep breaths. "That's your old name, isn't it? You run like you got something to be running from. Maybe you should be called Fontaya." Chased.

"You only get a name if you win, right?"

He tilted his head. "An official one, anyway."

"What's your name?"

"Henequen Aranthar." She knew that name. He had stories, legends. They called him The Strangler.

She took a step back.

He grabbed her hand. "You scared, Barli?" He stepped closer to her, leaning in till his lips were next to her ear. "Now that you know my name?"

Barli was forgetting the burn in her throat.

He laughed a little and stepped back. "I took you out, got you far away from everyone else, and you know no one will ever miss you." Henequen smirked.

She took a quick breath in and, when he leaned toward her again, she slapped him.

Henequen caught her hand the moment after, twisting it till she cried out in pain. "It's been a while since anyone's wanted to get that close to me." He took her hand and brought it to the cheek she had slapped. "I'm sorry. I just get so bored sometimes."

"I don't like guys. And if you touch me, I will hurt you."

He smiled wider, and his eyes twinkled. "Is that what got you in here then?" He dropped her hand and sat down on the rocky ground, perching on a small rock. He took off one of his shoes and cleared it of debris. "Did they ship your little girlfriend to another Island?" His eyes brightened as he pulled the shoe back on. "Wouldn't that be a dream—the two of you Black Sins, free to be together again, roaming the world and murdering demons."

"No. That's not why I'm here."

His eyes roved over her. "Any extra digits? Limbs? Got a penis? Seriously. What's your other demon?"

Barli straightened her clothes. "What do you care?"

"You're crazy, aren't you?" His eyes were kindled with an excited light. "Is that it?"

She hid her wrist. "Take me back."

Henequen smiled. "Fine." He set off at an easy pace. They made their way back down the mountain toward town. "This mountain, it's a volcano, or it used to be, anyway. This whole island around us only exists because it was built on top of great destruction."

"They teach history to us?"

Henequen shrugged. "I liked hearing it. It made me think the demon is just as necessary to our community's future as a whole as anything else. And maybe we shouldn't be destroying it all, if it's only to lay the necessary foundation. But then, when you think about how much destruction would be wrought if this volcano were to go off again…then I think it's right again."

"So…" Her breathing was getting tough again. It was just too much. She hadn't done enough work. "So what are you saying?" she asked between breaths.

"Why do I have to say anything? Maybe I'm just making conversation you won't shy away from." And showing off that he could still breathe just fine.

Barli rolled her eyes. They were coming off the mountain when she broke to little more than a tired walk.

"I'm crazy, you know. So it's not unreasonable to be scared."

"I wouldn't be if you didn't act like a creeper," Barli said. "Your demon keep you acting like a jerk?"

His gaze slid away from her. They were almost there and Barli found herself walking slower. She didn't want to go back to the darkness and confinement. "Something like that," he said.

Barli wasn't sure what to say, or whether or not he was lying. He said he didn't but how could she know if he'd been lying about that or not? Or what if this amused him? She didn't know the sort of thing that would or not.

The steady jingle of the keys around his neck paused as he took them out and let them both back into the building. It was dusk now, and getting steadily darker. "Now," he said, leaning closer in the darkness, "don't go banging that pretty head of yours against iron bars. You're not the worst running partner I've ever had. So I'll see you tomorrow, huh?"

"Um…" Her throat seemed suddenly tight. "If you…"

"You can even slap me again, if you want." He opened the other door, taking her back to the long hallway of rooms where all the contestants were held. "I hope no one kills you."

And he shut the door between them, and she heard the lock click, and she was alone.

Dried sweat lingered on the back of her neck as she stepped back into Lipa's room. It was hard for her to think of it as hers. Lipa was curled up in her bed and appeared to be sleeping.

Barli crept in quietly, checked her bag to make sure nothing was missing, and slowly drifted off.

Chapter Twelve

"WHERE DID YOU DISAPPEAR to last night?" Barli blinked away, staring up at the muscled Lipa towering over her bed. She scrambled backward, breathing hard. "Wh…I—what's wrong with you?"

"You weren't in the hallway. Whose room were you in?"

"I…Henequen. I was with him."

Lipa shook her head. "Shit," she said. "And he let you go?"

"You know him?"

"Took him in when he was fifteen. He won the first competition he was in. Never seen someone take to killing like that. They called him The Strangler, but that's only one of the things he did. The nicest thing he did. He got his target—and he killed four other people's targets before they even got the chance! He's crazy as the three kings. I would stay away from him, if I were you."

"Seemed fine to me," she replied. She pushed away from Lipa. "Anyway, aren't we all a little unhinged?"

"Some are more unhinged than others."

There was a bright whistle and Lipa jumped to her feet. "Are you ready, little girl?"

She felt something smoldering in her stomach, replacing the pangs and nervous energy she'd had before. Determination. Assurance. He hadn't done anything to her—*she'd* slapped him in the face. It had been easy. What did she have to worry about? If she could hit a Black Sin, she could do anything. Energy—life—flared up inside her and she found herself bouncing on her toes. It wasn't like it sometimes was, where she could feel her insides twisting painful, making her want to die just to stop it. But it didn't hurt so much now. Now it felt like a warm fire, kindling the beginnings of something greater.

"I'm going to beat all of you."

Lipa raised her eyebrow. "Cocky child. But maybe you will. You're the type they like for the job, ones that don't have any disabilities to slow them down, except the ones in their head that makes 'em just that much easier to control."

Barli barred her teeth, feeling a shot of hatred run through her veins. "What are you saying?"

Lipa stared at her hard as they stepped into the hallway—clearly the whistle was a notice for assembly. "Nothing's wrong with you, 'cept your mind. And that's the worst way to be messed up 'cause you never know quite what it is."

The other doors had opened too. Barli felt for her knives she'd slipped into the ankles of her boots and the one she'd carefully slid beneath her sleeve. With the arrival of the rest of the contestants, she was distracted from ripping into the entirely too haughty Lipa with one of her blades just to shut her up. All of them, this was her competition. She looked them over slowly, and she saw several of them doing the same. There were a dozen.

There was an even split between men and women, and between children and adults. The youngest she saw was maybe ten years old, a boy with one milky eye and a cleft lip. The oldest might have been Lipa, or maybe a tall woman with large breasts and splotched skin that was dark and light in all sorts of other random places.

Barli wasn't sure who she thought the most threatening one was. Some looked more scared than dangerous. The others were tougher. One of them, a broad male with thin lips who was likely in his twenties, definitely had eyes as chilly as some of those cold-hearted Priests. Him, she thought, he was likely the most dangerous of all of them.

The heavy iron door whined as it opened. It was not the girl from before, but another older female Priest. "Contestants, please follow me." She took them back through the passage to the main prayer room, then moved them past it until they were brought out into a main courtyard, very similar to the one in Hevon'i. She heard cheers coming from somewhere and followed one of the younger girl's gaze up to the second floor. She saw at least thirty people around the sides, leering down at them from the balcony of the upper floor. They must have been the usual occupants.

Across the way, on the ground level, she saw at least four Priests. Interspersed between them, she saw a set of five individuals, cloaked in black and bearing the heavy facial markings of the Black Sins. She recognized Henequen squatting on the ground so he looked half the size. She saw red welts on the back of his neck when he turned around. She frowned, fairly certain they hadn't been there yesterday.

"One of you will be chosen," the Priest she had met yesterday said. Vorain was standing there too. "You will get to stand among these great and other famous names: Poltona. Vikari. Ishane." The Priest smiled. "We'll have a day of this—sparring and skill work, just to see what you're capable of. A day of rest, where you can do as you wish, and then we'll send you on your missions. Is that understood?"

They nodded.

"We'll go to our stations then and make our marks. Listen to the Black Sins, they'll tell you what you need to do." He stepped away, and she realized the yard had been cordoned off into several different sections, demarking the stations the Priest had referred to.

One of the Black Sins stepped forward. "Listen up. Being a Black Sin is about being in control. It's about fulfilling our duty, it's about making up for what we are. Keep that in mind."

"But it's also about killing," Henequen broke in. "And even though we've got the legal backing for it, it's our job to keep it out of sight so the normal folk don't have to think about it."

"And people that see you coming, they don't tend to take to death easily," a middle aged man added. He was the oldest of the Black Sins she saw here—she knew these five were not all of them. There were rumored to be fourteen, one for each of the Islands, but Barli wasn't sure if anyone but the Priests and the Black Sins themselves knew the truth. Maybe the Black Sins didn't even know. "So it's in your best interest to be secretive and smooth," he continued, "especially since some targets are not citizens and are in the company of noncitizens and do not always understand our laws and customs."

In other words, sometimes they were supposed to off people from the mainland—the ones who didn't believe in demons.

"I'm Danerax. This is Kazini." He gestured to the first girl who had spoken, an older teen with lavish long black hair. She had an exceptionally flat chest, but otherwise seemed perfectly normal. "Henequen. Anelace." He or she—Barli wasn't sure—had a bland expression of practiced disinterest. Anelace's hood was pulled over the face, so Barli couldn't get a good look. "And this is Arbalest." She smirked at them, a pint-sized person no larger than a child but clearly with an adult's face.

Barli had her guesses about how the last three made their killings. And Kazini nearly meant manipulator. Danerax, on the other hand, was more of a tangential connection. The thing it sounded closest to was rat. Barli wasn't sure what to infer from that.

They broke them into groups. Barli didn't bother with getting close to any of the others. She was only grateful that Lipa wasn't in her group. The first station they did involved climbing, scaling the compound's walls to the second floor. They were then supposed to avoid being pushed off by the upper balcony occupants for as long as possible. Anelace sat back and timed them while one of the Priests made notes.

Barli watched the others go. The first could hardly get herself off the ground. Barli smirked. The walls here had nice veins and cracks, perfect for squeezing toes into.

The record was five seconds. The second floor was vicious, and you had to be careful about how you landed if you didn't want to damage an ankle. That would have certainly hurt her chances. Barli watched the offenders. They liked to pinch and try to pry fingers free – but those things took time. As long as she kept moving once she got up there, she'd have a fair shot at beating the timer.

"Ready?"

She stepped forward, shaking out her limbs and staring up at the wall. She took another deep breath and surged forward. Barli did not generally climb rock, and as she took her first pulls up the surface she found its hard unforgiving nature to be extremely irritating. The stone scraped against her fingers and her knee banged against the wall, but Barli kept going. She preferred rope. It was soft and had decent give.

She climbed higher. She had always liked climbing, though she wasn't a huge fan of heights. She never stayed in the crow's nest any longer than necessary. Barli reached the second floor railing. As hands reached out to shove her off, she set into motion, swinging from beam to beam like a monkey until someone got wise and kicked her hand instead of prying. She reflexively released, dropping to the ground fifteen feet, landing lightly as she straightened back up.

"Impressive," Anelace murmured.

She turned away so the Black Sin wouldn't see the prick

of tears in her eyes. She shook the pain off, grinning to herself. She was better than these other people and she would prove it too.

They switched stations. The next one, which Kazini was overseeing, involved knife throwing. Barli did okay, but it wasn't her best. She disliked throwing things anyway. It was unnecessary.

Henequen was stationed at the wrestling mat. Barli had never done much hand to hand fighting before Xinpaku and she glanced uneasily at her prospective partners: the well-muscled man, a club-foot woman, or a girl with something shriveled sticking out the side of her neck.

Henequen winked at her as he paired them, giving Barli the hobbling woman. She couldn't climb at all—Barli didn't think she had a good chance of winning. She had done well on the knives, however. If she could kill her target, Barli supposed anything was possible.

They faced off, and Barli stared into her face, wondering what it would be like to look into the face of someone marked for death that she would hand out. She would—because she was going to make it and she knew it now. It didn't matter if Lipa had more experience or the young man was stronger. She was better than either of them. The confidence infused with her blood and it made her strong. This was the feeling she was always chasing. It would come to her for weeks and then abandon her. She had always felt so weak and dour without it, but it had come back at the perfect time.

Barli wasn't above playing dirty or obvious. The fact that if she was a Black Sin she would have things like keys, like Henequen, was extremely attractive. She could go anywhere she wanted. Who didn't want that?

The minute they signaled the start, Barli moved away, forcing the woman to chase her. She was slow because of her leg. Barli waited for her to lunge and overextend herself before she went in and unbalanced her good leg, dropping the woman to her knees. Barli grinned. This was what she loved. She loved feeling like this, like nothing could go wrong.

Barli kicked her and went in for her neck, knocking her to the ground as she caught her arms and forced her down. Her eyes were bright when there was a whistle and they pulled away.

"Good," Henequen said quietly. "I like to see that you have real fight. You look better today," he added.

She grinned as she stood up, wiping sweat from her forehead. "I am better."

Henequen licked his lips. "Than a limp-legger? I'm *so* impressed."

She threw a punch at him, but this time he caught her hand, deflecting her blow. He shook his head. "Not now, girly. Tonight."

She wasn't sure what that meant, but the next minute the Priests were calling for their final rotation. Barli gave him a backward glance as she was swept away. A few seconds later, she fell hard onto the squishy grass, the dirt still unpacked from the last rainstorm. The club-footed woman sneered at her. "Better watch your back, baby," she said. "I've seen that arm of yours. Maybe you think about taking it a little harder next time."

Barli wiped mud from her palms. "Maybe I'll take it to you!" she replied, eyes stinging. She wasn't giving up just like that. She had the fire inside her now, and even she wasn't particularly strong, Barli knew she could think her way out of any of this. She always used to be smart, only her mind only seemed to work like firecrackers some of the time.

"Better watch your back, brack."

"Do I *look* like a brack to you?" Barli spat back. She wasn't sure she'd ever hated someone so much in her whole life. She rolled her eyes and headed for the next station.

Vorain was at this station. Barli felt his eyes on her and she tried to keep her temper under check as she continued to keep wiping her hands clean of the mud now stuck on her clothes.

Danerax had them stand in file as he looked them all over. "We have found at times that there are those ill-suited for the necessary tasks we undertake. So this is a preliminary task, before we send you to the outside world. We want to make certain it's worth it." He held up a large black bag, which was moving. Barli took a half step forward. "Now I'm sure some of you will have no issue with this, but we've discarded one of you for this already. This is the only test that, should you fail, will disqualify you in of itself."

Barli swallowed. What was in the bag? What did they have to do?

Her eyes widened as he pulled a wriggling creature out of the bag and handed it to the man.

A rabbit.

She took a deep breath and steeled herself as Danerax

gave her a rabbit of her own. The bunny was a soft brown color, with white accenting. Its long ears laid back against its head, as though it was trying to squish its ears into its flesh.

Once he had handed them all out, Danerax stepped back. "Okay," he said. "The task is simple: kill them."

Barli swallowed hard, looking at the small innocent creature. She was supposed to kill the bunny? Barli glanced down the rest of the line. To her surprise, the girl with the strange neck had already twisted the rabbit's head so severely that it was certainly dead.

She glanced down the line the other way. The club-footed woman narrowed her eyes at Barli and very slowly and deliberately, took the rabbit's small head and wrapped it in her palm, pressing slowly until Barli could see blood running down the creature's unblemished pelt, the rest of its body still.

And she had suggested Barli was sick.

Barli looked down at the rabbit, struggling to escape from her grasp. She stroked its back once. She couldn't afford to wait long. She grasped the rabbit gently and pressed her fingers against the rabbit's throat. It was a sensible test. If one couldn't kill an animal, it seemed unlikely they were suited to a career of killing people. But…but if it was true that the demon dwelt in the people, and not in the animals, well wasn't that actually quite different?

Barli closed her eyes as she felt the bunny's heart rate increase, beating faster and faster until it ultimately stilled and became nothing.

It wasn't that she cared about the rabbit's life particularly; it was just that it hadn't done anything. She hoped at least they would use it for food.

Barli handed the dead animal back to Danerax. "There you go."

Danerax smiles. "Everyone has passed. Good." He held out the bag for them to drop the carcasses back into. He glanced upward to all the watchers, currently consumed with someone else's attempt at the climb. "The residents will thank you for it."

Would they get something besides fish too? Barli couldn't remember the last time she'd had any type of meat to eat but fish. The Asylum always bought up fish that couldn't be sold to anyone else on the market. It was the cheapest food around.

They called them back together and Arbalest climbed on top of a large barrel. "Listen up! If you're going to be Black Sins, you have to know your place. You have to know what you're doing and what you're doing it for. Otherwise, the point is lost."

Barli sighed as Arbalest let one of the Priests take over, and the man launched into a story she had heard a hundred times. It was the tale of the demon, how the little pieces of the demon had been broken down and fled into humanity, how the Priests did their best to contain the demon, taking it in and keeping the rest of the world safe from the pieces of the demon, trying to gather them all up. The demon, that could not really be killed, but recycled again and again. They were gathering it, diverting it, never allowing it to get too strong.

The Black Sins had become the agents of the Priests generations ago, when evil had walked still more freely through the world, and plague and danger had marked the Islands with despair. So evil murdered evil, the only thing evil could do to try to redeem itself.

It was, as always, a compelling narrative. She wasn't sure what had grabbed her about it this time, though she had heard it so many times before. Maybe it was the hopelessness of who she was, and knowing there was nothing she could do but accept it. Maybe it was the feeling of purpose she had listening to the narrative and the mission the Black Sins were tasked with, when she had felt so utterly lost these past few months. Maybe it was having an explanation for the things she felt and the way she acted, and knowing this really was the only way she could fight it. There were too many reasons, all of them beautiful, and she wanted desperately to join them in that moment. It was not because she wanted freedom or escape from the confines, but because she wanted to be a piece of something great and meaningful, something more than she could ever be in her old life. It was the feeling, for the first time, that there was something better about this life.

The lecture stretched on until the sun had passed and was well into its descent. It was about that time they passed out coney stew. The crowd upstairs seemed to have disappeared.

She didn't want to sit. She had the same anxious movement, but it was still better now than it had been before. She wished there was an open stair here, but the design was different from Hevon'i and it seemed the only way to get to the second story was from inside.

They were taken back to their rooms after they had finished eating. Lipa returned to staring out the window.

Barli hated the sitting around. She did crunches until her abs ached. Then she slipped out into the locked corridor again, wondering how she'd done. She knew it hadn't been altogether an impressive performance, but she'd certainly done better than some of the others. Were they all right? Did she have to watch her back now?

She had taken two knives with her, and one of them she'd coated in one of the poisons Farren had distilled from his garden. She thought it best she be careful, just in case.

Barli lit a candle as she stepped into the dim hallway. She let her eyes adjust to the dim for a moment and scanned the other doors. They all seemed closed. Safe. But she had to admit it was too early to go on a murderous rampage. There was still daylight leaking in from on high, and taking on two in one room was stupid.

She hurried to the far door and knocked quickly on it, then stepped back and waited. She waited several minutes and knocked again. She knew the chances that Henequen was standing in that little passageway at that very moment were very low, but she knocked and waited anyway.

Eventually she sank down against the wall, watching the candle slowly burn lower and lower. When the door behind her suddenly pushed against her, she moved back quickly and gripped her knife until she realized he had finally come.

"Henequen!"

He smiled at her. "I saw the way you were climbing today. Like a fish to the sea." He held the door open and she passed into the dim corridor.

"You'll take me out again?"

He nodded. "If you want."

"Yes!" she breathed.

As he went to the other door, slotting his key into the shape, she heard him muttering something under his breath.

The evening was cooler than the previous one, and given the state of the sky they could expect rain that night. She did not love running, but she liked the ache in her chest and the way she couldn't take enough breath in. She liked the pressure and the heat. It was a low burn and it spoke of an undying fire. Still, she didn't desperately need it tonight the way she sometimes did.

Her energy however was unflagging. Henequen set the pace, moderate at first. It quickly became punishing and Barli had to work hard to keep up. Once again, they headed up the mountain. The ground was rough through the thinning soles of her shoes, but she didn't complain. Henequen didn't have to do any of this.

Eventually she had to stop. She wasn't as fast or practiced as Henequen, though she was sure if they'd had equal opportunity she could have schooled him. "Why do you run so fast?" she asked between breaths.

Henequen wiped a faint glint of sweat from his brow. "It drowns them out sometimes." He sat down on the ground, picking a stick up and drawing patterns into the thin layer of dirt. "And I can be out here longer. Away from the others."

But he'd brought her along. "Did they like me?"

"Sure. And a few others too," he said. "But yeah, you're in the running."

"Good."

They sat in silence for a while, until Barli leaned over to see what he was drawing in the dirt. "What is it?"

Henequen shrugged. "It's messed up, isn't it, how people can look at one thing and see different things entirely? Like, how are we supposed to even do anything together like that?"

Barli squinted at the rough stick marks, walking around the image to see if it helped. She still didn't see much of anything. "What's it like, being one of them?"

"It's…fun." He smiled, sharp teeth showing. "It makes you feel good, you know, putting the world right. And when they die…falls, yeah, it's good. And no one's going to touch you ever, 'cause they're so shatung scared."

Barli smiled a little, though she would have been terrified to hear such a thing not too long ago. And she wasn't sure she understood, but it didn't matter. Maybe the others in Hevon'i couldn't stomach it, but she was different. She was better. Stronger.

Henequen had stopped smiling. He straightened up, looking over Barli's shoulder with a troubled expression on his face. "It's not the same. It's not the same. Falls, gotta remember it's not the same," he said to himself.

"Henequen?"

"No, no…" His head twitched irritably. He took a deep

breath. "Come here." He grabbed her arm, jerking her off balance.

"What's your problem?"

"Shh." He put a finger to her lips and slowly tucked a bit of her loose hair behind her ear. Then he leaned even farther forward until their lips were a millimeter apart.

She pushed him back. "What the shatung did I tell you?"

His eyes were bright. "Do it."

What?

He lunged forward again and she slapped him. "Don't."

Henequen's sharp teeth caught the light. "Make me stop."

Barli knew how to fend off unwanted attention. It was an important lesson to learn as a sailor's daughter. Drunk men were stupid and had a tendency to get a little too handsy.

She lunged forward, grabbing and twisting one of his arms while she kneed him hard in the gut. He slammed into the ground, his head snapping back. She reached back to punch him square across the jaw.

But he wasn't fighting back. Was he unconscious already? Had his head hit the ground harder than she'd intended? She tempered her punch, redirecting the force so it merely grazed his nose. Exactly how much trouble would she get in for knocking out a Black Sin?

"Henequen!"

His eyes flickered and he took a deep breath in, coughing slightly as he did so. "That all you got?"

"What in the calcun is wrong with you?"

He closed his eyes and smiled slightly. "I'm a Sin," he said, as though that explained everything. "Now hit me again."

Chapter Thirteen

N O THANKS," BARLI SAID. She stepped back. "Wimp! You think you're gonna make Black Sin when you're so soft?"

She glared down at him. "You're right." Barli couldn't help it. She was feeling good, and when she felt like this, sometimes her thoughts just sort of skipped around and sometimes she did things that, looking back on it, seemed just a little crazy. But if everything turned out okay, then what did it matter?

She kicked him. Once. Twice. Three times. She sat down on his chest, knees pinning his arms. "You strangle them, right? That's why they call you Henequen. That's the type of rope you use."

There were tears in the corners of his eyes, but he was still smiling. Or was it a grimace? "That's right," he said.

Barli put her hand to his neck, pressing against his windpipe. "I'm not soft. Can you feel my fingers? Calloused. I've never strangled anyone before. It seems sort of soft to me, though. No blood. No guts. Is it painful? I guess your victims can't tell you, can they?"

She took her hand away. "Is that good enough for you?"

His breaths were ragged and gasping. "For now," he said.

She rose, looking at the darkening sky. She didn't fancy running on this uneven ground in the dark. Even walking on it would be risky. "Let's go then. It'll be night soon."

He stayed on the ground, lying on his back and looking up at the setting sun. As his breathing evened back out, he slowly stood. Barli kept her gazed fixed on him, wondering if he would lunge for her again. He was clearly some sort of insane person, but she supposed she should have expected that.

"Can you keep your hands to yourself now?"

He looked at the sky, back down at his scattered drawing that Barli had pushed him back into, and then at her. He smiled slightly, and as he took a step forward he grimaced and the smile faded. His head jerked for a moment and the smile slid back into place. It was less manic now. He almost seemed placated, missing some of the swagger she'd seen earlier.

"You messed my drawing up," Henequen complained. But he didn't seem too upset. He started back down the mountain without another glance in her direction. Barli rolled her eyes, groaning as despite the fact that she'd just kicked him several times, he broke into a slow jog. Barli sighed and, despite her aching legs and burning chest, she forced herself to keep at a steady pace behind him.

She didn't hear anything from him as he unlocked and

locked the doors into the Asylum. The jingle of his keys was the only sound, and he seemed strangely quiet.

"Quen, is that you, darling?" A faint glimmer of candle met them in the passageway.

Henequen stiffened slightly. "She'll know. She'll know. She always does," he whispered under his breath. He pushed Barli roughly behind him as Kazini stepped just into view.

"Not going to greet me, Quen?"

He wet his lips. "Hello, Kazini."

"What are you doing over in this part? Watching the competitors sl—" Her eyes widened. "What are you doing with her?"

He shrugged.

She stepped past him and Barli backed up against the wall as Kazini held her hand out, the sharp of her fingernail cutting into Barli's cheek.

Should she fight her off? Was she merely asking for it the same way Henequen had been? She didn't think so. Kazini's expression was almost angry, something she realized she'd never seen on Henequen.

Henequen took Kazini's wrist and pulled her away. "She's mine," he said.

Kazini stepped away. "Oh. Well then." She tilted her head. "I was wondering how long it would take you." She reached into her pocket and pulled out a set of keys, unlocking the door back to the hallway. "Go!" she said, pointing insistently with her finger at Barli.

Barli didn't fancy a fight with her. She hadn't heard of many stories about Kazini, but she assumed she was as fearsome. She stumbled back through the door, her eyes widening as she saw Kazini smash her face into Henequen's. She pushed him up against the wall.

"What're you doing, Quen?" she said, kissing her way down his neck. "Aren't I good enough? We've got to stick together, haven't we? I know you."

Henequen's eyes were closed, his lips moving quickly.

Kazini took a breath and glanced back toward Barli. Her eyes narrowed when she saw her watching through the still open doorway, and a moment later she had kicked the hefty door closed in Barli's face.

The hallway was impossibly dark. She stumbled through the darkness, feeling her way down the hall and counting the doors until she was at the correct door.

Her fingers closed around the doorknob and she pried it open slowly, still trying to absorb everything that had just happened—her increasingly bizarre encounters with Henequen, and this latest scene with him and Kazini. She didn't understand the nature of their relationship. Maybe it wasn't possible. They were both Black Sins, and since neither of them seemed to be at all physically disabled, chances were they were both insane.

"You went out again? You're more stupid than I thought."

Barli ignored her roommate, creeping back to her bedside and slipping onto the top of her cot. She slipped her pillow between her knees as she scrunched up into a small ball. "He doesn't scare me." Honestly, Kazini was more terrifying—especially since Henequen had told her she was a constant liar.

Lipa turned over. "Good for you."

"He's a Sin, I'm a Sin. We don't have problems with one another."

"Easy to say. Not necessarily true. The Black Sins kill Sins. It's simple like that." Lipa stretched out with a yawn. "They don't get in trouble for killing anyone classified as an official Sin—they could kill anyone in the Asylum, if they wanted, if for whatever reason they deem them a threat or annoyance. So you should be afraid, and if you aren't, you'd better be far better than any of them who might come after you."

Would she really do something like that? "Why would they kill me?"

"There have been them that died before, ones who got too close to Henequen."

Barli bit her lip. It seemed unlikely but…Barli wasn't sure. Kazini had seemed…possessive. She kept the club-footed woman's warning in mind, and she didn't really sleep that night. She dozed on and off that night, waking at the slightest provocation: whenever Lipa switched which side she was lying on.

The next day was free, and Barli wished there were locks on the doors so she could actually get some decent sleep, as she was pretty sure Lipa at least wasn't trying to kill her. The others she was less certain about. She wasn't sure why. She must have had enough of a killer instinct to have made it more than one competition. Maybe she didn't think Barli was a big enough threat.

When she felt like getting up, Lipa had already been gone several hours. Barli did her familiar morning workout.

Once she stepped out of her room, she walked up to the heavy iron door. There was one of the younger Priests standing on the other side.

"You want out?" she asked as Barli approached. When Barli nodded, she let the door swing open slowly, allowing Barli to pass through. It clanged again behind her and Barli jumped a little at the sound. The girl led her into the courtyard, where most of the other contestants were already gathered. Two of the men were sparring. One of the younger girls was climbing the wall, going sideways and spidering, showing off what tiny holds her smaller toes could wriggle into. She noted too that the normal occupants of the Asylum seemed to be around as well, going about their regular duties for the day.

She spotted Kazini with her feet hooked around the posts of the upper balcony, looking down over everything. Some of the other Black Sins were also watching their prospective members. Arbalest was doing so in a particularly hands-on manner. Henequen was sitting on one of the barrels, legs crossed and drawing in dirt with a long stick.

The day was overcast and the ground was soggy. As Barli had predicted, it had rained heavily last night. It looked like the pattern would continue. Barli felt the ground squelch beneath her feet.

She took out one of her daggers and played with it, twirling it between her fingers. Xinpaku's lessons skittered through her head. She found a board and set it up, practicing her throws. Barli sighed. Her performance was far from excellent. She tried to remind herself it didn't matter anyway. Besides, if she wasn't keeping one eye out for the club-legged woman she could probably do a better job of it too. Keeping one eye on her, Barli couldn't aim properly.

Once she got bored of hitting poorly, she collected her daggers back up and wandered over to Henequen. Maybe it was because he'd told her right out that he was crazy, but she couldn't help be curious about him. He was just so…bizarre.

Barli squinted at the drawing as she approached slowly. He was muttering under his breath again. Or maybe it was singing? Something about it sounded familiar. She got closer, wanting to hear better.

He looked up slowly. "You're ruining it."

She stepped back, looking down so she could see the pattern spreading out from the barrel reached her here, still several feet away. "How long have you been making this?"

He craned his neck, looking up at the sky. "Since it stopped raining."

Barli hadn't slept well, so she had a good idea of when that had been—far before the sun had come up. Crazy—he definitely fit the build. When people looked at her, did they see crazy so obvious? Was it lingering that close to the surface?

She looked down at the long drawings, marked apparently in the darkness. He would have been working on it for hours and hours. She still didn't know what to make of it. Maybe it was because she couldn't see the whole picture. Or maybe it was nothing at all, or something he'd just made up in his head.

"Why?"

"I couldn't sleep." He pulled up the long stick he was using to draw in the mud, balancing it on his knees. "Farren and I used to draw all night when I couldn't sleep."

"Farren? You were on Hevon'i?"

"Hevon'i?" He shook his head. "I've never been there."

Barli frowned. "How do you know Farren then?"

Henequen's head tipped upward, and she followed his gaze to Kazini, who was watching them from her perch on high. "I don't know what you're talking about."

Her eyes narrowed. "What's with you and her anyway?"

"The stars don't sing

and the birds weren't made

to fly without wings."

His hands beat against the barrel, tapping out the beat of an unknown song.

Yep. He was absolutely crazy. Why was she even trying? She rolled her eyes and walked away.

"Watch your back, girly. Sotza is eyeing you."

Sotza—was that the club-footed woman? Or was there someone else who wanted to sink a knife into her flesh? Barli glanced around and saw the woman looking at her. "I know," she said under her breath.

Barli sighed. She hadn't climbed much stone, so she decided to join the younger girl in her wall-scaling pursuits. She slipped up the wall, taking several different passes at a route up. The stonework was uneven and lent itself to presenting several different means of presenting herself.

"Hey, Quen's girl!"

Barli was halfway up the wall. She twisted her head upward and saw Kazini looking down at her.

"Come up here!"

Barli slinked up the wall, her arms aching a little at the sheer angle she was climbing. Spending too much time on the wall was definitely taking some of her boundless energy out of her. She pulled herself onto the balcony, resting on one of the railings.

The moment Barli was settled, Kazini slipped toward her, forcing an arm around her neck, leaning in next to her ear.

Barli's grip tightened on the railing. Her other hand went for a knife, though she knew there was no way she could get away with attacking a Black Sin in the middle of the courtyard like this, where everyone could see. And if Henequen wanted, he could probably get her kicked out in a second. Any of them could. So what did she want?

Barli's teeth were on edge. "Can I help you?"

Kazini's breath was in her ear and Barli resisted the urge to shiver. Although the action was clearly hostile, she couldn't help but feel a thrill of excitement running through her. It had been a long time since she'd felt a girl so close.

"I don't know why Quen's doing special favors for you, but listen close, girly: Quen is not for you. He's special, understand? You mess with him, I will fuck you up, Black Sin or no."

"I don't want anything to do with him. He came to me."

Kazini's arm tightened around her throat. "Listen to me, girly. I won't kill you, 'cause Quen would probably flip out. But don't talk to him. Do you understand?"

Kazini might have been the most over-protective

girlfriend Barli had ever met. "And if he talks to me?" She scowled. "Listen, I'm not interested in guys so don't worry."

The Black Sin leaned back for a second. The next moment she nipped her teeth against Barli's ear. This time she did shiver. "I see," Kazini said, her voice lighter. "You're not lying, are you?" she purred. "That's good. Because the other pretty girls Quen likes never make it. I'm looking out for you, as much as him." She kissed Barli's cheek and slowly released her, slipping away to a new perch.

Barli took several deep breaths, holding it in for a ten count before releasing it. Were all the Black Sins this insane? Did she even want to be part of a group so deranged?

But what other choice did she have? And just because they were crazy…well that didn't mean she had to be. She could be a normal crazy. Or were they only like that because of what they did? Had it turned them insane, or had they always been like that?

"Sin."

Her back straightened and she saw Vorain walking toward her. "Priest. Sir," she said politely, her mind still whirling.

"How are you feeling?"

She gave him a strange look. "Are you supposed to be asking me things like that?"

His expression darkened slightly. "Why are you so hostile? You've been given an opportunity."

Barli let out her breath with a huff. "I don't belong here. These people are crazy. I'm *not*. I'm…a little left from center, but not everyone's the same. Doesn't mean they're demonic."

Vorain looked at her for a long moment before sighing deeply. "I can understand why you would feel that way."

"No, you don't! You haven't seen what these…what these *people* are…" Barli shook her head.

"Hush," he said sharply. "And I'd like to remind you of something simple: you were brought in for a reason. I've read your file, Sin, and it's nothing prettier than any of these other contestants or the Black Sins themselves."

Barli's eyes crinkled. "Falls," she said.

Vorain folded his hands. "I know you can forget sometimes, when you see what other people are like. But I will always reassure you: you are not normal. Think about it, think about your relationships with everyone else in your life and you'll remember. And maybe you don't have it as bad, but you've still been touched and there's nothing you can do about it."

She swallowed.

"I was just going to check in," he said, "and see if you needed anything."

Barli blinked. "N-no, I'm fine."

"Because you'll be going out tomorrow, into the world. And I know you haven't been out there on your own since…"

She glanced over at Henequen. He still appeared to be absorbed with his drawing. He had moved to another barrel. "I'll be fine. And if I'm not, what do you care?"

"That's what you don't understand, Barli. You think we're just enemies to you. But most of these people we take in, they'd be dead if we didn't, or living terrible lives, or be on sprees murdering innocent people. Maybe not every single person we've ever detained was touched before they got there, but isn't it worth it all, for the betterment of everyone else?" He sighed. "We do care about you. Not everyone does, but a lot of the Priests aren't doing this just because of the dangerous. They want to have a home for you, keep you safe and relatively happy. And if doing this will make you happy, then we'd like to support you in that. And it's worked well in the past, people like you."

People like her? What did that even mean?

"I guess I should thank you then."

"It would be polite, but I don't expect you to," Vorain said. He did have kind eyes, and he had never been rude or treated her particularly like she was trash, even if other people did.

"If I…if I win, what happens?"

"What do you mean?"

"I…where will I go? How will I know what to do? How often will I have to…kill people?"

The wrinkles around Vorain's eyes deepened. "It would be up to you. Many Black Sins like to choose the Island they came from as their base, but some don't. And you'd have a Priest who gives you your missions. You can turn some down, if you want, and they'll be given to someone else."

She nodded, as if this was all perfectly normal. "Right. Well…thanks, I guess, for not sucking. You're the least annoying Priest I've ever met."

He laughed. "Thank you, I guess."

Barli squinted at him. "How are you liking this anyway? Being someplace new?"

He shrugged. "It's…different. You probably won't get a chance, but there's a weird formation for a mountain. The rock's different."

"Old volcano," Barli said.

"A volcano? Wow…how'd you know that?"

She shrugged, cheeks blushing slightly. "Someone told me."

"Some of the other Sins are young too. I could see it being nice to be around more people your age."

"Yeah…well, I don't think some of them like me very much."

"Oh. Well…give it time, right? I'm sure it takes them time to warm up." He gave her a half-hearted smile.

"Hey. What do you know about Kazini and Henequen?"

"What do you mean?"

"You said you've read my file and others, so…"

He shook his head. "I can't tell you anything about all that. The files are private, Barli." He put his hand up and wandered away.

Barli spent the rest of the evening with her back to the wall, watching Sotza and Kazini, even though the latter had promised not to kill her. Henequen had said she was a liar, after all. But was Henequen just as much a liar as he made her to be?

She couldn't sleep. It wasn't even because she was

particularly worried, or stressed about the fact that the next day she had plans to go out and murder someone. It was because she was in that state and she just had too much energy to even know what to do with.

Barli's eyes were closed and she was trying to take deep breaths and lull herself to sleep. Lipa was fast asleep, and she'd been complaining about Barli's tossing and turning before that. But Barli's mind was traveling a hundred different paths all at once, and sleep was not one of them.

Had he really said Farren? And how would he know that name if he hadn't truly meant it? And what had Kazini meant? Did he actually kill other girls he'd been with? But she was alive, and they certainly seemed as if they were together, to some degree at least. Why did Henequen try to kiss her at all? And if she'd been waiting for him that evening, would he have let her out again? Who would she have to kill? Would she be able to find them? Could she do it? Would Farren's poisons work?

Farren. It was weird. She had sort of missed all the people she used to know, but going this long without seeing Farren felt weird in a different way. It wasn't a longing for his presence, exactly, but more just a strangeness she felt surrounding her. And at the same time, she didn't miss him at all. He was, after all, awkward and sometimes rude, socially inept and positively accusatory.

Guilty—that was how she felt. She had things he didn't, and there didn't seem to be a good reason why. She was the one who couldn't figure her life out without drawing a little blood. He'd cut his hand and they'd taken what little privilege he had away. He hadn't wanted to get to know her because he'd known she would do this—she would leave. She would come here and do her best and she would leave. And she'd ignored all his wishes, gotten involved with him anyway…and his predictions were following through. Maybe she'd even made it worse, giving him a glimpse of the world he didn't know, and leaving him with only that, with just a taste of everything waiting beyond the walls.

The door creaked, or maybe it was the window. She thought for a moment she was back in Hevon'i, and perhaps it was Maigi. Oh yes, she'd taken that away from him too. Visea had been right: she was selfish.

Her throat constricted. She tried not to think about their last conversation, their last fight. Darling, sweet Visea…she had to find a way to apologize. There was no way she could unless she became a Black Sin and had the run of the Islands. She'd see everyone she used to know, she'd say she was sorry, and they'd take her back and things would be beautiful again. She'd touch her soft hair, kiss her gentle skin.

She shivered a little, remembering the way Kazini had nearly strangled her today. Especially how she had her tongue so close to Barli's ear. Kazini was pretty if you could get past the brands, though she had almost no breasts to speak of. Visea had been well endowed.

That was more than a creak.

Her eyes flashed open and she grabbed the dagger she slept with, instinctively stabbing up as she felt the briefest bite against her own neck. A scream ripped from both her and her opponent's throats, melding together in their share of pain.

Barli kicked her back, scrambling into a low crouch as she looked up. Sotza. She was holding her shoulder where Barli had forced her blade through. Red was already seeping up, staining the bleached uniform the club-footed woman wore.

They hadn't been lying. Somehow, somewhere, she'd thought it was all a joke. No one was that serious, right? No one wanted it that badly. That would have been insane. At some point, she'd forgotten what Vorain had just told her, what he'd reminded her existed inside her just as much as anyone else here: they were touched by a demon. They would do what they were driven to do.

She clenched her knife tightly and drew another one from her boot, tucked just beneath her cot. Her hand was shaking slightly and bright red dripped down from the blade she was not about to remove her fingers from.

"Falls," the woman cursed. She screamed again.

Barli felt blood trickling down her collarbone.

"Falls," Lipa grunted as she came awake. "Can't anyone get a decent sleep around here?"

Barli brushed the blood away with the back of her hand. More rushed to replace it, but it didn't feel too bad. It just stung.

"What did you do?" Sotza gasped. There was a clang as her own blade fell to the ground.

It all seemed to be happening in surreal slow motion. Barli watched her drop to her knees, crying. There were sounds beyond, and Lipa kept complaining, now about the mess and how she never got peaceful roommates when she came to these competitions.

Barli glanced down at her knife. She didn't think she'd struck the woman too deeply—only half the blade was bloodied. But she certainly wasn't acting as though that was the case. It was then she saw that the blade was still slicked.

Poison.

Well, she supposed it was a good chance to observe the potency, and whether Farren knew his stuff. It definitely seemed to be causing pain.

One of the male contestants entered the room, followed by the young boy. On instinct, he pulled the small boy away, shading his eyes—as if the boy wasn't here to become a murderer.

The absurdity of the action brought a laugh to Barli's lips, and she did not even try to keep it down.

"I-I can't—" Sotza wasn't screaming anymore. She had slid over sideways, panting up at the ceiling, hand over her chest. Her eyes were wide and frightened.

Barli pressed the back of one of her hands to her bleeding neck to stem the flow. She hadn't thought to ask Farren about that healing poultice he had been talking about earlier. It had never occurred to her she might need healing.

Finally someone wearing Priest garb entered the room. Barli didn't recognize the man, but he was relatively young, possibly even Vorain's junior. "Clear out!" he ordered the curious.

Sotza wasn't moving anymore. She wasn't making any sound at all. The barest drop of a tear slid down her face. The Priest knelt before her, pulling on gloves as he gingerly turned her. He beckoned Lipa forward. "Take her pulse," he instructed.

Lipa crouched beside the bed, her fingers sliding under the woman's jaw. Barli waited in the stillness, her stomach humming.

"Nothing," came the pronouncement.

The Priest nodded. "Very well then." He called the man back in and had him and Lipa remove the body. The whole time Barli kept crouching on her bed, blades still out, heart beating fast.

She wasn't sure how long it was before Lipa returned. She glared at Barli. "Try not to invite any other late night visitors," she said moodily. It couldn't have been five minutes later before she was asleep again.

Barli laughed again, quietly so she wouldn't wake Lipa. There was no way she could sleep now. She took Lipa's normal perch at the window and stared out at the night. Somewhere, she knew she should feel bad. She had just killed someone, after all. But she felt nothing but relief and humor that it had happened like that. It was her own fault for trying to kill her. Barli was just defending herself. And besides, she was a Sin, wasn't she? And they weren't even going to punish her.

It had happened so fast. It was so easy. If anything, it convinced her for certain she could do it. Sotza had been aiming to be a murderer, and Barli had killed her just like that. Easy. And that's what was so funny about it—look how much better she had been! Barli had never felt particularly skilled at anything in her life. She could climb and she could fish and she could do a hundred different things, but she could only do them okay. Everywhere there were people better than her. But look how good she'd been against Sotza! And she'd gotten slaps in on Henequen. Maybe she wasn't as good as Kazini, but that girl wasn't right in the head.

Her eyes had nearly glazed over when she saw a figure on the street outside the Asylum. When she squinted, she was pretty sure it was Henequen. What was he doing out there in the middle of the night? She leaned forward.

He was slinking down the street, glancing over his shoulder as though he might be followed. She glanced after him, but saw no one there. He stopped, leaning his back against one of the buildings, shaking his head furiously. He stayed that way for several minutes. Then he looked over his shoulder again and moved on. Eventually he passed out of sight.

Barli kept her daggers in hand the rest of the night.

Chapter Fourteen

S HE DRESSED HER NECK roughly in the morning. Lipa didn't talk to her, and when they were led out to the courtyard she saw the other contestants looking at her. She wondered what they'd heard.

Kazini was sitting on the barrel Henequen had been installed on the other day, her legs crossed. When she uncrossed them, her movement was jerky and stiff and Barli realized she had never really seen Kazini move very much, except to slip around her. Maybe she wasn't crazy. Henequen was nowhere to be seen.

The main Priest had a set of papers. He didn't say anything about the missing contestant and Barli wondered where they'd taken her body.

"Today is the day you will get your assignments. All of your targets are located here on the Island, and even better all have been seen in the city within the last day. You will be responsible for carrying out the hit. Be certain you kill the right person, otherwise you are disqualified from this and all future competitions."

That made sense. Barli hadn't even thought about the possibility, but she supposed it might not be as simple as she'd assumed. The world was full of an awful lot of people, and they were not all marked the way the people in the Asylum. They looked like anyone else, like how she'd used to. They might look normal, on the outside.

"Other than that, there are no restrictions. These passes should let you in anywhere that you may require entry to, but keep in mind the lower key the nature of the kill, the higher we will regard your efforts. We do our best to stay out of the way of common folk. They don't like to see us. It makes everyone more nervous."

In other words, do it quickly and quietly. She couldn't get arrested for killing anyone, but she could lose the competition if anyone strongly connected her to the event, or really remember her afterward.

She knew all these things. Xinpaku had told her as much, when he had been berating her and telling her to be careful. Barli just hadn't understood exactly what he'd been saying then. It had seemed much farther away.

They had them wait in the courtyard while the main Priest left with his stack of papers. Apparently they had to make sure everyone left at different times, just to help cut down on potential casualties.

Barli felt a laugh burbling up from inside her and she bit it down as the first of the contestants disappeared, gone to get his assignment and begin the task set before all of them.

The little boy sidled over to her. His eyes were wide as

he looked up at her. "That other woman, last night, did you kill her?"

Barli nodded, watching his face. It was a testament to the oddity of the Asylum and the way they were all raised that he did not in the slightest look horrified, but rather gave her an approving look with quiet respect.

Before long he had been called away too. As their numbers dwindled, Barli began to feel the beginning of nerves.

The next time the girl Priest came out, she pointed to Barli. Barli's feet lunged beneath her, walking with more energy than she would have thought possible for the thing her steps led to. But she had killed once now, and though it had been somewhat frightful, it had also brought with it a taste and sating vicious exhilaration.

Despite it being somewhat unsettling, she was going to take it in stride. It was simpler than she'd thought, and that might have been what stuck with her most. She supposed she'd never thought it would be particularly difficult, but seeing exactly how easily the woman had gone down had been a particularly strange experience. It made her own life feel so much smaller and temporary—and everyone else's too.

The Priest led her down to the prayer hall. The older Priest had his head bowed by a table. He gestured to the thick paper envelope resting on the table. She stepped up to the table.

"Your mission," he said solemnly.

Barli took the envelope. It was heavier than she'd expected. She slid her finger under the flap.

"Ah. Not here. Child, take the Sin to her room to grab her things. You can take her from there to the outside."

Barli clenched her mission close to her side. She waited once again for the heavy door to be swung open. She scurried to her room, digging through her bag. In the end, she just threw it over her shoulder. More weapons and poison couldn't be bad, after all. Plus she wasn't sure how long it would take. She would need a change of clothes if she didn't want to be easily spotted from her own stink.

"Ready?" the girl Priest asked blandly.

Barli nodded. Her chest compressed as the Priest took her out to the main hall and finally she was at the door.

"Go on. You only have three days. The most common issue people run into is actually not finishing in time."

Barli didn't need to be told again. She was free!

She nearly stumbled down the steps. Three days of freedom—that much was guaranteed. And beyond that, so much more was possible. The moment had arrived. She looked up into the dark gray sky. It was going to rain. She knew it with a sailor's certainty.

Barli tried to remember the path Vorain had taken to get to this point. She thought she could backtrack most of the way, so she could find the way back to the docks. On nearly every Island, the docks were the most important location. It was where the floating population lived, where deals went down, and where Barli had always hung out with her friends. It was also on the docks where she'd met Visea.

She found herself backtracking the roads she had so briefly passed. It felt strange somehow to not be heading up and away from people and into the rocky mountains with Henequen, despite how strange he was.

The people in the streets didn't notice her immediately. Without the Priest leading the way, there was not the same standout quality that had warned everyone away before. She didn't need to keep her head bowed, because she looked from a passing glance just like everyone else. A couple times she saw someone who did more than glance briefly in her direction, and when they did their gaze lingered on her face and they froze, took a step back, and hurried away. If they were with anyone else they tugged on their sleeves, pointed in her direction, and ushered the rest of them away.

It would be tricky, she realized. People didn't assume a random person might be a Sin, but once they did notice, they would take the opportunity to leave as swiftly as possible—and that would include whoever her target was, whether they knew she was there for them or not.

Her target! She hadn't even looked yet. She'd been too busy lingering outside the sweet-smelling bakery, wishing she had some money to buy fresh rolls.

Barli's fingers fumbled with the envelope as she slid her nail under the flap and ripped it open. There were more pages than she'd expected. On the first page there was a name of the unfortunate soul: Gaju Plon. Beneath that was a description, a general location listing both assumed living place and workplace. There was a rough sketch as well, surprisingly detailed. The skill of the artist was clear. The next several pages were maps of the city. Barli had not used such assistance often before, and it took her some time puzzling over the pages to discern an approximate location.

Who gathered all this information? She supposed she'd always known the Priests must do more than just lecture the citizenry and lock and unlock doors. Perhaps it was them who did all this work.

It didn't matter. What mattered was accomplishing her goal. Gaju Plon's days were numbered. Did he know? Did he know they had been checking up on him, that soon he would be no more?

She digested the information on her target quickly. The information was plentiful, but to her surprise it did not include any list of the reasons *why* the individual had to be disposed of. She knew adults were rarer additions to the Asylum, and she was likely one of the elder of such additions even at her own still-tender age. Perhaps it was because they were even worse at accepting the alteration to their situation than she was. Perhaps if she had made it a few more years, she could have never bowed to the confines of the Asylum at all...though she still refused to think she quite yet had done all that was necessary to acquiesce and adjust to such a place and form.

Barli checked her maps and found the closest of Gaju's likely locations. She pulled up her hood as she went so that it all but covered her face. She stepped through crowded squares, quite unnerved by the utter mess of people she had never met before pressing in on either side of her. She almost wanted to let her hood fall back as she got jostled around from side to side just so they would leave off and give her some space. She had gotten used to not being surrounded by throngs of people.

She stepped up, pressing her back against the wall as

she watched people go about their busy days. Slowly she readjusted to crowds.

It had always been that way, she recalled. When she had been on a ship for several days, surrounded by nothing beside the rest of the crew and the greatest body of water known to man. When she returned to town it always seemed overwhelming, until she let the energy slowly seep back into her until she was feeding off of all of them, never sleeping as she would race through the port cities and spend her time going from one late night pub to the next. She'd always been aimless, catching whatever caught her fancy, dancing when she wanted, sleeping when she didn't. It had been that way for years.

Visea had changed everything.

Her throat caught at the distance and longing as she surveyed the crowds, keeping her ear open for the name she needed, her eye for the face. Everything had moved like an impermanent dance before Visea. She'd had no aim and though people had always surrounded her, she'd been nothing but alone.

"Eh—Gaju! What's yer folly?"

She froze, but refused to look immediately. She had played games when she was a child, spying on her parent's conversations. They'd had a good relationship, but were still partial to salty words at times, however they attempted to keep it from her. She had gotten into the knack of sneaking down to hear their fights—though in all honesty they were loud enough she never had to get close. She'd listened at times also to the sailors in their cups, learning the matters of their hearts without even meaning to do so. She had been fascinated by their stories, the way they talked about the woman they were so enamored with, whether they be wives or girlfriends or daughters. Sailors were often reminiscent of their families, and late at night, she could hear the love in their words and over and over she loved to listen to their own descriptions, wishing devoutly for such a phenomenon to grace her. She knew from experience, when she looked too long, they snapped and glared at her, their mouths quieting. They used to look her over, fighting to remember the love they'd just spoken of, while those who had nothing to stay looked all the harder.

They wouldn't look the same way anymore. Though it had been at times uncomfortable, she would miss the way she used to turn eyes. Now they only turned away.

Her head turned slowly so it seemed as though she was looking at the older tattered sign swinging from the nearby cobblers. She caught sight of the pair, taking in both men's appearances. The sketch really was quite good—already she could easily discern from the sketch that this was certainly the Gaju she was searching for. What, she wondered, had he done?

She slipped closer, wondering if she could get bonus points for accomplishing her task in only one day. Her fingers brushed against the cold dagger at her sleeves. Barli looked to the side as she sauntered slowly closer.

They were talking shop. She'd seen in her information he was a local fisher, and from the conversation they were having it seemed confirmed. He owned a short-ranged vessel and was out on the sea most days. He was complaining about a broken net and was haggling the man down on fixing the matter.

She kept her head bowed as she drew closer, even though it made her look like a street urchin begging for free coin. Though she disliked being took for such street trash, she supposed it was still better than being recognized for what she really was: a Sin.

They spoke for several more minutes before he stepped away, thanking the man however grudgingly. He seemed perfectly normal. What had keyed the Priests in to the situation? Barli frowned. She knew, of course, that just because there was no physical mark that didn't mean someone was untouched by the demon. She was proof of that. When she looked down at her wrist, of course, there was evidence of what had occurred. So perhaps she could expect some physical sign, however it subtle it might be.

Barli stepped out into the street as Gaju hefted a large basket Barli assumed was full of fish over his shoulder, wandering down the pass. She swayed a little as she walked, moving from one side of the street to the next to be sure to keep out of his view. As he was on the move, she gained confidence in her following, staying not more than ten feet behind him.

As the streets emptied down the less well-traveled section of the wharf, Barli's pace slowed further and she let him gain more distance from her. Dinghies used only by the locals replaced larger vessels as she continued along the coastline, farther from the heart of the city. Barli did not tend to linger in this part of town. She tended to enjoy more fully the hustle and bustle of shore parties.

In time, the street grew so empty she felt quite conspicuous making her way after him. He was all alone, and there was barely another on the street. She could dispatch of him here and now!

But instead she stopped, looking out at the ocean stretching into the horizon. It was well past midday now and as she stood there the first raindrops began to fall. They would only press more thickly upon them soon, and Barli did not relish in the idea of being entirely soaked through. That was something she certainly did not miss about roaming the streets. If it hadn't been cold already, she would have taken a dip into the sea.

When she looked again, she had lost track of the man. He had walked out onto the docks and disappeared somewhere in the mess of ships.

She glanced around and, seeing a cargo shack not far, made for it as the rain began to beat more swiftly down. As she huddled in a corner, overturning a half filled basket of fruits to sit on, she felt her stomach clench.

She could have been done with this already. There was no one else around! She was certain she'd found the right man. Why had she let him slip away? She could have followed him closer—what could he have done about it? Barli could have easily caught him, and all she needed was a well-placed nick with a poisoned knife and he was as dead as Sotza or that rabbit. She hadn't been bothered by either of them in the slightest.

But the man was different. She had seen his retreat and unarmored back, so close she could have, even with her limited skill, thrown a knife into Gaju's back. But she hadn't.

Her hand banged against the splinter-filled wood.

She had to finish this. She had promised herself—and, beyond that, she'd told Farren she would. He'd refused her promises, but she saw it as such. And Barli didn't have much beyond her word anymore.

It wasn't like Sotza, though. Sotza had been coming for her. Sotza had been ready to risk her life for the sake of the competition. Even as much as Barli wanted to win, she didn't think she would have ever gone to such extremes. But in her mind, Sotza had more or less given up her right to life when she decided to try to attack and possibly kill Barli. She'd signed similar paperwork she recalled at the beginning of this venture. She had signed her life away, accepting that she might die. So perhaps there was nothing to guarantee her survival either.

Gaju was a fisherman. He was a widow, according to the paperwork, and childless. So perhaps he didn't have too much to live for, but how could she know that for certain? One could have certainly looked at her life and thought it must not have been worth much. And maybe it wasn't. Maybe there wasn't a huge need to preserve her life…but just because she hadn't had a chance to build it into anything yet didn't mean it could never be anything.

That was, she realized, exactly why she had needed so earnestly to take this competition. If she couldn't make it to Black Sin, she would be forced back into a room in a building with nothing to do but learn how to cook awful meals. If she couldn't make this, she might as well have Farren's life, which was no life at all.

Farren—that was what was giving her pause. He had nothing, he'd done nothing, but still he was confined to live a life that in her eyes hardly seemed worth living. If this simple man, perhaps having some inclination of a darker nature, was deserving of death then how could one argue to preserve Farren's woeful existence? Turning the argument around, for she was appalled at the idea that at any time the Priests might deem Farren's existence too troublesome and cut him off, how could she follow through?

She was beginning to understand what Ployame had been trying to tell her so long ago. She could understand why they might not all jump at the chance. The idea of having such power thrilled her—but was she truly in control of it?

She pounded her fist against the wood again.

How could Farren at once be her reason to do it and also not to do it?

And what if there was something about him so truly revolting that his death could be called for? Could she judge? In a way, the Priests had taken that issue off the table with their rules and regulations, with their careful systems that kept potential risks bound and sought out retribution against those that were beyond containment. She wasn't judge. She was only executioner. But she could not throw her conscience away.

She had already decided. Why was she wavering now? She had to kill him. There was absolutely nothing else to be done. It would cost her her own life and her own sanity to let him walk free, and someone else would be sent to kill him after her failure. His life was already gone, his body just didn't know it yet.

The rain came down in heavier drifts.

Barli hauled herself up, climbing a precarious bunch of crates until she could see out of a dirty window. Its only purpose was to pour some daylight into the room so it was possible to see through the ranks of storage and it hadn't been cleaned since its installation. She brushed dust away, hissing a little as she found a splinter had found its way into her palm.

The rain and the thick coating on the thin glass made it difficult to see, but smudges rocked back and forth with the waves and she saw no extra figures making their way from the dock. She doubted she would, with the rain coming down the way it was.

She picked at her hand, prodding the splinter from its roost as she waited for the weather to abate. When had her hands gotten so soft? She had never had such soft hands before. They had been hard and calloused from the saltwater and rough thick ropes.

It was several hours later when the rain began to turn into a normal fall drizzle. Barli's stomach was beginning to growl when a dark blot of movement caught her attention.

She quickly slipped off her stack of crates, cursing the creaking sound. Thankfully the continuing downpour would no doubt cover most of the sound. Barli eased the door open, her eyes lighting on the dark figure. She hadn't seen anyone else in the vicinity, but that wasn't odd on a day like this. Most who were going out would have done so already, making certain to catch what fish they could in the prosperous weather. There were fish that only surfaced when it rained and they were common fall prey. They wouldn't be back till nightfall. For his ruined net, Gaju had lost a good day's fishing. There was no point in going out after the storm had set in after all.

She darted after him, heart racing slightly as she followed him. She spotted a few others about, and, unnerved, she did not get any closer. Firmly, with every beat of her heart, she commanded herself not to lose heart. She had already decided. All she had to do now was carry through on her agreement.

Why did it seem so hard?

He was getting away! Already the streets were becoming more crowded. She swallowed. The next day he'd likely be on his skip and it would be far more difficult to catch him.

Maybe if it was too much to stab him, she could manage to slip something into his food, or something he was sure to touch. The issue was, of course, that nothing could be certain with what happened next: whether someone else, someone undeserving, suffered the same fate. She was no expert at such things—perhaps she had best not try it. Farren would likely have some ideas on how to limit anyone else's exposure, but evidently she was not as brilliant as him.

But if she had missed her chance to catch him on the skiff, she'd have to do it in town. Otherwise there would be too many other people around. Barli's jaw tensed as he slipped up a crowded street.

If she got to the food right after he collapsed…

She wasn't sure why, but the idea of having him unconsciously come into contact with what would end his life was something more comforting than approaching him herself, where she might see for a moment the panic of his life leaving his body.

He stepped into a tavern. The evening had nearly come and while the local fishermen weren't quite back yet, the sailors in port for the day had already begun their carousing. Barli made sure her hood was cresting heavily over her forehead, waited several long seconds, and stepped inside.

She had three days, she reminded herself. She didn't need to accomplish this today. But she was afraid—what if she hesitated too long and lost her nerve? She had proved she could kill people but…things were more complicated than simple murder. Was murder ever simple?

Barli clapped her hands in time with the music, avoiding other people's wandering hands as they threatened to dislodge her carefully construed cowl. It was stuffy inside, despite the outside chill, and it wasn't long before Barli wished she could remove her cloak, if just to breathe. She also wanted to join in the dance in the center of the tavern, where half a dozen people were kicking their legs up in keeping with the merry jig.

She used to dance.

Barli's eye focused on Gaju and she found herself wondering again what he might have done that the Priests found so offensive. It didn't help that, despite Vorain's assurances, Barli could not help but feel they were inherently *wrong* and that people didn't deserve to be locked up the way they were. Maybe it did help some people…even so, was it worth it?

She watched him order food and she swayed closer. It was as well she was wearing such a thick and concealing cloak. Though girls could wear trousers as easily as men, a place like this invited a long skirt to use in the high energy sweeping dances and she would have looked out of place as she was now.

"Hey, girl," a man said, "little shy, are we?"

She ducked her head further, feeling her cheeks heat.

"Come on now, dance with me. I have a little flit like you at home." He was drunk on his liquor and Barli gently extracted herself from the hand that was quickly coming down to her shoulder. She couldn't be unmasked here. It would ruin the night for all of them and certainly make her target wary.

"No, thank you," she said sharply.

He raised his hand and took a step back. "Well, if you feel like a little fun…I've a great lift."

"I'll keep it in mind," she said, moving away.

The hood was terribly inconvenient. She could hardly see behind her—not unless she turned her head incredibly far. She couldn't see the ceiling either. But she had to keep it up. She didn't have another choice.

Barli barely managed to sidestep two men having an intense row about their latest drop of cargo, stumbling into a corner. She had been pushed farther away from her mark. As she watched, a steaming plate of food was delivered to his table. He was eating alone, although at the same table three other men were playing cards. She watched his quietly, keeping track of him between the swirling skirts of the dancers.

It was too crowded. She wasn't sure she could get close to him without too much jostling. If she didn't have to keep her face hidden she could have slipped by easily…but keeping her identity under check was a new problem, one she wasn't used to dealing with. She used to talk up men when it suited her. Many of her old tactics for the barroom were now impossible. Would she ever be comfortable in a space like this again? The pang of loss tightened her throat. It hit so suddenly she felt almost dizzy for a second.

As she sat, studying the man, she noticed that his eyes were far from idle. He gazed surreptitiously around the room, and when he glanced her way she quickly diverted her gaze. Was he already suspicious then? As she watched him longer, she realized he too seemed to be marking at least one other person, though from her vantage she couldn't tell who it might be.

Barli bit her lip. She had three days, but she couldn't afford to have it take so long. She was too afraid something would go wrong or change her mind. Her stomach whined. If she'd had money, she would have bought something. Unfortunately, she did not. How did the Black Sins get around? Did they receive stipends for their missions? Or did they just not eat? They all had seemed particularly lithe.

Several hours passed and Barli began to sweat profusely from the heat in the room. Her target was still in his cups and the tavern had gotten still more crowded once the fishermen had all returned. One of the barmaids was giving her a look—she'd been here too long and still not ordered anything. The cloak gave her a foreboding air in of itself and wasn't good for business.

When the woman started coming toward her, Barli took her leave. She ducked out into a cloudy night. At first the chill was a relief to her hot face and she even considered taking her hood down for a few seconds before she was certain that several individuals were also loitering on the street.

She stepped across the way so she would have a good view of the tavern's entrance. Barli shivered a little as the hot air in the tavern faded away. She wrapped her cloak more tightly around her shoulders. Most of the strangers kept moving, two of them were having a spitting contest.

Another man was loitering nearby. He started walking toward her, slinking more than walking. She swallowed hard, neck stiffening as she fumbled to pull out one of her daggers.

Why was she afraid? She never used to be afraid. There was really very little crime on the Islands and Barli had only heard a couple stories about unsavory things happening. What was it that had her staring at the man coming toward her fearfully, instead of bemused interest?

His hood was pulled over his head and it had a familiar cut to it. Wait—now she knew why she was afraid.

Who was it? Which of them still wanted her dead? Why would they work this hard to hunt her down instead of their own quarry? Or was it just chance that they their marks had found the same tavern to frequent?

Chapter Fifteen

IT TOOK HER ANOTHER second and he was close enough not to wrap his skilled hands around her tender throat when she knew the Sin for sure: Henequen.

"Farren's on Hevon'i now. You know him."

"What are you doing here?" she hissed.

He folded his arms against his muscular chest. "Have you done it yet?"

"No! And what do you—what are you talking about Farren for?"

Henequen sighed. "We have to get out of here."

"We? What? I'm supposed to—to kill someone."

"Get it over with already then! You've found him. What else is there to wait for? It's a simple matter."

He was so callous. "It's not that easy."

"Do it now and meet me at the fifth pier," he said quietly, moving past her.

She grabbed his arm. "Wait. What are you even…why? And what did this guy do anyway? He seems normal."

Henequen's eyes met hers, and something seemed

deeply unsettled in his face. It almost made her heart stop. "That man is far from good. I would have killed him several days ago if we hadn't been told to stave off for the test. Who knows who else he's harmed in that time? He'll come out of there drunk and stumbling, but not quite as drunk as he pretends. He'll have a boy with him, someone he's convinced to help him back to his home. He'll lead him down the back alley and then he'll take him." Henequen said. He broke her grasp. "So dispose of him and be done with it. And meet me at the pier."

He was gone before she could call out in protest again. She trembled a little from the description he'd given her, even the spaces between his words left too much to the imagination.

She wrapped her cloak even more tightly around her. What did Henequen need from her? Why would he have sought her out?

Barli's feet shuffled against the hard-packed dirt streets, kicking up against the wall as she waited impatiently. Even though she had no idea what he wanted, she knew she would follow after him. That was exactly what she always did.

It couldn't have been more than an hour when Barli spotted Gaju leaving the tavern. As Henequen had predicted, he had a boy at his arm, fifteen or sixteen. She felt a small squeeze in her stomach. Gaju turned down a darker hallway. The music from the tavern was loud enough to cover the smaller noises of the night.

She followed after them, blade in hand. They did not go far. Before long, Gaju had ceased his inauthentic sway, new strength seeming to fill his limbs. The boy was actually drunk and even as he seemed to realize slowly something wasn't quite right, Gaju had already pressed him against the wall.

Barli darted forward, moving so quickly her hood drifted off her face. She caught the distracted and still not exactly sober man by the arm. She wasn't strong enough to pull him away from the boy, but she shoved him partially off as she took the knife in her hand and drew it across the man's exposed arm.

"Hey, girl—what do you..." His voice, which had started out fierce and angry, wavered suddenly when he beheld the marks on her face. "Y-y-you..."

She stepped back, watching as the poison quickly took hold. It took longer than it had with Sotza, but she hadn't cut the man quite as deep.

"Devil's spawn!" he spat as he dropped to his knees, clutching his chest. "What right do you have? You think you can judge life and death? Or are you so feral you need an excuse to kill?"

Barli's heart rate accelerated and she stumbled backward, nearly stumbling over the back of her hem. "I-I..." she shook her head uncertainly.

The boy stepped away from the wall. His hands were shaking slightly. He looked down at Gaju who was struggling to breathe on the ground and kicked him. "Shut up, bastard!" He glanced at her. "Are you going to finish him off?"

"He's already dying," she said softly.

He readjusted his clothing, looking awkwardly at her.

"Thank you," he said awkwardly. "I...well, thanks." He turned away.

Barli swallowed. For a second, the boy had looked her in the eye. And it hadn't been the fear or discomfort she had learned to expect, but honest and earnest gratitude. Barli swallowed for a second. "Wait—"

He folded his arms across his chest. "What?"

"I...I just wanted you to look at me a little longer."

He lifted an eyebrow. "You're a strange and scary girl," he said, "but I'm glad you're here. What's your name?"

"I'm not supposed to have a name."

"What?"

Barli finally realized what was odd about this boy—he wasn't from the Islands. She gave him a closer look, trying to gauge his country of origin. It was either Belin or the Trikingdom, she concluded. His skin was surprisingly light and his hair! Her eyes widened. She'd never seen hair like that, a golden yellow nearly like the sun. "Um...I should...my friend's waiting for me. But...it was nice meeting you."

Her face was hot, though she couldn't say why. "I should go."

"You're the one who told me to wait. I'd really like nothing better than to get out of here..."

"This place. It's not always like that."

"Good. All the same..."

"I'm going to the pier," she said, "I could take you back to your ship."

He smiled slightly. "I'd be glad for the company, mystery girl."

They didn't walk too close, and they didn't talk much, but it was nice for a moment to not feel like she was judged. He didn't know what she was or what she was trying to become. He knew she'd killed a man and left him in the street, but he didn't seem to mind. When they parted ways, she hadn't even asked his name. But it didn't matter. He was one normal person who hadn't looked at her like she was a monster. It meant more than she could say.

Once she was alone, she allowed herself a brief moment of reflection: she had completed her duty. She had at least a decent chance of becoming a Black Sin…unless she did something that would jeopardize her position. Meeting Henequen might well be one of those things.

The lanterns hanging from the long poles were flickering dimly. Half of them had been already put out by wind or rain. She flipped her hood back up and stepped up to the fifth pier.

A figure popped out of the darkness. "Took you long enough," he said, leading her up onto a small vessel. "You have to hurry."

She hesitated as he boarded the ship, newly resting waves lapping gently against the dock. "Where are we going? Is this some weird part of the test?" She remembered he was crazy. "Where are you taking me?"

Henequen grabbed her hand and pulled her onto the boat. "We have to go. I have to go. I have to go," he said insistently.

Henequen cast them off into the deep. Barli fought against him as they swiftly pulled away from the shore, stamping on his foot.

"Let go of me!"

He kept murmuring the same thing under his breath, ignoring her until they were well away. He released her then, and sank to his knees at the stern of the vessel. She followed behind.

They were going back the way she'd come. She didn't quite remember what other Islands lay in that direction, but the largest one was definitely Hevon'i.

"Henequen, why are you taking me back to Hevon'i?"

He was rocking back and forth slightly, not in time with the gentle ebb and fall of the ship. His hands held his closely shorn head.

"He didn't do anything. They want to kill him and he didn't do anything. He didn't do anything!" His sudden shout carried across the waves, but there was no one but her and whoever was steering the ship to hear it.

"Who? Henequen, who are you...Farren? They're going to kill Farren? Is that it?"

"He didn't do anything."

Barli sighed. "Henequen, I can't leave. They'll know, and they'll never make me a Black Sin then. I'm going to get him out eventually, okay? Just wait a while, please. Take me back!" She couldn't go jeopardizing this. What would they say if they found out? And what did Henequen think she was going to do anyway? Why would he take her with him?

"He didn't do anything!"

She was attempting to reason with a mad man. Who in their right mind would give someone like him this sort of power?

She could still swim back. She was a strong swimmer. She didn't know Henequen—only that Kazini had clearly warned her away from him with more than a few concerning words, and that Henequen's behavior sometimes seemed to turn on a dime. None of it was very reassuring.

"I have to go back, Henequen." If they found out she'd left—if she wasn't back in time…she was almost certain they'd send the Black Sins out to end her too. They wouldn't want someone wild like that loose on the streets. Even if she went back…the Priests had never seemed particularly forgiving.

She stepped up to the edge, climbing the railing.

"Wait. Please. I-I'm sorry. I'm sorry I don't make sense and I'm messing everything up but it's Farren and please. I'm trying to hold on to it, but I can't and it's so red but I can't but I need to, please. I know you can help me. You hit me. You can do it and I don't know and he wouldn't anyway."

Barli's shoulders fell. "Fine," she said, with no idea how she was going to accomplish whatever Henequen thought needed to be done that he couldn't do himself. "We get him and then I come right back, before they know I've gone."

He closed his eyes and nodded, rocking. "Thank you."

She watched as the shore slowly disappeared beyond the horizon. After watching Henequen rocking and quietly muttering things for several hours, she couldn't stand to watch it any longer. He was the only company she had. "Henequen?"

He ignored her.

She swung down from the railing and marched up to

him. "Henequen! I don't know what's wrong with you, but you'd better tell me what this rush is all about that can't wait a few more days—and why you need me—and how you know Farren."

Henequen was sustaining his incessant chatter.

She swung down in front of him and gripped his chin, pulling his face around so she was staring into his eyes. They darted away, trying to escape her gaze, but she held his face firm. "Henequen. Pull it together!"

He scratched his arms. "It's my fault. I'm not…I'm not normal."

"I know. None of us are."

"No it's…it's different. I…please, can you hit me?"

"What?" She let go of him, startled.

"Please. It helps shut everything up. Kazini fucks me when I get like this but I don't like it."

Barli's words got stuck in her throat. She…what?

"Please. I can't think. I hear all these things that aren't there. It gets so confusing."

She didn't want to think about everything he was saying or what it implied. Barli leaned back and quickly slapped him hard across the face, sending him sprawling onto the deck.

"Again."

It felt wrong to brutalize him like this, especially when it was evident he was far more insane than she was. But she needed answers out of him, and if he said this would help her get them, she was willing to try it. She beat her hand against his chest and gut.

Finally, she sat back and waited for him to, wincing

slightly, return himself to an upright position. His lip was bleeding but his hands were finally still, not pulling at his body.

"Can you ask your questions again? Slower. One at a time."

She took a deep breath. "Why do we have to go?"

Henequen took a deep breath. "They've been talking for a while and they've decided to kill him. They just decided. They'll send the message tomorrow."

Falls. They didn't have much time. He'd been right. "Why did you bring me?"

"I didn't even know where he was anymore, if he was even alive. I've never been to Hevon'i. I don't know the layout, how I might get in. And he…he and I…I don't think he'd trust me."

It did seem to be working, slapping him around a little. He was giving her actual answers. "Why? How do you know him?"

Henequen swallowed, eyes darting around. "I met him when I was younger. We were locked up together. Then things got messed up and they took us both away. They wouldn't tell me what happened to him."

"Well. He's been okay, if not exactly happy. Alive, anyway."

Alive. He was still alive for the moment—and they were going to keep it that way. Barli sighed. "Are you going to get in trouble for this?"

"If I get caught," he said. "I don't know what we'll do, once we have him. But Farren was always smarter than me. He could figure something out."

He was smart. He knew about poisons and other things. She hadn't even given him the chance to be smart. Barli nodded slowly. "It's…better than nothing."

"I'm sorry. I just…I get messed up sometimes."

She sat down next to him. "Do you really hear things that aren't real?"

"So they tell me." He shifted uncomfortably. "I don't feel like I can know for sure, though, you know? What if everything else, everyone telling me I'm making things up, is the real illusion?"

She didn't know what to say to that. Even if she felt like her mind got wild sometimes, it was really nothing compared to that.

Eventually she fell asleep.

Henequen woke her in the morning. He looked tired, as if he hadn't slept at all. "We're here," he said.

A young man stepped toward them. "Sin, sir. Is that all?"

Henequen frowned. "Wait for us here. We should be back within the day. Thank you for your service."

The man tipped his hat. "Always willing to help you, Henequen."

They disembarked, Barli barely remembering to grab her pack before they were standing on the dock.

Henequen looked around and pulled his hood up. His lip was slightly swollen. Barli found herself tasting her own lip. Maybe she would deal with Henequen's oddities later.

For the moment, they had more important matters to attend to. She followed his lead, pulling up her own hood.

She didn't know these streets any better than she'd known the last city. Still, she remembered the way to the Asylum. She took the lead, leaving Henequen to follow her. Sometime between first and seventh street, he started murmuring things again. Barli tuned him out, realizing he was not going to get any better—unless maybe she hit him. But she didn't think that was something she ought to do lightly, nor in broad daylight in the middle of the street.

Once they got close, Barli began to really think about what they were doing. She'd fallen asleep without coming up with a plan, and judging from Henequen's current countenance, he hadn't come up with anything and wasn't about to either. At least he'd been smart enough to know this was going to happen. He was right—she'd needed to come. He couldn't do it on his own. He was just too crazy.

She couldn't see him up on the roof. It was a clear day and so his absence surprised her. The way he'd taken to the roof…what if he was locked inside? How would they get to him?

Something brushed against her leg and she glanced down, startled. "Maigi!"

The tiny black cat looked larger than she remembered for all that only a few days had passed. At least she hadn't starved to death. Barli had been a little worried about letting her loose like that.

She glanced up at the high walls. They looked slightly more scalable from this side. They didn't need to try to keep people out. They already knew to stay away. Barli glanced down at Maigi, wondering if the cat could possible climb it. She knew most cats were good climbers, but she'd never seen Maigi climb much of anything…probably because she'd been confined indoors most of her life.

She glanced at Henequen. He had folded himself up against the far wall, drawing in the dirt with a stick. No help at all.

Barli picked up a large pebble from the ground and chucked it at the upper courtyard's window. It took her several minutes to launch it right, but she finally managed to get one to strike into the courtyard.

A minute later, she saw a shadow at the window.

"Farren!"

The figure pressed closer, squeezing a little through the small window. "Barli?"

She stepped closer, neck straining to look up at him. "Hey," she said, relieved. She hesitated for a moment and walked up to the wall. It would be too obvious if they were shouting for long—she knew others would be outside too. Her fingers slit into the cracks and she kicked off her boots to help her grip.

It took longer than she'd wanted to shimmy up the wall, but eventually she pulled herself up the window and was staring at Farren's hollow black eyes, a little wider at the moment.

"What are you doing here?" he asked.

"I heard they decided to kill you, so, of course, we've got to get you out."

Farren blinked. "How are you going to do that?" he

asked. "There's no way they'd let me out of this place. Not alive."

"I don't get it. What's so dangerous about you? Henequen said you've never even done anything."

"Henequen?"

"Actually he said it over a hundred times."

Farren's head tilted and he frowned. "It's because of who my parents were – both Sins. They generally don't encourage that type of thing, but before they knew it, it was too late. They think I'm terribly dangerous. They've only kept me alive this long because they think maybe they've contained more of the demon in just one person."

"That's idiotic!"

Farren shrugged. "I haven't done anything yet. But maybe I touch people and make them worse, like it sort of oozes out of me."

"Why would you think that?"

Farren sighed. "It's not important. The point is, it doesn't matter. You can't get me out. I'm going to die now, I guess. So what?"

Barli wished she could have grabbed and shaken him, but she was having a hard enough time holding herself up on this wall. "So Maigi would miss you—she's still down there right now! And Henequen would feel bad and probably be more crazy than normal, which already seems to be pretty messed up. And I came all this way, just to try to save your life, and if we don't figure out something quick I'm going to be in plenty of trouble. So you're coming with me and you are not dying!"

He swallowed. "You'd do that for me?"

The strain on her arms was getting worse. She wasn't sure how much longer she could hang on. "Yeah, Farren. We're friends. That's how it works."

"Fine. Well. I still don't know how I'd get out of here. I can't climb like you. The only way I'm getting out of here is as a body."

They didn't really have enough time to make some sort of contraption that might lower him down more easily. Barli sighed. Wait. "That's it!"

"What?"

"You've got all sorts of plants, right? Can't one of them make it look like you're dead—just for a while?"

His empty dark eyes seemed to lift slightly. "Yes. I don't know how long it'd take them to find me but…I could do that." Something like a smile slid onto his face, though it quickly faded. "You'll watch? You'll get me, when I get out?"

"Of course."

"Because I've never been out there before. The last time, I was eight or nine and they had me sedated and blindfolded nearly the whole time! I don't know what it's like out there or how to act or…anything."

"Hey, hey. It's okay. I'll take care of you. I've lived in the world a long time." The burn in her limbs was getting stronger. "I have to go. I don't want anyone to see us. We'll wait, okay?"

He swallowed and nodded. "I'm trusting you, Barli."

"I know. I made a promise. And I keep them."

Arms trembling, she slowly made her way back to the ground, dropping the last few feet as her weary arms gave way. "Well, that's settled," Barli said, rubbing her shoulders as she walked back over to Henequen.

"Hey."

Henequen glanced up to her. "Did you see him?"

She nodded. "He's fine. It's going to be fine."

"So what do we do now?"

"We wait." Barli sat down next to him. "What are you drawing, anyway?" She had stepped in it again, of course.

"Does it matter?"

"I'm curious. About a lot of things, actually. Because it seems like we sort of have to be friends now, doesn't it?"

Henequen's eyes narrowed. "I draw the things I see. It doesn't make them go away but it makes my mind clearer."

Barli looked at the drawings again. She still couldn't pick out real shapes. "Does the stuff in your head always look like this?"

"Well, it's not exactly right. I should say I don't have any skill."

She laughed. "I've never been good at drawing either, so I just stopped. I...don't like to keep doing things I'm not good at."

"I keep hoping I'll have done it enough sometime and get good, but it's never happened. Maybe there are things you're just good at and things you aren't." He grew quiet after that and shortly began his murmurs.

Barli sighed. The day was nearly warm and she wished she were in a position to remove her hood. Instead she managed to get Henequen to at least move into the shade.

The sun slowly sunk lower and lower in the sky. Barli sighed, bored. She even picked up the stick Henequen had abandoned and began to make her own drawings in the dirt. They were hardly better than Henequen's efforts, but she found a simple joy in her terrible creation all the same.

She entertained herself with those simple means until the sky grew dark. Henequen had devolved into quiet murmurs and he only broke out of it when Barli asked if he had any money for food. He shook his head but stood up, brushing dirt from his cloak. "What do you want?"

Barli shrugged. "Fresh fish?" She hadn't had anything truly fresh in a long time. The Asylum only ever seemed to have fish on the edge of expiring and wilted greens. "Anything fresh…fruit!"

He walked away without a word, returning half an hour later with his arms full. He dumped several bright orange fruits into her lap and laid out a pretty spread of fish and rice. It smelled delicious.

Barli bit into the sweet fruit and grinned, wiping the juice from her chin. "Mmh."

They took their time with the food, though Barli noted she ate far more than Henequen. He did more playing around with the food than actually eating it.

"Aren't you hungry?"

Henequen shook his head. "He was okay though, right? Did he seem mad? When is he coming?"

Barli stared at him. "I don't know. Hopefully soon, but they don't pay that much attention to him so it might be longer. And I told you he was fine – why would he be mad?"

He stiffened up. "You better be sure he's doing something," he said with a tense nod toward the street. Barli glanced around him and saw a man in Priest's robes bearing down the road.

"Is that…the messenger?"

Henequen nodded. "It took longer than I thought. He must have set out late."

"We needed all the time we could get."

He didn't say anything, but she assumed he was thinking about how Barli could have been so much faster if she hadn't been as timid and untrusting.

"Hey, before, when you were antagonizing me, you were doing that on purpose? So I'd hit you?"

Henequen stared at the ground. "I had to guess the first time. I wasn't sure what you'd do."

"You could have just asked."

Henequen sighed. "Really? Do you think that would have gone better?"

"No. I would have…I don't know. I'd think you'd use it as an excuse to get me thrown out or something." Barli smiled a little. "You're pretty smart for being so crazy."

"But I am. Too crazy."

"I'm crazy too. Not so much but some." She held her arm out to him, revealing the scar there. "That's why I got in here."

Henequen's shoulders hunched. "You don't know what it's like to be really crazy."

They sat in tense silence, waiting for something to happen, for a Priest to appear, for any sound from the Asylum that might suggest their plan was in progress. The Priest they had seen before came up to the Asylum. Barli watched as the door slid open and he was admitted. It was only a matter of time before Farren's death was sealed.

After what seemed an unbearably long time, she saw movement in the upstairs windows. Few actually connected to anything but empty rooms, but she did see something. What, she wasn't sure.

Barli stood up at the first sign the doors were opening, but Henequen swiftly pushed her down again.

"You need lessons in being inconspicuous."

That was an odd comment coming from the guy who had spent the whole day drawing dirt pictures and muttering under his breath. "You're one to talk!"

"Even though I—"

The door opened, and somewhere above a heavy bong echoed from the tower. Barli hadn't known they had a gong, but hearing it she was certain that it was at least believed that Farren was dead. It was, however, entirely possible they had actually killed him.

What if they hadn't done enough? What if he hadn't had enough time? Should she have tried to get him through the impossibly small window?

Four shrouded Priests stepped slowly through the open doors, carrying a wrapped body between them. Barli felt her stomach drop. They couldn't know until they got to him whether he was already gone or not. The gong echoed out a slow beat, sweet and gentle as they stepped forward.

This was one of the simplest of funerals Barli had ever seen. It was entirely impersonal, hardly interested at all, acting nearly as though it was a bother. They carried the tattered sheet to the foot of the steps and began their descent to the shore.

All funerals ended at the sea. They were born to the sea and they returned to it. Usually there was full procession, where everyone who knew the deceased followed in parade down to the shore. They would tell stories and sing songs and light a bonfire, staying together until it burned out.

Barli and Henequen slipped after the procession. "Do you think he's getting enough air?" Henequen fretted.

"Probably," Barli said, "if those are his sheets, they've been worn to nearly nothing." That didn't stop the squeeze in her heart.

The walk to the sea took too long. Her head ached as the sea breeze finally blew over them and the bright blue expanse spread before her. They were returning him to the sea—but he'd never even swum in it. He'd never…what if he couldn't make it? He was already tied up and he certainly didn't know how to swim.

She took off at a run, disappearing behind one of the nearby buildings as the Priests slowly entered the water.

"Barli—"

"Shh." She shed her cloak as she ducked under the water.

It felt good to be underwater again. The water slipped around her, kissing every inch of her skin. She slipped deeper into the sea, the familiar salty taste pulling at her lips.

She surfaced momentarily, spotting the Priests again, trying stones to the blanket as they gently released the load. Barli took a deep breath and dove down, slithering along the rocky bottom toward the sinking body bag.

The Priests stepped away, load released. There was no further ceremony. How callous!

She grabbed the body and pulled it away from the Priests, popping up under the dock and hauling the body with her.

"Farren!" she hissed. She took out a dagger and stripped away at the bedding, pulling it away to reveal a cold and expressionless face, eyes closed, body damp.

The Priests were stepping out of the water now, unaware that anything had happened at all. They were turning down the road and leaving without a second thought. They wouldn't discover anything strange had happened. But maybe nothing strange had.

She dragged his unmoving body to the shore, keeping low to hide from the Priest's retreating backs, though she doubted any of them would care to look back. "Henequen!" She didn't see him.

She felt Farren's cold skin and pulled more of the dirty old blankets from his body. He seemed untouched. She couldn't know if it was whatever he might have taken, what they had done, or effects of drowning.

She knelt beside him and began compressing his chest, looking for signs of movement. "Come on, Farren." Carefully, she tilted his head back. Barli swallowed, fighting the ever-increasing dread. She brought her mouth to his and gave him two short breaths before returning to her compressions. *"Kitadu!* I am not getting in trouble for nothing!"

Chapter Sixteen

HIS EYELIDS SLOWLY FLUTTERED open and he coughed. Barli sat back immediately, putting a hand on his shoulder.

"*Kitadu*, Farren. You alright?"

He took several haggard breaths, blinking up at crisp cool moonlight. "Wh-what—where am I?"

"You're outside, Farren." She helped him sit up, though he reflexive fought her. Barli had expected as much. He'd never gotten used to casual touch—much less meaningful, helpful ones.

"Outside?"

"What happened? Did you fool them?"

"I guess. I don't remember. I started waking back up after they'd wrapped me up. Then there was all this water and I couldn't breathe and—"

"Hey, it's okay. I've got you now."

Farren was looking past her now, at the water that extended out into the distant horizon. He rubbed his eyes and his mouth fell open. "Wh…is this all real?"

"Of course it's real! Falls, I was so scared you were dead." Barli glanced around. "Come on, we should get out of here. Someone might see us." Where was Henequen anyway?

Farren was still staring at the water. "It's…there's so much of it. I've read about it, but…it's endless."

Barli took a deep breath and hauled him to his feet.

"What are you doing?" he asked, struggling.

"I'm trying to help you! And it's about time you got used to people touching you. You're in the real world now, Farren."

The Priests were not the type to waste anything, and Farren was naked underneath his blankets. It was already a cold night and now everything he had was soaking. "Henequen!"

"Who is Henequen?"

"He…he said he knew you, that you were together for like two years or something."

Farren frowned. "The only one…" He looked past Barli and his eyes widened slightly. "Tane!" And then Farren did something Barli had never seen him do before. He stepped up the bank and wrapped his arms around Henequen.

"You're not mad, Farren? I-I tried to tell them, but they wouldn't…"

Farren hugged the taller boy tightly, only half dressed in tattered bed sheets. "I told them it was me, Tane. I thought…" He seemed suddenly to realize what he'd been doing and jumped back nearly a foot, stumbling over his blanket's train. "Kitadu, Tane, what have they done to you?"

"They call me Henequen now."

He physically recoiled. Farren studied his branded face. "They made you into a killer," he said softly.

Barli glanced around and noticed a couple people were giving them strange looks now. "Henequen, give him your cloak." Farren was already freezing. "People are looking and we need to get back."

He untwined his cloak and put it around Farren's shoulders while Farren kicked the rest of his tattered blankets from his body. "Barli's right. We need to get out of here, and hopefully get back to the competition."

"How?" Farren asked.

Henequen stepped up the bank and they followed. Farren seemed like he couldn't decide where to stare—at Henequen, the sea, or the port around him. Barli stepped up behind him and forced the hood over his head. She had to keep pushing him forward as he wanted to stop and stare at everything they passed.

Barli heard a quiet mew and looked down to see the black feline pawing at the back of Farren's cloak. She smiled a little. That was an interesting cat. "Hey Farren, it's Maigi."

Farren bent down and coiled the cat in his arms. She climbed up and laid across his shoulders. "Barli?"

"Hmm?"

"What are we going to do? I...I'm not supposed to exist."

"First things first," she said. "I get back to where I'm supposed to be, and then we figure out what we're going to do about you."

Henequen nodded. "I can get most things we'll need, as long as it's still warm enough to stay outside."

They reached the same skiff Henequen had mysteriously commissioned last night. Farren stayed with Barli, studying the boat uneasily as Henequen left to talk with the captain.

"What's he doing?"

Barli shrugged. "It's a perk of being a Black Sin, I guess."

Farren glanced at her. "Is it true? All the things they say about him?"

"I don't know what they say," Barli said carefully.

"Come on."

The two of them embarked. Farren's face quickly went to shocked as his hands cast out, searching for balance. "Why's it *moving* like that?"

"It's floating, Farren. You'll get used to it."

As they began to pull away, Farren shook his head, gripping the railing tightly. "This is a mistake. I should go back. I'll tell them I was faking and they can kill me for real and it'll be fine. I can't do this. I can't do this, Barli!"

How did she get involved in madness like this? "Yes, you can!" She took him by the shoulders, wondering if it would help if she slapped him across the face too. "Listen, Farren. I couldn't live in that awful locked up ward. The fact that you've survived this whole time in there is amazing! So, of course, you can handle the real world."

He took a deep breath and swallowed. "Thanks, Barli."

Henequen had taken up his post at the stern, knees pulled up to his chest.

Farren watched him. "It is him, isn't it?" he said softly.

Barli leaned on the railing. "He came to get you. I don't

know how much of everything he really understands, but he's fought it all to do that."

"It's my fault. He was doing okay, I think. And we were friends and I knew I wasn't supposed to, but I touched him." Farren swallowed. "He went crazy not too long after. His delusions got real bad and a new guy came in and totally freaked him out. He thought the guy was seriously after him. I don't really know what happened—I wasn't there or maybe I could have done something but…the guy was dead, Tane had a knife, and there was blood everywhere.

"I took it from him and said it was me. I already knew I was never getting out. Tane, though, he wasn't anything special. They might have killed him. They thought he was freaking out 'cause he'd seen it and was so scared or traumatized. I never knew what happened to him. I never thought he could turn into this."

Barli shrugged. "I only met him a few days ago, but I don't think touching him messed him up, Farren. It never messed me up. Henequen's just…well, I hardly think a hug from you is the worst thing he's had to deal with."

"What do you mean?" His empty black eyes fixed on hers.

Barli tried not to think about Kazini. "He hears and sees things that aren't there, Farren. He can't trust his own senses. Doesn't that seem worse to you?"

He pulled the cloak around himself, shivering. Barli hoped they could get him some clothes before long. "This is so weird."

Barli smiled. "Enjoy it, Farren. Things are going to

quickly stop seeming so lovely and new. Soon enough you'll be mad and upset just like everyone else."

"Why would I want that? It doesn't sound that great."

Barli's eyes narrowed and then she laughed a little. "You're teasing me, aren't you? It's rubbing off on you already." Although she'd never get to show him what things were really like. They could walk through the real world, but they couldn't be truly part of it, not with their faces marked the way they were.

She hadn't given much time to think about what would happen to Farren after they got him out. But anything was better than dead, wasn't it?

The mark on her wrist told a different story.

She'd been out of her mind then though, right?

Where would he go? And what if she didn't win—they might well have discovered how she'd fled…Henequen had found her easily enough. Would they take not finding her by a similar token? If she got sent back to Hevon'i's asylum, how would she get out? Farren could hardly rescue her.

Even if she made it, where could Farren go that would be safe? There was nowhere on any of the Islands he wouldn't be regarded with disgust and suspicion. There was nowhere that, if his existence was revealed, the Black Sins would not be sent after him. Unaccompanied Sins were unheard of, and she was sure it would be reported should it ever happen. The only way he could be seen in public would be at the side of someone either in Priest's robes or with the marks of a Black Sin.

They had to get back in time, didn't they?

She sat uncomfortably on the dock. Farren lay on his

stomach and watched the ripples in the water. As time passed, the sky lightened. Suddenly, Farren gave a start and scrambled backward, calling over the attention of her and Henequen.

"What is it?" Henequen asked, scanning the horizon.

"T-there's something in the water."

Henequen and Barli exchanged amused glances. "There's lots of things in the water. That's where fish come from."

"B-but it's so big!"

Barli glanced over the side of the boat and laughed. "They're dolphins, Farren."

"What are those? Are they dangerous?"

She shook her head. "They're good luck," she said. "They're usually following fish. Sometimes it's like they drive them into the nets. Did your books not mention them?"

"No," he said sourly. He inched back toward the side and looked over carefully. "They don't have scales," he said, surprised.

"Just don't get in the water until you learn how to swim." Henequen, seeing there was nothing dangerous about the situation, walked away without another word.

Farren watched him leave. "Does he seem mad at me?"

"No?" Barli shrugged. "Then again, he's very confusing. He tried to kiss me so I would punch him. I wouldn't know what he's thinking."

"I really don't know him at all anymore." He watched the dolphins leaping through the waves, listening to their clacking chatter. "I don't know anything." He looked at her suddenly. "I can't believe I haven't even asked—how was it? The competition? How are you doing? Do you have a chance?"

"It's okay, I suppose. I found him quick enough, my target. I had some doubts though. It sort of scared me, too. I sort of annoyed this other contestant and she broke into my room the night before. I couldn't sleep, my mind was too wild, so I was still up or she probably would have gotten me. I had the poison you gave me, and I struck out at her." Barli lifted her cloak and showed him a slight red line on her throat. "She got me a little too. But the poison you gave me did its job. After she died, I sort of thought the next one would be easy, but it wasn't."

It was strange, talking to him. At the same time, it felt perfectly natural. She had missed this. She used to talk to Visea about things—although with her it had been whatever her mother had said to irritate her, or a new dress she'd spotted window-shopping. Murder was a slightly heavier topic. It felt nice, the breeze on her face, and her heart lightening as her voice loosed the things she had held so close. Farren didn't say much, but he commented when she needed him to.

When she had finally run out of things to say, they were approaching the shore. It was then of course that Farren caught her eye and asked the thing she'd been trying to forget about since she got here. "What happened, Barli? Why did you do that?" he asked, pointing to her wrist.

She stared at the shore, swallowing, wishing the boat was moving much faster and she could have brushed his question away with the excuse that they would be there soon. But she knew they still had enough time. It really wasn't that long of a story. Maigi meowed at her, moving her head to cover up the scar. Barli reached out and scatched her gently.

"I don't always know exactly why I do what I do. My mind gets funny sometimes. I have all this energy I don't know what to do with. Sometimes I get really mad when I feel like that, like everyone else is too slow and *wrong* and I can't stand it. Other times, it's like I can't do anything wrong, you know? I could do anything."

"So?"

Barli sighed. "I don't know if I told you this, but I…I like girls. And there was this one, pretty and sweet. She lives on Gozab. That's where my family mostly is too. That's where we stay over on our trips. Used to, anyway." She ran her fingers over the mark. "My folks were mad at me…that's not entirely unusual, but it was really bad. I think they suspected how I felt…it made it worse than usual. So I met up with Visea and then we fought. She said I was selfish and a whole bunch of other things and she didn't want anything to do with me anymore." She swallowed. "I…I didn't know what to do with myself. I'd never really been alone, and I was so furious at all of them and I couldn't do anything about it. And without anyone I cared about, I didn't know what the point of any of it was…"

Farren looked out over the horizon. "People are more important than they have any right to be."

Barli took a deep breath and nodded. She had been trying not to think about the way she'd left everything. She was sure things would have blown over by now, they'd probably be sorry about all of that. Except she was different now. She'd drawn a line that couldn't be undrawn, and it was plastered on her forehead.

They were nearly there now. Farren stood up and moved around to get a better view of the shoreline. "Perspective makes things look really different, doesn't it?"

She nodded quietly.

As they got close enough to make out individuals, Barli put the hood of her cloak back up and told Farren to do the same. When they docked, Henequen had a few more words for their captain before he joined them.

"So what's the plan?" Farren looked between the two of them.

Henequen's gaze narrowed. "Barli should head straight for the Asylum. You stay with me. I have a few ideas of where to stash you for a little while."

"S-stash me?"

Henequen nodded. "You can't be seen—not by anyone. Or they'll get you. They'll get you. You and me and you and me. Gone. Gone. Gone." His fist bumped against his leg as he walked. "Barli, they'll be wondering where you've been since they've found the body."

"Will they wonder about you?"

His fist kept beating against his thigh. "You never saw me. I disappear for days. Sometimes Kazini finds me— falls!" He grabbed Farren's arm. "Let's go," he urged.

Barli stepped out into the street, her stomach twisting. "Wait! How will I find you? What if—"

"Then I'll come for you," Ferran said, his arms wrapped around Maigi.

"Are you promising me something, Farren?"

His face reddened and he gave a little smile. "I guess I am."

An hour later she found her way to the Asylum's double-door entrance. She stepped up quietly. When she got within two feet of the doors, they swung open. Barli pulled her cloak more tightly around her, as though she could hide from accusing words that questioned where she had been.

The Priests said nothing, merely ushered her inside. She stepped into the darkness of the hall, blinking slightly as her eyes readjusted. One of them stepped up and urged her to follow. She stepped into the head Priest's office, glancing around anxiously.

Even though her fate would soon be decided, she couldn't help but think instead about Farren and Henequen, and whether Henequen could keep himself together long enough for Farren to adjust and learn how to keep out of sight.

She looked down at the heavy wooden desk and slowly looked farther up, to the long black beard and beaded eyes of the Priest.

"You've finally returned, Sin. Your target's body was found yesterday."

Barli bowed her head. "I wasn't sure if I could come back too quickly, or if one of the others might come after me."

The Priest sat back, looking thoughtful.

"I mean," she said, continuing with her lie, "I already

had to deal with one assassination attempt. I don't want to kill another one unless I have to."

"How pertinent of you. You seem to have given this quite a bit of thought and patience. This bodes well."

"I'm sorry if you were concerned."

"You have fair skills since Kazini and Arbalest couldn't even track you down."

"Thank you." They'd sent two Black Sins after her? What would they have done to her if they *had* found her?

The Priest nodded. "I'm glad we've come to this understanding. You'll be confined to rooms until tomorrow when the winner will be announced. If you wish to use the yard in that time, Mirch will be at the door."

Lipa had not returned yet and so Barli had the room to herself. She took up Lipa's spot at the window, longing to spot some shadow of Henequen skulking along the alleyway. At least she wasn't in trouble. They'd never know she had taken an unsanctioned journey to a whole other Island to rescue a dead man…unless Farren got caught. If that happened, they were all going to be at the end of their ropes.

She couldn't fall asleep and she didn't try. She just stayed at the window, knives still close by. She doubted Lipa would do anything, but someone else might get involved if they knew she was here.

Barli wondered if any of the other Sins had returned. She hadn't had too rough a time finding her target—not with all the knowledge provided. Had they had more trouble? Or had they lost their nerve, as she almost had? Or were most of them already back?

The door slammed open and Barli's hand immediately jumped for her knife, flashbacks of Sotza filling her head. She whirled around as a compact force slammed into her, a flash of long black hair whipping across her face as Kazini pinned her against the wall, twisting her wrist sharply so she couldn't help but drop the knife.

"Do you think your story will fool me? I don't know where you've been, but you are not as good as me, understand?"

Barli's head pressed against the wall, dislike coloring her expression. "Whatever. Get off of me! I don't know what your problem is."

"Where's Henequen?"

"I. Don't. Know. Now, get off of me!" She thrust back against Kazini and stamped on her foot.

"This is serious. If you know where he is, you have to tell me. If he's off in his head, he'll…listen! This is important." She released Barli slightly, stepping back. She took a long strand of her hair and twirled it gently. She looked worried. Was it genuine? Did she actually care about him?

"I'm telling you the truth. I don't know where he is."

Kazini's eyebrows pinched together and she stepped further away, heaving a sigh. "I'm sorry. He just tends to have issues when he doesn't have a mission. I think the guilt gets to him or something, and since he's seemed so interested in you lately I thought you might know something."

She almost felt bad for keeping it from her. "Are you two together or…what?"

Kazini folded her arms across her chest. "Does it matter?"

"I was just wondering if…that sort of thing is common between Black Sins?"

She glanced back toward the door and bent forward. "Technically, it's not illegal. It's not encouraged though. But…Quen's a special situation. We all try to look after him, but I'm the best at it. I know where he goes and how to calm his mind." Kazini bit her cheek. "He's going to end up dead someday, done in by his own suspicious mind."

Barli turned back to the window, hoping he knew some places where even Kazini could not find him. "I don't really care," she said. "I've enough crazy already for just myself."

Kazini gave her a long stare. "Fine. Well, if you do end up joining the team, just keep me informed if he seems to be acting particularly odd. We don't want any trouble from the local people. Even with our power, if they were to think him unstable…well, that's not the sort they'd ever take to wandering their streets."

Their streets—as though they did not belong to Kazini or any of the rest of them. And she supposed they didn't. They would not pay for their maintenance. Like the streets, their work was funded by the people themselves. "I'll keep it in mind." It seemed safer to turn her attention elsewhere. "Do you think I have a chance then?"

Kazini swept her hair back, braiding it with quick fingers. "A good one, too. The others haven't been quite so quick. I suspect it's a boon to have spent as much time in the world. Perhaps that's why so many of us Black Sins didn't grow up in the Asylum."

She found the door again. "Well. I should look for him, I suppose. If you haven't seen him…" She ducked out, frowning and pulling at her long hair once more.

Barli stared at the door for several long seconds, wishing devoutly it had a lock on it. She started when it opened again, clutching her hastily retrieved knife. Were they all out to kill her? Or was it Kazini hoping to catch her in her lie?

But it was Lipa, looking grim but satisfied. She barely glanced at Barli, falling wearily into her bed. "I'm surprised to see you. I thought you might have fallen in a ditch somewhere."

Barli blinked. "What? When did you finish?"

"Well, I've done it tonight, but most everyone's came back to sleep. No one's seen you since that morning."

"Oh." She hadn't had to consider where she might spend the night if she'd had a normal night to spend—but both of them had been spent on a ship. "I…thought it better not to return. Already I've had unwanted visitors here."

"Ha!" Lipa snorted. "You've finished, I assume?"

She nodded, not wanting to talk any further. Lipa looked dead on her feet and she quickly pulled her boots off and slipped into sleep. Barli turned back to the window.

If she didn't make it…what should she do? Run from Vorain when he escorted her back? But where would she go? She wasn't Kazini—she didn't know the first place to search for Henequen. And maybe she shouldn't get any more deeply involved with him. If it was a warning so often repeated, there had to be something behind it.

Maybe she shouldn't have left Farren with Henequen, particularly with what she'd heard from Farren. He was clearly dangerous. No one was making that up. But he'd never seemed so to her, just strange and confusing.

She had to find him, somehow. There was no way she could leave him with Henequen long term—and Kazini would be on the search for him too. Yes—the best was to run from Vorain. He was a sweet boy, but he didn't know the streets as he should. She could outrun him quick, even if she hardly knew the city herself. She knew how to weave between people.

"Hey, girl! Get up now, it's time and past." Lipa shook her foot.

Barli kicked her away lazily, feeling strangely at peace with the motion. It was how her mother had used to wake her, she realized. Alertness followed shortly and by the crick in her neck she realized she had fallen asleep taking her vigil at the window. Bright light streamed through as she roused herself, splashing a little water on her face before joining Lipa in the hallway.

Everyone else seemed to be present as well, some looking more downcast than others. Barli breathed deeply as they waited to be ushered into the courtyard. The boy had found her again, slipping beside her as she walked. She did not trust something about him and kept a close look at his hands.

Assembled in the courtyard were a half dozen Black Sins and twice as many Priests. The upper balconies were full again of the normal residents of the Asylum. Kazini was lounging on one of the barrels. She didn't see Henequen. No—there he was. He was sitting in the windowsill, not making eye contact with anyone. The bruise on his face had yellowed.

"You have all done well," the head Priest said, "to have come this far."

Arbalest's brow lifted. "Not that all have done what they ought."

"Now, now, Ara," Danerax cautioned. "Not everyone's cut for the job."

"It's only more for us. I can't complain," Kazini said, taking out a knife and cleaning beneath her nails.

"Enough!" the Priest snapped. "Quiet down or they'll think you all have no discipline at all." He placed small spectacles on his nose. "Now there's no great ceremony for such a thing. It is a duty, after all."

He cleared his throat. "But I will wait no longer for all of your sakes. It is past time this competition was put well into the past. The new Black Sin will be the Sin from Hevon'i, for her quick dispatch of any competition that proved too dangerous, and her slick disposal of her target. Step forward, girl."

Barli's heart pounded. She wasn't sure what she had even been hoping for at this point. She was going to stay tied to the Asylum. But, she had beaten everyone else. She had proved it with all certainty: she was better than these other people. She was one of the really crazy ones.

Was did that say about her?

"Girl."

She stepped forward slowly, feeling the young boy prodding her back. She glanced toward Henequen, but even now he wasn't looking. He wasn't drawing either. He was just sitting there.

Why was she looking at him?

She took a deep breath looked up at the Priest.

"Your new name will be Cassava, for your effective use of poison, after the food staple and general deterrent." He lifted his hand and two of the other Black Sins approached her. They gave her little nods, not particularly encouraging. The next second they had grabbed both her arms.

"The rest of you will return to your Islands. If I see you again, perhaps you will prove to be more impressive. Cassava, it is time you were marked."

Her eyes widened and she fought against the swiftly tightening grasps of the two Black Sins, knowing now why they held so tightly to her. She had forgotten about that. If she was one of them now, she needed the brand.

Barli only vaguely remembered her last branding. It was a nightmare of pain and burning flesh she knew was hers. She'd already been nearly unconscious, recovering from the slicing she'd given her arm. This time, however, she was wide-awake.

She was wide-awake as they took her down the stairs to a quiet hot room where a furnace burned, bright red embers sparking up from the pit. Long prods rested in the bright orange glow, themselves a bright color that signaled the excessive heat they were exposed to. She was wide-awake as they forced her onto the table, laid her down, and bound her. Thick leather straps pressed against every other five inches of her body. She was wide-awake when Kazini brushed her hair out of her face, her touch almost tender. She was wide-awake when Danerax wrapped a thick glove around his hand and poked the fire twice more, sending another shoot of sparks up. He pushed the long iron deeper into the fire. She was wide-awake when Arbalest pushed a thick strip of leather between her jaws.

"It's not consolation that this is the worst part," the Black Sin said.

She was wide-awake when Danerax lifted the steaming orange tip from the fire and brought it down. Over her muted scream, she heard Danerax's voice. "Now you are one of us," he said.

The pain overpassed her and she was no longer awake.

Chapter Seventeen

CASSAVA WOKE IN NEW quarters. They were nicer than any she had been partial to before, whether in the Asylum or before when she had lived another life. The bed was surprisingly large so she nearly felt as though she was swimming in all the space. She had a chest and a desk and a table. The plethora of furniture nearly confused her.

She raised her hand gingerly to her face, feeling the tender marks. They were painful to touch and if she moved her face too much they pained her too. But if she stayed still they were not too bad. The swelling she knew would go down in a few more days, and given time the redness would fade to something less offensive. She had already been made ugly, so it was really no loss.

She rose, opening the chest to find new clothes, nicer than any she'd had. She pulled them out slowly, reveling in the softness of the fabric. It was perverse that she had earned these treasures by being that much more cruel. But was it cruel?

Cassava twirled in her new deep blue wool skirt, heavy and warm for the coming winter. Her shirt was plain brown, but it matched and it was *clean*. If only she could go dancing…

She slipped into the hallway, realizing she was on the third floor. It was lighter up here, more sunlight streaming in from skylights in the overhang. The day was crisp and cold.

"Settling in, Cassava? Oh, don't you look darling like that!" Anelace gushed. Up close, Cassava was even less sure what gender Anelace was. "Here, some ointment for your face." Unscrewing the cap swiftly, Anelace proceeded to apply the cool paste to Cassava's burning visage. She sighed at the feeling.

"Cassava!"

She whirled around. Her posture tensed immediately as she realized it was Kazini.

The girl raised her hands. "I apologize, okay? I've been stressed is all. But we're on the same team now. Anyway, congratulations. And if you need help or have questions, we'll tell you what we can. The Black Sins stick together…some of us, anyway."

Cassava gave her an untrusting nod, not quite able to fake a smile at Kazini's cheer. Maybe she did mean well, but Cassava certainly didn't trust her. Her moods seemed to swing worse than Cassava's ever had.

"Have you decided where you're going to live?" Anelace asked.

"It's early yet, you don't have to pressure her, Lacey." Kazini snapped.

Anelace snorted. "Touchy as ever, Kazini. I wonder why?" The Black Sin stepped away without another word.

Cassava thought about walking after Anelace—it seemed safer than staying with Kazini. But... "Can you change where you go?"

"Sure," she said. "Whenever you want." Kazini flipped her hair back. "I'm just glad this tedious competition is over and we can go back to killing like we ought to. So I'll be off again and you won't have to worry." She smirked. "I know you're afraid of me—"

"I am not," Cassava replied fiercely. She could handle Kazini just fine. She'd beat everyone else, why couldn't she beat Kazini too? "I could take you any time."

Kazini lifted an eyebrow and then started laughing so hard she ended up holding her side. "Oh, that sounds good," she said. "We'll have to have it out sometime. I'd like the challenge. But I do have a mission now so I've got to be going." And she flounced away.

Cassava rolled her eyes and continued down the hallway. She had yet to see who she really wanted. She glanced down into the courtyard. The ground was smudged up again, like someone had been messing with it. She found the staircase and went down, hearing a strange jingling as she hit the steps. Patting herself down, she found a ring of keys in her skirt's pocket.

Keys! Freedom!

It took her some time, but she found the right key to give her access to the courtyard. She walked through the grass field, frowning as she looked at the lines drawn into the mud. It had been raining since she'd last been awake.

The disjoined lines, smooth but crisscrossing and unalike, assured her that Henequen had left them.

"Henequen?" Where was he? And where was Farren?

The mud squished under her foot and she looked down again, stepping carefully as she lifted her skirts. Was there something in the mud?

"Black Sin Cassava."

She whirled around. "Vorain. Sir," she added quickly.

"Congratulations."

She nodded. "What…what do I do now?"

"Well, you've a few days still to recover. You can go where you want, do what you want. And then you'll get your next mission. They won't be going easy. Events on the mainland have the Priests concerned…we might have some quite long missions coming up soon, and they'll want to evaluate your rate and general methods."

Cassava shrugged. "So a few days to myself first?" Maybe she would go dancing. So what if she ruined the party? Or perhaps she could find some mask…though she'd get as many strange looks for that. "Sounds good."

"Enjoy yourself, Cassava."

"I will." She had a few days to figure out what to do with Farren. "Vorain…have you seen Henequen around?"

"Henequen? I think he's in his room."

She glanced up at the third floor. "And which one is that?"

"I believe it's the fifth down." Vorain gave her a strange look. "He's a precarious one, Cassava."

"Believe me," she said, "I know."

She investigated his abandoned drawing a little longer

before scrambling back up the stair. She smiled every time she felt the jingle in her pocket. She hadn't realized quite how much she envied Henequen that small possession. It might mean more than anything else she'd ever owned.

She knocked on the suggested door. To her surprise, it gave under the weight and swung open slowly. Her chest tightened as she looked around, closing the door carefully behind her. Like Farren's room, the most prevalent piece of décor was the pages and pages of drawings. Some were plastered to the wall, but most of them covered the wood floor like a second layer of supporting pulp. Unlike Farren's room, none of them were discernible as anything in particular. But when she saw them all at once together, she felt deeply uneasy and found herself looking over her shoulder.

She approached the bed slowly, where Henequen was spread out. She looked away quickly when she realized he was naked. "Henequen?" she asked, studying the table with sudden interest. On the table were still more pages, but these ones were not drawings. Instead, they were phrases and rhymes and instructions, written over and over again. She recognized some of them from Henequen's ramblings.

There was soft rustling behind her. "You're up." He breathed out. "Good."

"Where is he? Is he safe?"

"He is safe. I…you should talk to him." Henequen's voice was oddly quiet and his speech unhampered by his usual tics and oddities. He gave her directions. "I don't think he can stay here forever."

"Henequen, how did you get that boat? And the food? You didn't have money, did you?"

"Of course not. I asked. Politely. The captain owes me his life, he's generally very happy to accommodate me. The other one, I just went in, showed my face, and asked politely. That's usually enough."

Cassava tucked that bit of useful information away, final turning back around. Henequen had partially covered himself, but he was still lying on the bed. "Are you not coming?"

"No. Right now, everything's quiet."

Cassava followed Henequen's directions to a dusty-windowed building set back from the main streets. It had taken her half an hour to get there and she wasn't sure she quite knew how to retrace her steps. She stepped up to the door and eased it open slowly, moving to the back room.

"Farren!"

"Barli." He let out his breath into a wide smile. "Tane said you won, but…" His smile dimmed a little as he stared at her face. "I see it's true."

"Are you hungry? Do you need anything?"

He shook his head. "Tane left me enough for a week. I just want to go outside!"

"And I'd probably never get you in again!" she said. But she grabbed his cloak off the ground and threw it at him. "Come on. We've got things to talk about." She glanced around the little sanctuary. Henequen had brought him more than just food. He had new clothes, and paper. Several sheets were already full of vivid new drawings. There was one of Henequen, another of the dolphins, and a spread of three pages that recorded the coastline and the view from the ship.

"They'll put me on jobs soon. If we work it right, Henequen and I should be able to keep you stocked on what you need, and as long as you're careful, you could go out on the streets. Just nowhere crowded, okay? And you'll have poison if you need it, right?"

He nodded.

"And we'll see how it goes. It's not...I couldn't take it. It would be so lonely but I don't know what else to do. You can't know anyone else."

"I've done with less for a long time. Two whole people? That's nearly crowded. I have Maigi too." The cat purred at the sound of her name, moving to stand beside them. "And I'll go out, draw maybe."

"They're really good, you know. I bet you could even sell them."

He stopped. "Do you really think so?"

She laughed a little and nodded. "Especially if you have some new objects to try out..."

"There's so much! I don't know what to draw first," he said.

"And I'll have to teach you to swim sometime. It's simply inexcusable. It'll have to wait till it gets warmer though...I nearly got a chill that night."

They walked quietly together, Farren asking questions about the oddities of the world and Cassava doing her best to answer them. She wasn't sure she'd felt so at peace or simply…happy in a very long time.

They reached the shore and Farren had to stop again just to take it in. Barli climbed across the rocky shore and pointed out shells and starfish, enjoying the way his face lit up at each new discovery. Eventually it grew too cold to be out and they turned to go back to Henequen's hideout.

Farren broke the comfortable silence. "Are you going to go back home now? I mean, you could see them if you wanted. You wanted to see her before, didn't you?"

Cassava sighed. "Farren, you'd never say you didn't want anything to do with me, would you?"

"Only if I was lying."

Visea. She was beautiful and smart and lovely. If she went back… "Even if I'm wild and crazy and sometimes I think my body can't possibly stay in my skin and my job is killing?"

He swallowed, looking out toward the horizon. "Even then. I promise."

"Then there's not really a point. Besides, I can only keep promises to so many people, and I've already promised you."

About Jacyn Gormish

Jacyn Gormish (they/them) is a queer Jewish nonbinary disabled superhuman. They enjoy writing, metalsmithing, and weaving. They live in the Twin Cities with their wife, their cat, their service dog, and a whole bunch of medication.

Twitter: @JacynGormish
Website: http://www.jacyngormish.com

More From Deep Hearts YA

The Mixtape to My Life
Jake Martinez

Justin has always been comfortable in his skin, even if the world around him wasn't. A junior simply counting down the days for when he can leave for college, Justin's life is thrown for a loop when the one thing that helps him feel like himself suddenly slips away from him. But an unexpected blast from his past puts summer on a new and exciting path, one as random and unexpected as a mixtape.

Squishy Crushy Something
Kieran Frank

Jayden never expected he'd be the type to develop a squish on a boy, never mind a full-blown crush. But now he has two.

L.I.F.E.
Felyx Lawson

Rider is a closeted high school student and would be happy to stay that way, if not for two obstacles in his path: an assignment about love, and Cameron Walker, a new student who is so much more than the jock he first appears to be.

9 781998 055531